PRAISE FOR BONE

THE GREAT DECEPT

'Delicious' – Stephen Booth

'Political intrigue is mixed with gritty urban crime, conjuring a potent cocktail where violence, scandal and betrayal go to the very top of the British establishment' – Fantastic Fiction

WHAT YOU DON'T KNOW

'A story rich in resonance' – Cathi Unsworth, *The Guardian*

'Belbin's novel is fast-paced, combining Westminster intrigue with local politics… two plots entwine in a smart novel that recreates the heady atmosphere of Labour's first months in power' – Joan Smith, *The Time*s

BONE AND CANE

'Spare, uncompromising and very well written' — Nicola Monaghan

'Bone and Cane are an appealing pair. Definitely worth seeing what they do next.' Laura Wilson, *The Guardian*

DEATH IN THE FAMILY

ALSO BY DAVID BELBIN

The Pretender
Student
Provenance (New and Collected Short Stories)

THE BONE AND CANE NOVELS

Bone And Cane
What You Don't Know
The Great Deception

DEATH IN THE FAMILY

A Bone & Cane Novel

DAVID BELBIN

Printed by imprintdigital
Upton Pyne, Exeter
www.digital.imprint.co.uk

Typesetting by The Book Typesetters
us@thebooktypesetters.com
07422 598 168
www.thebooktypesetters.com

Cover design and photography by Graham Lester George
glgimage@me.com
07967 558275

Published by Shoestring Press
19 Devonshire Avenue, Beeston, Nottingham, NG9 1BS
(0115) 925 1827
www.shoestringpress.co.uk

First published 2022
© Copyright: David Belbin

Limited edition
ISBN 978-1-912524-64-8

For Trevor Griffiths –

comrade, teacher.

PROLOGUE

'Ahmad! Your daddy's going to be late for work. Wake him up, please.'

He wasn't meant to go into Daddy's bedroom but as Mummy was asking it was OK. He hurried to the door, half-opened it, knocked, then called inside.

'Daddy?'

Silence. Daddy's bedroom was at the front of the house. Mummy slept in the spare room, next to Ahmad's. When he was little, Ahmad used to climb in with her. She had her own room because, she said, Daddy's snoring kept her awake.

Ahmad knocked a bit harder. Again, no reply. He opened the door. The curtains were shut and the gloomy room smelt like old farts.

'Daddy!' Ahmad didn't know what to do. Daddy didn't like being woken suddenly. It was too dark to see him properly. Ahmad crossed the cold floorboards. He knew he'd reached the big window when he felt Daddy's plush prayer mat beneath his feet. He pulled one curtain open. The light had no effect on the sleeping man.

'Daddy, time to wake up.'

This was no fun. It should be Mummy's job but she and Tamazur were busy. A letter had just come, telling them all about his big sister's new school. She and Mum were girls together, making lots of plans. Ahmad felt left out, as usual.

'Daddy?' Ahmad pulled the duvet open a little. His father slept in a white vest. Ahmad squeezed his shoulder. Gently at first, then a bit harder. The shoulder felt cold. He shook his father's arm. What was wrong with Daddy? Should he go and fetch Mummy? He looked around the bedroom, hoping for an answer.

He didn't like what he found.

BOOK ONE

Bilal

Sarah

ONE

Uncle requested Bilal's presence at his terraced house in Hyson Green. This was the poor part of the city where Uncle and many like him found lodgings when they arrived from Pakistan. Uncle was the family patriarch, Bilal's dad's older brother. Bilal could barely remember his father, who'd died of cancer when he was five. Since then, Uncle had kept a close eye on him and his sister, Nazia, especially after Mum died. Brain clot. That happened when Nazia was eighteen and Bilal fifteen. Nazia had delayed university and looked after him until he left school.

Uncle, to Bilal's surprise, already had company. Fucking Fahd was there.

Fahd wasn't a blood relation, but Nazia's brother-in-law, a surly, bearded figure sat beneath a framed print of the Kaaba. Bilal hardly knew Omar's younger brother and had never liked him. What the hell was he doing here?

The old man waved him to sit. Uncle's cramped front room, made smaller by dark flock wallpaper, was dominated by two cream, mock-leather sofas, facing each other. Bilal sat next to Uncle, diagonally opposite Fahd. Uncle explained the situation. When Bilal heard what he had to say, he wished he hadn't come.

'It's your responsibility,' Uncle told Bilal. 'She's your sister.'

'My older sister. I have no control over her.'

'She's shaming our family.'.

'Have you spoken to Omar?' Bilal asked Uncle.

'Omar will say it's not our business.'

'Then don't get involved in his marriage.'

'Our family, our shame,' Uncle said. 'Your generation, you don't take honour seriously. All you care about is money, money.'

'That's not fair.'

Uncle was still an imposing man. Bilal had always been wary of him. Not scared, the way he used to be with Nazia, big sister

5

and surrogate mum. Naz was the only person in the family who could stand up to Uncle. Five years ago, when Uncle made noises about Bilal marrying a white woman, Nazia put him in his place. Uncle had been forced to swallow his resentment. Was this a delayed reaction to the way she'd hurt his pride back then?

Fahd spoke for the first time. 'You have to tell her. It stops. Or she will be punished.'

No need for Bilal to be polite to Fahd. These days, Fahd wore a Shawar Kameez most of the time and talked about Allah a lot. Yet, by all accounts, he used to be wilder than Bilal or Nazia had ever been. His newfound piety pissed Bilal off. Two could play at that game.

'The Koran says you need four witnesses for what you're accusing her of.'

Fahd sneered. He knew that the community didn't need witnesses. A woman accused of adultery was ruined the moment the accusation was made. Now Bilal was sure: Fahd must be the source of this gossip. He had always been jealous of his older brother, who had married a beautiful woman much younger than him. Fahd was a sometime preacher and a sometime politician – a full-time nothing, far as Bilal was concerned. Nazia should have known better than to give him any kind of ammunition. Bilal had to warn her. He gave Fahd a hard stare.

'Do you know the guy's name, at least?'

'I know the car he drives. It's been seen parked near the house.'

'That's it, is it? A car parked near the house once too often. Has anyone even seen him go in?'

'You can ask your sister. I expect she knows his name.'

'What shall I say? "Who have you taken to bed while your kids are at school and your husband at work?" She'll tell me that this is madness, Uncle.'

Uncle frowned. 'You want me to go to Omar instead?'

Bilal considered the threat. 'Do that, and you'll poison the marriage. I'll speak to Nazia, see if she can put your mind at rest.'

Next day, Bilal called Nazia to say that he was bringing round a present for Ahmad, her youngest. His nephew would be nine in a week's time. His niece, Tamazur, had recently turned eleven. Once, Nazia was going to train to be a social worker. She'd meant to establish her career before having children. But Omar was over forty when they married and keen to be a dad. After they were both at school, Omar had told Nazia, you can go to university then. But she never did, and Bilal had never asked why. Nor had he asked why the couple stopped at two kids.

He parked his taxi on Nazia's wide road in The Park. At the top of her steep drive his big sister kissed him on the cheek. 'As-salāmu'alaykum.'

'Wa'alaykumu as-salām.' Bilal gave her the gift. 'It's the game he wants.'

Ahmad had been given one of the new Playstation 2s for Christmas.

'That's generous of you.'

He followed her inside.

'Some tea?'

'I'd rather have a beer.'

Nazia came back from the fridge with a Becks, which was surprising. They normally only had Kingfisher in. Nazia liked wine, while Omar drank spirits. Beer was for guests. His sister, at thirty-eight, was still a striking woman. Like him, she nearly always wore Western clothes. Today, blue jeans and a loose cotton top with a scarf for modesty. This was one of the more modern houses in this affluent, tree-lined part of the city. Its décor was equally modern. A few books and a framed scripture on the wall were the only suggestion that the household practised Islam.

Bilal drank from the bottle to give himself Dutch courage. The beer was dryer than he liked. He'd decided not to mention how the gossip came from Fahd. Naz's dislike for her brother-in-law would make her dismiss the story regardless of whether there was any truth in it.

'How's Samantha?' she asked.

'Sam's good, thanks. Looking after herself.'

'No change…?'

'Nothing at all.' Bilal and Sam had been trying for a baby for three years now.

7

'My offer's still good.'

'I appreciate it, sis. But think what Omar's family would say.'

'This is the twenty-first century. Things change. People, too. Omar would come around.'

'Actually, it's his family and your marriage I'm here to talk about.'

Nazia straightened the silk scarf around her neck.

'My marriage?'

'Uncle asked to see me. He's heard gossip that you're having an affair.'

The way she laughed, high-pitched, then looked away, told its own tale. Bilal had heard that laugh before, when he was a little boy. Nazia used to fight with Mum. Mum spoke hardly any English, which embarrassed them, but had a sharp mind and a sharper tongue. She could always tell when her daughter was lying.

'Ridiculous,' Naz said.

He looked at her for a long time, and she corrected herself.

'It's a misunderstanding.'

'Who is he?' Bilal asked.

His sister was silent.

'Did you buy this beer for him?' He couldn't believe she would let a man be alone with her in the house, but Fahd claimed to have seen his car parked outside.

She didn't reply.

'Are you doing it with him here?

She slapped his face. 'Never speak to me like that!'

'I want to protect you!' Bilal protested, face smarting.

'Then persuade Omar to go on a diet. He's put on so much weight, when we share a bed I'm afraid he'll roll over in his sleep and smother me to death.'

Bilal half-laughed. That was a thing his sister was good at, diverting the conversation, using a joke to lighten the mood.

'They've seen the guy's car outside the house.'

'Impossible.'

'You mean he's not been here?'

She sighed and sat down. 'There is a man I've spent time with.

An old friend from before Omar. Strictly platonic. I thought I'd kept it well hidden.'

'Who is he?'

'You don't know him.'

'You can't see him any more.'

'Omar and me, we're not like you and Sam. We hardly talk. I get lonely.'

'You have two kids. If you get bored during the day, get a job, don't start an affair.'

'I told you, it's not an—'

'—I don't want you to lie to me,' Bilal interrupted, before she could dig herself in deeper. 'I'm going to tell Uncle exactly what you just told me. It's an old friend from before your marriage. Nothing happened, but you understand how gossip can get started, so you won't be seeing him again. Are we agreed?'

His sister looked away. 'Agreed.'

TWO

This time it was just to be the two of them, in Uncle's office. Uncle rented two rooms on a road near the Arboretum and both High Schools, easy walking distance from Hyson Green. These Victorian houses were too big for modern families. Most had become flats, student houses or office buildings like this one, where Uncle owned the ground floor. He still handled a few accountancy clients, despite drawing his old age pension.

Bilal began his shift early and made sure to arrive after the morning school rush had cleared. Uncle, who only drove in when it was wet, lent him his parking pass. The old man's office was painted dull magnolia and had no pictures on the wall. Bilal took the leather upholstered chair opposite Uncle's desk. This was where he sat once a year, when Uncle went over his tax return. Bilal began his rehearsed report, unsure how well he was selling his sister's story.

'She didn't tell you the man's name?' Uncle asked when he was done.

'No. She said I didn't know him. I believed her on the rest.'

'Why would you know him?'

'There was a guy,' Bilal explained. 'Used to be my teacher. Nazia got to know him at parents' evenings – after Mum passed. Anyway, they were… close. Before Nazia married Omar.'

He didn't mention how Nick Cane had subsequently gone to prison for growing weed and possessing several grams of cocaine with intent to supply. Nazia knew about that. They'd discussed it when Nick was in the papers. She'd expressed dismay at Nick's eight-year sentence. Bilal had never known how or why the couple finished, but it wasn't long after they parted that she met and married Omar.

'You must still keep an eye out,' Uncle said. 'Omar is a proud man. Word of something like this…'

He didn't need to finish. Omar would be crushed if his wife had an affair. No telling what he might do. But there was something Bilal needed to say.

'Fahd's always been jealous of Omar. I've seen the way he looks at Nazia.'

'That's as may be but if he's right about the affair, your sister will be ruined. Make sure she knows that.'

Uncle was keeping a careful balance. He was the head of Bilal and Nazia's family and their family's honour was more important than his loyalty to Nazia. Bilal wasn't close to Omar. There was too big an age gap between them. Also, Omar worked long hours and wasn't around as much as he might be. Omar was a decent man, a good father, an observant Muslim, but he was also boring. He had few interests outside family and work. He couldn't even talk about football. Bilal often wondered what – if anything – his sister found attractive in her husband. Why had she agreed to marry him? There must have been something there, once.

His mobile rang. Nazia.

'I'm at Uncle's, on Newstead Road,' he announced in answering.

'You need to come,' his sister said. 'Omar had a heart attack in his sleep. The doctor's here but there was nothing he could do. An ambulance is on its way.'

Shocked, Bilal muttered a few words of condolence. 'I'll be right there.'

He told Uncle what had happened. The old man groaned.

'Perhaps best if I break this to Fahd,' he said.

Bilal didn't argue.

Ten minutes later, Bilal was in The Park. The paramedics had already moved Omar's covered body. Bilal rang Hassan, Omar's GP. He was a Muslim and an old family friend, nearer Bilal's age than Omar's. Hassan would sign the death certificate. There should be no need for an inquest or post mortem. Hassan spoke frankly about the deceased.

'Omar was on medication for his heart and insulin for his diabetes but he was badly overweight and drank too much. What happened last night could have happened at any time in the last two years.'

'Omar knew that?'

'Knowing something and acting on it are not the same thing. I'm afraid that, despite the diabetes and the angina, he didn't find time to exercise or go on a diet.'

Death dictates its own rhythms. As a blood relative, Bilal was the only man allowed to be alone with Nazia for the next four months and ten days. This stricture, *iddah*, was there to ensure that any child she carried was fathered by her late husband. Fahd, as Omar's younger brother, was the dentist's most senior male blood relative. It was his right to take control of the funeral arrangements. Tradition dictated that burial should take place quickly. In hot countries, that had to be within 24 hours, because of the risk of decay. In the UK, tomorrow afternoon was the earliest the funeral could be arranged. Which barely allowed time for relatives to fly in from Pakistan.

Luckily, Sam didn't have a shift. She was able to take care of Ahmad and Tamazur, who were each distraught. Nazia, by contrast, seemed unnaturally calm. Probably the shock before grief set in. She kept the silk scarf wrapped around her head, preserving some modesty in the face of the polite officials for whom death was an everyday job.

Later, when they were alone, Nazia told Bilal she thought Omar had brought it on himself.

'He used vodka to get to sleep. I made him give up smoking, but the drink, he liked it too much. Only after the kids were in bed, though. He never let them see a drop pass his lips.'

Tradition required that Nazia surround herself with women. But his sister had never had close female friends, not even at school. She and Sam got on OK, but Naz was several years older than Sam, and Sam found her hard work. Sana, Naz's closest friend from university, lived an hour away, in Birmingham. Bilal got her number from Naz. Sana offered to come at once. After the funeral, it was agreed, Naz would stay in Birmingham for a while.

Bilal rang Uncle, told him what had transpired. Uncle didn't bring up the lies that Fahd had been spreading. Earlier, he'd seemed to accept the explanation Bilal had relayed. Bilal didn't, not entirely, but Nazia's four-month *iddah* should ensure that she didn't see the other man – whoever he was – again.

THREE

In fields throughout the country, cattle were burning. Sarah saw four pyres from her first-class train seat. She was spared the smell. There wasn't a single farm in her Nottingham constituency, so she was also spared having to visit one.

She spent the weekend on constituency business. Two surgeries, one fete and a whole morning delivering leaflets for the local elections. Pub lunch with the workers, microwave meals in the evening, alone. On Sunday evening, the expected text message came. She called Tony Bax, her constituency chair, to tell him.

'It'll be announced tomorrow. Local elections postponed due to the foot and mouth crisis.'

'Bugger.'

'This throws your wedding plans, doesn't it?'

'To put it mildly.'

The local elections were due on May 1st, with the General Election expected to be the same day. Tony's wedding was booked for May 10th, when the elections should have been all over, with a fortnight's honeymoon in Tenerife to follow.

'I'll have to postpone.'

'I don't see why. The General Election can't be any earlier than the start of June, and you'll be back by then.'

'How can I stand in an election if I'm not around to campaign?'

'Easily. Your council seat's safe, whereas I'm going to lose my seat in the Commons, whatever happens.'

'Not necessarily. Though you should have gone for Chesterfield.'

'Don't start that again.' Sarah's hometown party had selected former MP Reg Race to replace the retiring MP, Tony Benn, as their candidate. Benn, a totem of the left, was standing down, because he 'wanted to devote more time to politics'. Race used to be a Bennite, placing him on the hard left of the party, but these days was a Blairite, putting him to the right of Sarah. She saw

14

herself as being of the left. However, she'd never even joined the Tribune group, the party's main broad left grouping. When asked why this was, she'd usually say she didn't like being defined by any group narrower than the party itself. Fairness, imagination, intelligence and honour were what mattered most in her politics, not dogmatism or ideology. Honour was the reason she remained doggedly loyal to Nottingham West, where she had been an MP for six years. It was why she hadn't put herself forward for Benn's safe seat, despite having been approached. She was, after all, the obvious choice: a Chesterfield girl, granddaughter of the town's most famous previous MP.

Was she being foolish? She might have spun the decision to leave West in a way that didn't look like a defection. Yet walking away wasn't in her nature.

'And don't even think about cancelling your wedding,' she told Tony. 'I've bought a new dress. Show your fiancée where your priorities lie. With her.'

Tony didn't concede the point, but Sarah knew he'd do what Eve wanted. Tony always put other people first. In retirement, he remained a cornerstone of the city council. She wondered what job he'd take on after the election. He might put himself forward for one of the council cabinet posts, or he might want less responsibility, give himself more time to spend with his new wife.

What would Sarah do when she lost her seat? She'd be all right for money at first, though she hadn't been an MP long enough to qualify for a large redundancy pay-out. She needed to find something that paid fairly well and provided a pension. You had to consider such things when you were on the cusp of forty.

Which reminded her, it was Nick's 40th birthday before hers. She wondered how he'd take it. Forty was less of a problem for a man. Nick was entering his prime, while she... what was she? Entering limbo. No job. No man. No kids, not that she'd ever been particularly keen. Moot point, when there was no man in the picture. When she and Nick were a couple, best part of twenty years ago, Nick had wanted kids. He'd talked about them as being part of their future. She'd played along. She wondered if he still felt the same.

Stop! She was meant to be thinking about jobs. She'd had one offer. The man who'd made it had since retired and gone off her radar. Time to fix that, now that she had a free month. She'd call Eric Turnbull, Nottinghamshire's former Chief Constable. Not from the train. There were things she didn't want overheard.

When she got home, Sarah took a microwave lasagne out of the freezer and picked up the previous day's Nottingham Post, turning the pages while she waited for the meal to defrost. She resisted the temptation to open a bottle of Chianti. In her job, wine was constantly on offer, but it piled on the calories. She always meant to take two or three nights a week off the booze. Most weeks, she managed one.

The story was buried at the bottom of page six. *Sudden death of much loved city centre dentist.* Her dentist. Omar Khan, 55, had been feeling fine when he went to bed on Monday evening, but died in his sleep. A heart attack was suspected. Omar was survived by his wife, Nazia, and two young children. Poor sod, Sarah thought. He'd been her dentist since she became an MP. A quiet, family man, who seemed dedicated to his job. Just before Christmas she'd phoned with a bad toothache. He didn't berate her for a missed appointment earlier in the year, but found time to fit in two emergency appointments. His poor family.

And patients. These days, a good NHS dentist was hard to find.

The funeral, at Wilford Hill, was men only. Bilal glimpsed the casket before it was closed. Brilliant white cotton robes could not disguise their wearer's sad state. Omar had not been embalmed. That was against tradition. The men read from the Quran, then drove to the house in The Park, where the women had prepared food. In the old days, people stayed until late. Close family might stay the whole week. But no longer. Nazia and the kids were among the first to leave, heading to Birmingham in a car driven by her friend, Sana.

Uncle and Fahd remained to see the last mourners out. The younger man, clad in white, had trimmed his beard for the occasion. It was three quarters grey, giving him the air of a wise Imam. Provided you didn't look too closely.

'Did Nazia seem OK to you?' Uncle asked Bilal, who was about to leave.

'Except when she was around Fahd. Bad atmosphere then.'

'Have you told her everything Fahd's accusing her of?'

'I didn't say who the accusations were coming from. She has enough to deal with without...' Bilal heard footsteps. Nazia's brother-in-law appeared in the doorway, his eyes cold and heartless, his tone sanctimonious.

'Where is Nazia? I wish to talk with her again.'

'She's taken the kids to stay with a friend in Birmingham.'

'The widow is meant to stay in her husband's house after his death. Her *iddah* isn't over for four months and ten days.'

'It's an old-fashioned rule. Naz has mourned at my home for two days. She's staying with a friend whose kids her kids can play with. Where's the harm in that?'

'Does her friend have a husband? That is against-'

'-They split up, so another man's presence isn't an issue.'

'She is with a divorcee? An adulteress?'

Bilal tried not to sneer. 'I don't know Sana's marital status. From what I heard her husband didn't like how Sana earned more than he did and wasn't willing to take care of their kids, so he pushed off back to Pakistan.'

'When is Nazia back?'

'I don't know,' Bilal told Fahd. 'When she's ready.'

'We need to talk about what we discussed before Omar's death,' Fahd said.

'I'm not sure that we do,' Bilal replied.

'Have you spoken to the man?' Uncle asked.

'No way. Omar's death makes it impossible for her to see him. I think we should let this go.'

'*Let it go*?' Fahd repeated with contempt. 'It's too late for that.'

'There are things I would like to know,' Uncle said.

'Such as?' Why would Uncle be taking Fahd's side?

'Omar's diabetes. Did he always inject himself or did Nazia do it for him?'

'I presume he injected himself,' Bilal said. 'Most people do, don't they?'

'And his will. What does it say?'

'I expect he left everything to Nazia. Why wouldn't he?'

'Is there a trust for the children or does she have total control?'

'Why are you asking this?' Bilal asked, speaking to Uncle but looking at Fahd, whose eyes remained cold.

'Fahd showed me something. If Nazia is arrested, the family will have to make arrangements for the children, and we need to know the legal position.'

'Arrested?' Bilal said. 'What are you on about?'

Fahd reached into the pocket of his dhoti and brought out a syringe, which he'd wrapped in a handkerchief. 'Don't touch it.'

'Where did you find that?' Bilal asked.

'Hidden at the bottom of the wardrobe in Nazia's bedroom.'

'What were you doing in Nazia's bedroom?'

'Looking for something like this. Proof.'

'What? Why?'

'She could have injected him in his sleep,' Fahd insisted.

'With insulin?' Bilal shook his head. 'This is nonsense. I'll ask Nazia about the needle when she's back. There'll be a simple explanation.'

'Or you'll give her time to make one up.'

'My sister is a grieving widow. I don't know why you have it in for her.'

'Because she's an adulteress! She won't get away, I promise.'

Bilal shook his head. There was no arguing with Fahd when he was like this. He needed to talk to Nazia before these two did something stupid and irrevocable.

'Don't slander my sister,' he told them. 'Or you'll answer to me, and to Nazia's lawyers, to the full extent of the law. I will sort this out.'

'You won't,' Fahd said. 'It's too late for that, anyway.'

'What do you mean?'

'I've already phoned the police.'

FOUR

It was a clear morning. Sarah was determined to get fit before the election. She'd lost a stone so far this year but still wanted to burn off a few more pounds. Rather than walk down Friar Lane and through the Market Square, therefore, she took a longer route into the city, striding up Standard Hill, across Regent St and down into Wellington Circus, where a six-metre-wide, concave, stainless steel sculpture had been installed the day before.

Anish Kapoor's Sky Mirror stood directly in front of Nottingham Playhouse. From behind, the concave dish's function was hard to grasp. When Sarah joined the gathering of onlookers in front, however, she had to smile. She'd seen a maquette of the planned sculpture, but the effect of seeing the city mirrored, back to front, in ten tons of polished stainless steel, was mesmerising. This city was on the up. Hard to take in that, soon, she'd no longer have a reason to remain here.

The phoney war was under way. Unless the foot and mouth crisis suddenly got a whole lot worse, the election would take place on June 7th, though this had yet to be declared. Yesterday, Sarah had been out canvassing. Today, she ought to be in the Commons, where the dregs of business took up the extra time suddenly available. Instead, she was chasing a new job.

Sarah crossed Derby Road onto Upper Parliament Street. She turned left before the venerable old Theatre Royal, where the road was being dug up for tram tracks. She got to the Labour offices on Talbot Street at a minute past nine. Her agent, Winston, was already there, waiting to ambush her.

'You need a website.'

This was Winston's current bee in the bonnet. MPs needed to embrace what they were calling *New Media*, reach out to the hip young internet users.

'I don't see why,' Sarah said for the fourth or fifth time this year.

'It's cheap advertising. Much cheaper than those four-page newspapers all the candidates are putting together. Newspapers are last century. Also, with a website, you can get supporters to sign up and give you their email address. After which, it doesn't cost you a penny to contact them.'

'I get free mailshots anyway.'

'Not an infinite number. Email's virtually free. It's fast and modern. I'll put out feelers to find a Labour supporter with the technical savvy to do a decent website. We'll make good use of this unexpected extra time.'

Sarah spent the morning making and taking calls. Just before lunch, when the Nottingham Post was delivered, she scanned the news pages. Cars were to be banned from the Market Square between 8AM and 6PM. People were protesting that the Odeon cinema on Angel Row, where The Beatles and Stones performed, was to be turned into a six million pound 'super club'. Nothing she needed to comment on.

Sarah met Eric Turnbull for lunch in French Living's basement restaurant. This had been their regular lunch spot when they were each exploring possibilities. Since then, Eric had remarried. Mary Harris was a solicitor, about Sarah's age. Sarah had been invited to the wedding, found an excuse not to attend. Nothing to do with envy. She liked Eric, just not enough to be in a relationship with him. He was intelligent which, for her, was the biggest turn on in a man. His cultivated blandness concealed the hard edge he brought to his job. Today, the former Chief Constable was dressed more casually than of old, in a brown, soft leather jacket with open-necked shirt and chinos. Eric was nearly handsome. His face was a little too thin, his chin a little too weak. He was also, at fifty-six, ten years too old for Sarah. That had been the determining factor in her gently rejecting his advances.

'Today, lunch is on me,' she said.

'Taking pity on a pensioner?'

'I don't suppose your pension's too shabby and I'll bet that Mary earns more than I do, but I'm here to ask a favour.'

''twas ever thus,' Eric said. The waiter came over and Eric took charge, even though she'd said she was paying. He ordered a jug of tap water and two glasses of Pineau des Charantes as an aperitif. Sarah got straight to the point.

'Last year, you said the Police Federation were interested in recruiting me.'

'They wanted to look outside the force for their next General Secretary, yes. Given your years in the police, and seven years as an MP, I'd say you were perfectly placed for the job. As far as I know, no decision has been made, although I am out of the loop these days.'

'Did you also tell them I worked as a Trade Union research officer before I went into parliament?'

'They don't like to think of themselves as a trade union but, you're right, I'd forgotten that. Makes you an even stronger choice. I expect they could be persuaded to bump up the money for somebody of your calibre. You would have to move to Surrey.'

'After I lose the election, there's nothing to keep me here.'

'I can't see you settling in Leatherhead. Still, shall I make a call or two?'

'Please. Obviously, it's dependent upon-'

'-obviously. And we're all hoping that you do get back in and continue doing the fantastic job you have been doing.'

'Appreciated,' Sarah said, not questioning who 'we all' were these days. They discussed foot and mouth, the changes taking place in the city and a couple of plays Eric had been to see recently. Theatre-going was a new thing for him. Must be down to Mary.

'You still see plenty of people from your old job?' she asked, after they'd each polished off the *onglet* of beef with fried potatoes and salad.

'A few.'

'Have there been any changes with the drugs gangs since last year's... horribleness.'

'That's one word for it,' Eric said. Andrew Saint, an old university friend (or, to be precise, the onetime best friend of her university boyfriend, Nick Cane), had been murdered. Worse, he'd been killed in a Majorcan villa that Sarah had inherited from her father. Saint had been coordinating some building work for her, but Sarah had no idea that Andrew and his girlfriend, Nancy

– also killed – were hiding out in the villa, where she'd never lived. Nor – until he fled the UK – was she aware that Andrew was involved in drug trafficking.

Her ownership of the death scene had been kept out of the media. Eric might have had something to do with that.

'You know how these things go,' Eric said. 'Any vacuum that Saint left was quickly filled. The turf divisions change from time to time, with sporadic violence between rivals. For the most part, there's an *entente cordial*. Supplies are steady and the city has enough custom to keep all of the gangs in clover. Word is, there's a new player, but the police can't get near them. Never could. Occasional fleeting successes is the most they can hope for.'

Sarah noticed how the police had become *they* since Eric's retirement. He'd never made a secret of his belief that the War on Drugs was doomed to fail.

'Did you manage to sell the villa in Majorca, by the way?'

'Not yet. I'm renting it out until its reputation is less… current. A double murder has a tendency to reduce house prices. You and Mary aren't looking for a holiday home, are you?'

'Not in that part of the world. Tell me, what are your canvas returns saying?'

Whenever Sarah mentioned Eric's wife, she noticed, he steered the conversation in a different direction.

FIVE

Bilal had known Fahd and Omar for more than a decade, yet each remained a mystery to him. Omar was a quiet man, a workaholic who lived for his wife and kids. Nazia had done her best to get him to take up squash, then badminton, then golf. No joy. Omar took the kids swimming at the new university pool. That was it.

Fahd, by contrast, had dropped out of Wolverhampton Polytechnic after failing his first year. He'd tried for the council in the late 80s, but was narrowly beaten by a Tory, a defeat which he (probably with justification) blamed on racism. Not long after that, Fahd and some of his cronies tried to take over the local party in an inner-city ward, a safe Labour seat. The way Bilal heard it, there was a scuffle at a meeting. Fahd was said to have been seen carrying a weapon, maybe even used it, reports varied, with the result that the ward was closed down for months. After an inquiry, Fahd was expelled from the party. He hadn't been involved in politics since, though some of his former allies had ascended to positions of power.

Omar, Bilal recalled Nazia telling him, had tried to persuade Fahd to go back to university, but his younger brother wasn't having it. He professed an ambition to become a preacher and began to study. Omar arranged for him to marry a girl from their home village in Pakistan. Fahd seemed to be turning his life around. But when the couple met, they did not get on. The wedding was called off.

Once, Bilal had collected Fahd from a Forest Fields brothel. The older man should have known better than to use the cab firm that Bilal worked for. They had pretended not to know each other, and never spoken of it. What you did with white girls didn't count, that was how some Muslim men felt. Bilal, married to a white woman, thought that was a crock of shit. But people believed what they wanted to believe, particularly when those beliefs allowed them to have guilt-free sex. When he'd mentioned her brother-in-law's behaviour, Nazia had not been surprised.

'Who but a whore would have him?' she'd said.

There was nearly a decade between Omar and Fahd, with a sister in between. Jameela had died of leukemia when Omar was a student. That loss must have had a big effect on both men, but she was never mentioned. Their parents had each died in their late sixties. This left Omar as the head of the family, an orphan married to an orphan. Because of this position, Omar felt bound to support Fahd from time to time. He'd helped him buy the modest terrace in Sneinton. The terrace stood in stark contrast to Omar's home in one of the most expensive parts of the city. Bilal had only been inside the place once. It was scruffy and cramped. His and Sam's semi in Wollaton was luxurious by comparison.

Strange that Fahd was making such a fuss about Omar's death. The brothers had had little time for each other when Omar was alive. But that was families for you. Even if you blamed them for everything that had gone wrong in your life, it didn't matter. Family remained family.

'Have you spoken to Nazia since yesterday morning?' Sam asked at breakfast.

'Not yet. She said she'd call when they were settled in at Sana's.'

'Something's clearly bothering you. You came home late the other night.'

She'd been in bed when he got in.

'I was with Fahd and Uncle.'

'You let me think you'd been drinking. But when you kissed me goodnight, there was no whisky on your breath.'

'We weren't drinking. After we'd done, I drove around for a while.'

'What did Fahd say? Something bad about Nazia, I'll bet.'

Sam was a year older than him and worked as a nurse in A and E. When they met, in a club, he'd thought she was too good for him. Too pretty, too practical. Two years later they were married and, with family help, scraped together the deposit on a modest house in a good part of town, near Wollaton Park. A house big enough for a small family, should they prove able to have one.

'Fahd has always had it in for Nazia,' Bilal muttered.

'From what I've seen, Fahd has always lusted after Nazia and hated the way she could see through him and his pretensions. What did he say?'

Bilal told Sam about his visit to Uncle and subsequent discussion with Nazia.

'You reported this back to Uncle?'

'Yes. Before we could discuss the situation further, I got the call saying Omar had died. I thought that put an end to the gossip. Then, yesterday, back at the house, after Nazia had gone to Birmingham, Fahd went snooping, and claimed to have found something hidden in a wardrobe. A hypodermic needle.'

'So what? Omar was a diabetic.'

'This one was hidden, in a wardrobe, and it had been used. Fahd has this theory that Naz deliberately overdosed Omar with insulin so that she could be with her lover. Is that a real thing – overdosing someone with insulin?'

'It's a thing. But very hard to prove. Remember that nurse in Grantham, Beverley Allitt? She used insulin to kill her victims. It took a good while before staff noticed an unusual pattern of heart attacks and the police investigated. That said, murder's a fanciful idea. And you only have Fahd's word for it that he found the needle where he said he says he did. Has he gone to the police?'

'He says he called them. I've heard nothing. I haven't told Nazia yet.'

'Oh, Billy…' The personality drained from his wife's face. For a moment he saw, plain as day, how she would look when she was older, and life had worn her down, the way life always did.

'You believe him?' she asked, finally. 'You don't think he's creating trouble because he wants to exercise control over Nazia and Omar's money?'

'I don't know what he wants. I don't know if he knows. Nazia repeated the offer, by the way. Just last week.'

'After you accused her of having an affair? That makes me suspicious.'

'Honestly, it didn't come out that way. She wasn't worried. She said she'd not been having an affair, just revived an old friendship, and she'd put a stop to it. I can't remember how the surrogate thing came up, but it did.'

'Today isn't the day to talk about that. The first thing we need to work out is who Fahd thinks she's having an affair with. If it isn't true, and we can show that, then maybe the business with the needle will go away. Have you any idea who he suspects her of seeing?'

'No.'

'She's not a saint, Billy. Didn't you say she had a boyfriend before Omar?'

'Sort of, but that was never going to work out. He was white. Used to teach me. He ended up being a bit of a legend at school. The one who got sent to prison for growing caves full of weed.'

'I remember you telling me about him. Rick something?'

'Nick. He must be out of prison by now. Nick Cane.'

Sarah was running late for her train. She hurried through the dingy underground tunnel beneath The Broadmarsh centre, her least favourite thoroughfare in the city. Charging into the station, she all but bumped into Nick.

'Sarah!'

They hadn't seen each other for over a year and it was awkward. Before she knew it, the moment for an impromptu hug had passed.

'I'm sorry we haven't...'

'Don't be daft. You have an overwhelming job. Be nice to see you properly, though,' Nick added. 'And thanks for the offer of work, by the way.'

Sarah didn't know what he was talking about. 'Pardon?'

'Your agent, Winston, rang. He'll explain, I can see you're in a hurry.'

She considered saying sod it, she'd catch the next train, but this was not the way she wanted to encounter Nick again.

'You're looking really well.' She leant forward and kissed him on the cheek. 'It must be your birthday soon, and I'm not far behind. The official start of middle age. Can't say I'm relishing the prospect.'

'You're looking good on it,' Nick assured her. 'Go on, get your train.'

She made it to her seat with a minute to spare. Seeing Nick for thirty seconds had given her more of a sexual buzz than a two-hour lunch with Eric. She spent the first hour of her journey daydreaming about getting back together with him. Not impossible, after she lost her seat. Nick had nothing going on in Nottingham. There was his internet business, but he could do that anywhere. He'd spent five years in prison for cultivating cannabis and possessing cocaine, then three years out, most of them on license. As of this year, however, he was officially rehabilitated. Sarah's about-to-be employers might not appreciate her being with a man with his past but they had no say in the matter. There was no promotion for Sarah to muck up, either, since she'd already be in the top job.

At Market Harborough, she got out her mobile and called Winston.

'I bumped into Nick Cane. He said he was working for me...?'

'He's the best person we could find to set up your website. Tony Bax vouches for him. And I've had a look at his work. It's varied. A taxi firm. Two NHS practices. A gambling site. A variety of companies, not just in Nottingham. The quality's consistent. A lot of these internet people just do coding, or use prepackaged software that makes every site looks the same, but this guy can code, do lay-out and copy edit. He writes pretty well, too.'

'I should hope so. He used to be an English teacher.'

'Then can I get on with it? Thing is, if we pay him to do the set-up work soon, it doesn't count as an election expense.'

'Would he be working just for me, or all four Nottingham MPs?'

'You're the only one with a marginal seat, so your need is greatest. I suspect the others will want to see how your site goes before jumping on board.'

'That's agreed, then. Can you negotiate the price?'

'You'll need to meet him to discuss content. Or I can, if you prefer. He said you two had history, implied there might be some awkwardness.'

'Not awkwardness, exactly,' Sarah insisted. 'Nick spent five years in prison. I used to go out with him, when we were students. I've kept the connection quiet.'

'He's *that* guy,' Winston said. 'Now you mention it, I did hear about him. I don't think it's a problem. His name won't appear.'

'If it's not a problem, commission him. He's usually good at what he does.'

'Agreed. Back in the day, I smoked some of his weed. It was excellent.'

SIX

The police came to see Bilal on Tuesday. He was ready for their questions.

'How might a needle have found its way into the wardrobe?'

Omar had lots of needles.

'What was the state of their marriage?'

They often slept in separate beds but, as far as Bilal knew, that was because of Omar's heavy snoring. 'I know that my brother-in-law has a theory, but...'

'Fahd claimed that your sister was having an affair.'

'Nonsense.'

'Do you know who Fahd accused her of having an affair with?'

'All I know is that he was meant to be a white guy. Not who. But the idea that my sister would...'

The officer told him that wild accusations were quite common after sudden deaths. 'Bereavement takes people in all sorts of ways. Old resentments surface. People get paranoid. They want somebody to blame. It's natural.'

'Thanks,' Bilal told her. 'That's helpful to know.'

It was no good, Bilal decided. If he were to set his mind at rest, he had to find out who his sister had been seeing. Which meant he had to find Nick Cane.

When the police were gone, he opened the phone book. There was only one Nick Cane. His address was on Waverley St, near the city centre. A third floor flat. He would go there after work.

Sarah got an email from Nick on Tuesday morning and replied with the information he needed. Her fantasies about them getting back together were just that, she told herself, fantasies. This was how they would communicate from now on. At least with email there was no character limit. There was only so much you could convey in a 140 character text. Sarah, unlike some of her colleagues, wasn't afraid of the internet. Most days she remembered to check her electronic inbox.

29

She didn't use the web for pleasure, not unless you counted the web-searches she carried out late at night, after a drink or three. Surfing the net, they called it, although the metaphor didn't work for her. You couldn't surf a net, only get tangled up in it. She had learned not to put her own name into Yahoo. There, intermingled with the news reports and guides to British MPs, were sites where men talked about women, and what they'd like to do with them. What most of them wanted to do with her was pervertedly predictable.

Sarah attended the third reading of the International Development bill, a set of sensible measures on the path to delivering the government's promise to devote 0.7% of Gross Domestic Product to Overseas Aid. Clare Short, the minister, was away, so it was left to the junior minister to introduce it. Should Sarah get back in, this was the sort of junior role she might be offered: somebody's deputy. Would such a job, combined with constituency casework, satisfy her? At forty, you ought to be entering the most important phase of your career, not biding your time. She had worked hard for seven long years yet had little to show for them. Regular small achievements, all of them to do with casework, not policy. No big ones.

If she got the Police Federation job, would the role satisfy her? In some ways, it would be a retrograde step, taking Sarah back to a career she'd left in the late 80s. It meant working closely with police officers. Not the more genteel, civilised ones, but the kind who got involved in federation affairs: the police equivalent of the trade union activists at Labour Party meetings. She got on with them without being *of them*. She had more in common with an MP like Gill Temperley, even though she was on the other side.

Back in her office, she worked through a pile of correspondence with Hugh. Now and then, their shoulders touched. At one point, his thigh brushed hers, and she felt a little sexual *frisson*. Not the first time he'd fuelled her middle aged urges. She used to think he was gay, which made it fine for her to fantasise about turning him. Recently, however, he'd made a point of talking about women he found attractive, even solicited her advice about asking one of them out. Hugh was good looking and very clever. He kept his political cards close to his chest but was probably to the left of her, as you'd expect, given his age. He'd be a great catch for someone. But he was ten years too young for her, just as Eric was ten years too old.

Another message from Nick flashed up on the screen.

'Who's that?' Hugh asked. He'd dealt with Nick before, couldn't have found him memorable. Either that or he was being tactful, not letting Sarah know that he knew.

'It's the guy doing my website. Can you send him the stuff he's asking for?'

'A website? That's brilliant. I've always said you should have one.'

Now that she thought about this, he had mentioned it a couple of times. Sarah decided to flatter him a little.

'And you thought I wasn't listening? Oh ye of little faith.'

He gave her an affectionate smile. 'What's the URL?'

'Sarah Bone dot com. But I don't know if anything's up just yet.'

Hugh found the prototype web site: *SarahBone.Com is still being constructed, but please come back soon.* There was a little box in the corner. Sarah typed in the code she'd noted from one of Nick's emails and pressed 'enter.' There was a short biography accompanied by the photo she'd just had taken, wearing her favourite white dress with a red scarf. The photographer had wanted her in a red dress. She didn't own one. Too much red didn't suit her.

Hugh scrolled down the page and brought up a photo of Sarah outside the Commons. It was accompanied by a paragraph about her year as Prisons Minister. Next down was a photo of Sarah addressing a decent size crowd in the Market Square, titled *Campaigning for You.* Her best-known campaign, sadly, had been for Ed Clark, a double murderer who, she discovered after his release, was guilty of at least one of the murders he'd been sent down for.

No matter how many individuals you helped, there would never be enough of them to make the difference. Last election, she'd been lucky: a scandal engulfed her Conservative opponent.

This time, her opponent was a GP with three kids. She was also a lay preacher. Margaret Powell. Little chance of scandal. If anyone was prone to a damaging news story in this campaign, it was Sarah.

There were tales that would cost her if presented in a salacious way. None had yet become public. Not the murder of Andrew Saint in her Majorcan villa, now being rented out for her by a Spanish holiday company. Not her affair with married former County Councillor and government drugs advisor Paul Morris. Three years ago, she'd been in Paul's flat mere minutes before he was murdered by a person or persons unknown. Nor the espionage allegations about her late father and grandfather, a cabinet minister under Harold Wilson in the 60s. The evidence was due to be released under the 30-year-rule. She'd managed to get it suppressed.

Sir Hugh Bone MP was remembered for his knowledge of the Security Services, and for being a steady hand at a time of great political paranoia. What would Sarah be remembered for, were she to die tomorrow? Nothing substantial. Interested in Justice issues but only lasted five minutes as a junior minister. She'd been an MP since '95. Several of the '97 recruits had already outshone her.

'There's something missing,' Hugh said.

'What,' she leant over him, letting her chest accidentally brush his shoulder.

'There's nothing about your politics.'

Sarah pointed at the logo in the top left-hand corner. 'There. Labour.'

'Not what I meant. A website's the ideal place to position yourself for the future. This says *New Labour* rather than *Old Labour*, but that's about all.'

'What would you have me do? There's a picture of me in the '95 by-election with Tony Benn on one side and Clare Short on the other. Or there's one of Harold Wilson holding me as a baby, back when he was seen as left wing himself.'

Hugh gave her an incredulous look.

'Yes, I really am that old.'

'You're a decade younger than Tony Blair. You ought to be selling yourself as Labour's future.'

There was only eight years between her and the PM, but Sarah decided not to correct him.

'What kind of future did you have in mind?'

'That's what I'm asking you. Can I talk frankly?'

'I should bloody hope so. We've worked together long enough.'

'I can't work out what kind of a socialist you are, or if you're a socialist at all.'

Sarah stood back, stung. But she'd asked for this and he deserved an answer.

'I'm a pragmatic socialist, not a revolutionary or a Marxist. I understand the inherent contradictions that came with arguing for socialism in a capitalist society.'

'A reformist?'

'Mostly, I'm campaigning for social justice, making it up as I go along.'

'That's the big question, isn't it? How do we achieve social justice while still keeping the votes of the better off? That's the question Blair thinks he's answered.'

'We're not moving fast enough. Labour governments never last that long.'

'You don't think we'll win this time?'

'I don't think I'll win, but that's a different matter.'

Foot and mouth had peaked. The election would be called soon. In June, her six years as an MP would be over. She could start again. At forty.

'I hope you're wrong,' Hugh said. When she didn't reply, he returned to her website. 'You know, I like the idea of a photo of Harold Wilson holding you as a baby. With the right caption, it could be funny and touching at the same time. Sarah Bone – born into the Labour family.'

'I'll see if I can find it. Also, I think the front page needs more text.'

'We could link some policy documents and sections from speeches.'

'I'm more interested in giving people a way to donate.'

'What about a form for people to join Labour, maybe sign up to canvas?'

'Get all that written down.'

He flashed her the admiring smile that made her suspect he had a crush on her. Without thinking, she mirrored it, then quickly looked away.

What would happen if she gave Hugh the come on? The election would be called any day, and their working relationship would no longer be an issue. It would be nice to go out with Hugh, nice to be with anyone, after the long drought that had followed Paul Morris. But Hugh surely saw her as a boss, not a potential bed-mate. She wondered if he'd even noticed that she'd lost weight.

'Look at the time,' she told him. 'Christ, I need to get something to eat. What about you, got anything on tonight?'

'I have a date. That Lib Dem researcher I told you about.'

'Oh, right. Going anywhere nice? Sorry, I sound like a hairdresser.'

Hugh smiled and she felt like his mother. What had she been thinking?

'Her local. Just for a drink or two. And whatever ensues from that.'

SEVEN

Nick Cane had changed in the twelve or more years since Bilal last saw him. He was heavier. The skin around his square jaw was a little looser. But he still had all of his hair. The faint lines around his eyes bestowed character rather than age.

It took Nick a moment to recognise him. Bilal expected Nick to use his anglicised, schoolboy name, which was also the pet name that Sam used: Billy. Billy Goat, Bilal used to describe himself as: gruff and argumentative, determined to get his way. He'd been a brash fifteen-year-old, angry at a world that had taken away both of his parents. Mr Cane was the only teacher who knew how to handle him. Especially after he met Billy's sister at a parents' evening and took a shine to her.

Recognition dawned on the former teacher's face.

'Bilal! It's been a long time.'

'Hope you don't mind me turning up like this.'

'Not at all. Come in. I'm on the top floor, I'm afraid.'

Nick led Bilal up to his flat. Without asking, he put the kettle on.

'Tea?'

'Please. Some computer set-up you have. Is that a CD burner?'

'For work. I make my living off the internet. Not teaching these days.'

'I heard what happened.'

A wry smile, not embarrassed. 'Thought you might have done.'

'Used to like a bit of wacky baccy myself. Someone has to grow it.'

'They do, but that's not me any more.'

'I've come about Naz. Hear about her husband?'

'I saw the paper.' Nick took a couple of mugs from a cupboard. 'How is she?'

'OK, considering. You know what Naz is like, she keeps it all in. The kids are taking it hard, as you'd expect.'

Nick poured boiling water onto tea bags. In his living room, he took the armchair, Bilal the sofa, beneath a Grateful Dead poster.

'So come on, then,' Nick said. 'To what do I owe this visit?'

'You and my sister.' Bilal began.

'That was donkey's years ago.'

'I heard you started seeing her again recently.'

'You heard wrong. I haven't seen Naz since not long after you left Stoneywood in – when was that?'

'1989. You'd been going out with her for the best part of a year.'

'We'd become friends, but she was always going to marry a Muslim, not me. We didn't want anyone to get the wrong impression, stopped seeing each other.'

Bilal kept his smile friendly but sceptical. 'I was young and stupid back then. Not so stupid I couldn't see you were more than friends.'

'I would have liked us to be more, sure, but Nazia was a good girl. You know what I mean.'

Nick was protecting Naz's honour. There had defo been more to it than that. One time Bilal had come home from school early, seen his sister's bra on the living room floor. He'd cleared out quick.

'There's no need to fib, Nick. Nazia told me she's seeing you again.'

'Somebody's wires are crossed, Bilal. It's been nearly twelve years. I was out of circulation for five of those, and I haven't once run into her since I got out. What difference does it make, anyway?'

Nick was looking him straight in the eye and it was this that made Bilal blurt the whole thing out. 'Her husband's brother accused Naz of having an affair and murdering Omar so that she could be with her lover.'

'Jesus. And you think I'm part of this?'

'I couldn't think of anyone else it might be.'

'Do you believe me?'

'I want to. But if you're telling the truth I'm going to need your help.'

*

36

Sarah owned three properties, but only the Nottingham one bore vestiges of her personality. Her London flat had just two pictures on the walls: a framed poster for Huston's *The Misfits*, with Montgomery Clift, Clarke Gable and Marilyn Monroe as jigsaw pieces that did not interlock, decorated the living room. Above the kitchen counter, in a clip-frame, was an A4 flyer for her first election, the presidency of the University of Nottingham Students Union. *Sarah Bone: working for you.* There was a black and white image of her, wide-eyed, with awkward hair. She had not long since ditched her NHS glasses and been persuaded, by Nick, to let her hair grow out from the feminist short back and sides she'd favoured since starting uni. In the photo, her hair hadn't yet grown to the length that she had worn it ever since, sweeping around her shoulders. Beneath the image were the words: *your anti-Thatcher candidate.* They had worried that Sarah's gender might, in some way, associate her with the Prime Minister. The word *Labour* only appeared once, next to her name in the mocked-up ballot paper at the bottom of the flyer.

What would she do with this place when she lost in June? A London flat had its uses, but not one in Westminster. Were she to move to Leatherhead, she'd need to sell both flats in order to afford somewhere decent. The villa in Majorca should be first to go, but its recent history prevented that. She could sell Nottingham and rent this place out to another MP. That way, were she to get back in next time…

Stop being so fucking defeatist, she told herself. Tempting to reopen the bottle of red she'd begun the previous night, but she needed a clear head. She booted up her computer. This block had recently, at huge expense, been fitted with broadband internet. Broadband was the future, the MPs in the building had been assured, but Sarah was pissed off about having to sign a long-term contract. So were the other MPs who represented marginal seats. Most of them barely used the internet. In the end, they'd compromised on signing contracts that were renewable every six months. Thus far, the system worked. Pages loaded quickly and emails went off in a flash, much more quickly than when she used her computer at home.

There was a new email from Nick. Her website was 'nearly good to go'. Since when did he use such Americanisms? The site looked cleaner and stronger, but didn't have everything she'd asked for. She decided to call him.

He answered on the second ring.

'Hallo, stranger. What do you think of the web-site?'

'It's fantastic, thanks. Only...' She explained what was missing.

'I put in as much of that stuff as I could without messing up the design. The thing is, you can have all the content you want if you don't mind it looking crap. But then nobody will read it. Or you can have a smart looking site in a font big enough that people are comfortable reading it online and they'll leave with a warm, *you know what, I think I might just vote for her* glow.'

Sarah laughed. 'I've missed your frankness. Still, I'll need to talk to Winston before I sign off on it going live.'

'When are you back in Nottingham?'

'Tomorrow night.'

'Maybe we could meet, look at it together after you've talked to him. Work out whatever tweaks you want to add.'

'Maybe. I mean, I'd like that. Only...'

She didn't need to spell out how she couldn't be seen socialising with him in the run up to a tight election. He was still potentially toxic.

'There's something I want to discuss. A friend in trouble. I could come to you. After dark. You have the internet at home?'

'Only 14.4.'

'Mine's 56.6. If you want to work on the website, best come to me.'

'Or we could meet in London. I've just had broadband installed.'

'Broadband? I thought that was a fairy tale. Can I come now?'

She laughed. 'From your point of view, what tweaks does the site still need?'

'The campaign page is a bit out of date.'

'That's because I haven't done much campaigning lately.'

'Pity. A popular campaign would help your vote.'

'I'm not sure that anything will help my vote sufficiently to get me back in. Last time was a fluke.'

'I remember. I was there. I remember how the evening ended, too.'

Sarah gave a soft laugh. They had gone to bed together, her too drunk and exhausted to worry about the consequences. Too exhausted to stay awake, either, so nothing had happened.

'It'll be different this time,' she told him, and they ended the call.

Should she have told him that she had a job interview tomorrow, on the other side of the country? No point in getting his hopes up, then putting an obstacle in the way. If they did get back together, whatever they still had might fade as quickly as warm breath in winter air. She was not the woman she used to be. While Nick, as far as she could tell, had hardly changed at all.

EIGHT

B ilal was surprised when, a couple of days after he'd visited, Nick rang.

'I've been doing some reading on the internet.'

'Can you believe anything on there?'

'Most newspapers have a website these days. Even the Nottingham Post. You can't believe everything you read in newspapers, but facts are still facts. Anyway, when I put *insulin murder* into Alta Vista, one name kept coming up.'

'Beverley Allitt? The nurse who killed the kids, Grantham way.'

'She used insulin for some of her killings. But the most famous case is Claus Van Bülow. Early 80's – remember?'

'I saw the movie. Jeremy Irons played him.'

'He was accused of murdering his wife by injecting her with insulin, putting her into an irreversible coma. Found guilty, but the medical evidence was sloppy and he was freed on appeal. The judge found insulin played no part in the wife's coma. Seems it's very hard to murder somebody with insulin. Cyanide's far more efficient. Or some form of morphine, wasn't it, Shipman used?'

Harold Shipman, a GP who'd grown up in Sherwood, had been convicted of multiple murders the year before. 'Have you told Nazia what she's accused of?'

'Not directly, but I know the police have been to see her in Birmingham. They didn't arrest her or anything.'

'From the little I've read, insulin murder's hard to commit, but even harder to prove. Also, when Fahd found this so-called syringe and removed it from a wardrobe, he tainted it as evidence. There's no way the police would be able to use it in court. Didn't the post mortem say that Omar died of natural causes?'

'There was no post-mortem. The family doctor signed off on the death as a heart attack. Nazia affirmed to the funeral directors that death was due to natural causes. Autopsies are against Islam. Omar suffered from angina and the doctor's a family friend. He knew that the funeral had to take place very quickly.'

'Seems to me that Fahd is stirring the pot. He has it in for Nazia.'

'Fahd knows powerful people. If he wants to create trouble, he can.'

Nick scratched his chin. 'Why do I know Fahd's name? Was he a Labour councillor once?'

'He was active in the late 80s. Stood once, but didn't get in. Then got himself expelled for violent conduct.'

'It comes back to me now. As I recall, he waved a big stick around at his local party's AGM and got the whole branch suspended.'

'I don't know the details,' Bilal said. 'I wasn't old enough to vote.'

'I'll find out. If Fahd's going to slander Nazia, we might need some ammunition to fight back with. I'll talk to my friend Tony. He'll remember.'

Bilal thanked his old teacher. They arranged to talk the next day.

'I hope Nazia will be back by then.'

'Give her my best,' Nick said. 'I'd like to see her but, given the gossip you've told me about, that might be tricky.'

'Not tricky, impossible. Nazia has to mourn for four months and ten days, during which she's not allowed to be alone with men, aside from blood relatives.'

'Islam doesn't trust women much, does it?' Nick said, then thought better of the comment. 'Sorry, you don't knock a person's religion. Please forget I said that. By the way, do you know if Fahd's still in the Labour Party?'

'I don't think so. Did you rejoin after you got out?'

'I didn't. I'm not much of a joiner these days.'

'We understand that the circumstances of this interview are to be kept entirely confidential and will, of course, respect that.'

'Appreciated.' Sarah was wearing her soberest, most expensive outfit, a grey suit she often chose for speeches as Prisons minister, along with a pale silk blouse to enhance her femininity and a silver dragonfly brooch, because she liked it.

'Your loyalty to your present seat is admirable. You must have had offers.'

41

'One or two.' This wasn't strictly true. There'd been the Chesterfield approach, which she had considered carefully before rejecting it. She'd even had a word with Tony Benn, the retiring MP. He'd told her he'd been facing a reselection battle. Moreover, there was no guarantee he'd hold onto the seat even if he were to be reselected. This had made it easier for Sarah to follow her instincts and stick with Nottingham West.

'We understand that, in four or five years' time, you might wish to return to the Commons. We would not hold that against you, or stand in your way.'

'I can assure you that I'd give this job my all. I'm not looking for a stop-gap.'

Smiles all round. 'Perhaps you could tell us why you left the force?'

The toughest question. She decided on an approximation of honesty.

'It was a different force then. Institutionally racist and sexist. Worse, we were being politicised by a government that I profoundly disagreed with.'

'You're referring to the Miners' strike?'

'Not only that. I wanted to make a difference but wasn't prepared to keep my mouth shut while I worked my way up the ranks. That's why I became a trade union research officer and prepared myself to become an MP.'

'And got in at the first attempt. Very impressive.'

'It was meant to be a dry run. I was hoping for a safe seat in '97. But there was a big swing my way in an unexpected by-election. I got lucky.'

'The force is still dominated by men much older than you. They're very set in their ways. As is the federation. Are you up to dealing with us?'

'I wouldn't be here otherwise. Anyway, I'd be the one giving the orders. So the question becomes *are you up to dealing with me?*'

The interview only got easier after that. They'd made up their mind in the first five minutes. Sarah waited outside while they made it look like they had to discuss their decision. Five minutes later, they came and offered her the job, subject to a successful salary negotiation and her losing her seat at the imminent election.

NINE

When the website went live, Sarah called Nick to thank him. 'Looks great. Sorry, we haven't been able to meet. We'll have time to catch up once I've lost this election.'

'You're not going to lose. The polls are excellent for Labour.'

'For Labour, yes. For me, no. I only got back in by a fluke last time.'

'What's the point of having a website if you're resigned to losing?'

'Losing battles are the ones you need to fight hardest. By the way, can we install a web counter so I can see how many visitors it gets?'

'Sure,' Nick told her, 'but you don't want one that's visible to the public. It looks embarrassing when the figures are low. I'll make sure we harvest the stats.'

Sarah was impressed. 'You internet people have your own language, don't you? Where did you learn to do this stuff?'

'I took a course, two years ago. A… friend twisted my arm.'

'Do you prefer it to teaching?'

'It's less sociable, but less tiring, too. At least, being self-employed, you know your boss won't hold your prison record against you.'

The minute she'd put her phone down, it rang. Eric.

'I owe you lunch,' she said.

'I think you might owe me a little more than that.'

He told her what the federation were offering. A big salary bump.

'It almost makes me want to throw the election,' she told him. 'Perhaps we could manufacture a juicy scandal to scupper my chances.'

'I'm not sure your new employers would like that.'

'Point taken. Please tell them I accept, subject to my availability after the election, and am looking forward to the job immensely.'

'Is that really true?'

'Of course.'

'You'll be missed. By me, not least of all.'

'There's nothing to keep me here, Eric. We had our chance.'

She heard him sigh. They arranged to meet for lunch in a few days' time.

The police phoned to request that Bilal come to the Central Police Station at his earliest convenience. He parked in North Sherwood Street and was shown to an austere interview room where a young female Detective Inspector joined him.

'We need to speak to your sister. When will Nazia be back?'

'I don't know. She's mourning and needs space.'

'We're aware of that, but we also need to talk to her again.'

'Why? Fahd's talking nonsense.'

'You don't think there was anything suspicious about Omar's death?'

'Not to my knowledge, no. He was not a healthy man.'

'Nevertheless, his brother has accused your sister of having an affair.'

'He made that accusation shortly before Omar died. Naturally, I told Nazia. She assured me that there was no truth in it.'

'Who did Fahd accuse Nazia of having an affair with?'

'He didn't know.' Bilal wasn't going to throw Nick's name into the pot, not now that he had met up with him and concluded that nothing had been going on. Twelve years ago... that was a different matter.

'How well do you know your sister's brother-in-law?'

'Not very well. Fahd and I are very different kinds of people.'

'How do you mean? Religiously?'

'I don't talk religion with him. I don't really know him. I suppose you could say that I don't like him much.'

'And is that feeling mutual?'

'I don't think Fahd likes many people.'

This brought a smile from the inspector.

'What you're saying is that his allegations about how his brother died are the result of grief.'

'I think that Fahd has a bad side, a malicious streak, call it what you like, and that he's decided to take it out on my sister, who is a decent person.'

'Understood, but we still need to talk to Nazia.'

Bilal tried ringing Nazia again when he got home. Once again, she didn't pick up. Nor did Sana when he tried her landline. He decided to go for a walk in nearby Wollaton Park. He often went there to think things through. The place became busy on warm weekends but even then there were acres of space. This afternoon it was just him and a procession of dog walkers. Bilal did a circuit of the lake, which took twenty minutes, then visited the deer nearby. Two hundred red deer were allowed to roam wild in the park. A large sign said they'd been there since the Fourteenth century and warned the public to steer well clear of them during calving season, which was imminent.

With Omar gone, Bilal knew, there was nothing to stop his sister becoming his and Sam's surrogate. Nothing, that was, apart from Fahd's absurd accusations.

He wandered too close to the roe deer. One of the stags raised its horns in unambiguous threat. Bilal stepped back in acknowledgement of the magnificent animal, then turned and increased his pace, wanting to get home before his wife finished her shift. He would prepare Sam a nice late lunch, then they would have an afternoon nap, as they often did on a Friday. He wanted to make love to her and give nature another chance to take its course. A slim chance was still a chance, just ask any of the poor suckers who bought lottery tickets week after week. Although, in their case, somebody, somewhere was bound to win.

TEN

S arah went down to the chamber to hear the Foreign Secretary answer questions about nuclear defence. She'd belonged to CND in the 80s but become agnostic about nuclear weapons. She saw them as a rhetorical device rather than a real one.

'We are the closest ally and one of the oldest friends of the United States,' Robin Cook concluded. 'Plainly, that will be reflected in any judgment that we make if we are asked to be helpful.'

One Tory teased Cook about this being his last day as Foreign Secretary – as though Labour were likely to lose the election – and cited a time when he'd described Britain's pretence of being a nuclear power as 'nonsense on stilts.' This brought a good laugh from his own side but short shrift from Cook. Accusing politicians of hypocrisy was like accusing a mother of not being a virgin. The main qualification for a senior political role, Sarah had come to believe, was a willingness to tell lies for the greater good. When she was in the police, they had a phrase for this: *noble cause corruption*, where you framed someone who you knew was guilty but didn't have sufficient evidence to convict. In the police, if you were caught, it got you sacked. In Politics, sacrificing principles for power generally got you promoted.

Sarah had a train to catch. She expected the election to be called over the weekend. Today was her last chance to make a speech during this parliament, possibly her final speech in the Commons. But the debate was ending, with little business to follow. She had constituency correspondence to finish.

In her office, Hugh handed her a bunch of letters to sign. Lately, some of her constituents had started to use email. Sarah dealt with those personally. If the internet kept expanding at the current rate she'd have to give Hugh her log-in details for parliamentary work and set up a private account for friends' emails.

Hugh put the kettle on and made them both a mug of tea. He leant over to lift the boiling kettle from the floor. She admired his

47

bum. Gill Temperley sometimes teased Sarah about having her wicked way with Hugh. The Tory MP had no compunctions about having discreet flings with the pretty young men she hired. Gill's husband knew about her dalliances, and presumably had his own affairs. Old school Tories like them saw promiscuity as part of life. Fidelity to one partner was a boring, bourgeois social construct, fit only for the *hoi polloi*. Intellectually, Sarah accepted this argument, but she'd never been drawn to sleeping around. She only wished she had one partner to be faithful to.

'Out with your girlfriend tonight?' she asked Hugh.

'Tania, the Liberal research assistant you helped set me up with?'

'Uh-huh.'

'She thought I was gay and we were just going out as mates.'

'Did you put her right?'

'Oh yes. However, sadly for me, turns out she *is* gay.'

'Sorry about that.'

'Never mind. You keep me too busy to have a love life.'

'Rubbish. But what do you say to a works' outing? Let me take you to dinner, a thank you for all of your hard work this last four years.'

'That'd be a pleasure,' Hugh said, brushing back his long fringe. 'Long as it isn't your way of telling me that I'm getting the chop.'

'It's my way of warning you that the voters are likely to give *me* the chop.'

'They wouldn't be so stupid.'

'How little you know.'

She was flirting with him and he was responding. Why hadn't she tried this before? They agreed to have dinner on Monday evening.

The third time that Bilal called, Nazia answered her mobile phone.

'Where have you been?' Bilal asked.

'I needed some time alone, so I've been back in the house. Sana is bringing over Ahmad and Tamazur tomorrow afternoon.'

'You haven't been with them?' What had she been up to, back in Nottingham all this time? Meeting her lover?

'They preferred to be in Birmingham. They understand how I need to be at home for a day or two to sort things out.'

'OK, fine.'

It wasn't fine. Bilal couldn't see how Nazia had it in her to leave the kids in someone else's care only days after their dad had died.

'There's something I need to warn you about,' he told Nazia.

'The police? They want to question me again. They left a message, too. I'm seeing them in the morning, before Sana brings over the children.'

'Did they say why they wanted to talk to you?'

'Routine, after an unexplained death, they said. I told them that Dr Shah put heart attack on the death certificate and I'd gone over it all with an officer who came to see me in Birmingham. They said they needed to be on the safe side.'

'Fahd has been in touch with them, or so he says.'

'Fahd? What's it got to do with him?'

Bilal took a deep breath. He would rather be having this conversation face to face, but she needed to be warned.

'He claims to have found a hypodermic needle in your wardrobe.'

'In my wardrobe! What was he doing in there?'

'He thinks you deliberately gave Omar an insulin overdose.'

'That's...' His sister went quiet. Bilal heard a bell ring.

'Nazia?'

The bell rang again.

'Someone's at the door. I've got to go.'

She hung up.

49

ELEVEN

S arah liked to wake in her Nottingham bed on Friday mornings. She spent more nights in her London flat, but that wasn't home. She'd rarely shared the flat's three-quarter bed with a lover. It wouldn't be much of a wrench to sell it when she'd lost the election. Whereas she'd lived in Nottingham, on and off, since Autumn 1979. The city felt more like home than Chesterfield, where she'd grown up. Everything she cared about was in this ground floor flat, ten minutes' walk from the centre.

The day ahead was full. At least she didn't have a surgery until Saturday afternoon. If an election was called, tomorrow's would be her last. Surgeries did carry on during General Elections, but local councillors took them so that the MP could get on with electioneering. Pity, because Sarah preferred doing surgeries to knocking on doors. She'd rather give people practical help than pander for votes.

She was finishing her breakfast muesli when the doorbell rang. Before answering it, she glanced through the window to check who was outside. A bloke in a rusty brown leather jacket. Not many men wore short leather jackets these days. Even Nick, last time she'd run into him, had forsaken his for a formless, brushed cotton thing. This would be a builder or a journalist, most likely. She used the door's chain. You could never be too careful.

The man on the other side looked familiar. He was around her age, with a receding hairline and an ingratiating grin that confirmed her suspicion: journalist.

'Sarah. Peter Carlson. Remember me?'

'Didn't we talk for… *The New Statesman*?'

'When you were Prisons minister. Well remembered. Sorry to turn up out of the blue. I'm in the area. You might be able to help with a story I'm working on.'

'This isn't the way to go about it, Peter.'

'Call me Pete, please. I know, and I'll go away if you want, contact your office, all that jazz. But I reckon they'll be calling a General Election on Monday and, after that, your time will be circumscribed.'

'That does seem likely. I can have a quick coffee with you but, before I let you in, you'd better tell me what this is about.'

'I'm with the *Sunday Times Insight* team now. I'm doing a story about someone you used to be friendly with.'

Later, she would reflect that she knew who he was going to name even before he got the next two words out. She'd always known this was coming.

'Andrew Saint.'

Bilal decided to drive to Omar and Nazia's place in The Park. He wasn't happy about how they'd left things. Suppose last night's interruption had been the police, come to arrest Nazia? He'd called her back a few minutes after she hung up on him. Her line had been constantly engaged, or off the hook. Which worried him.

The night before, he and Sam had discussed the surrogacy again. He'd had to tell her about Nazia's offer. She'd offered before, a year ago, but, back then, they'd doubted whether Omar would stand for it.

'Maybe it'd be good for her,' Sam said. 'Take her mind off Omar's death.'

'Before, the family would have freaked,' Bilal argued. 'However, if Omar had given permission, they might have had to put up with it. With him gone…'

'Nazia doesn't give a shit what the family thinks. Why should you?'

Bilal knew that Sam was right. Trouble was, he did care. He wanted Uncle's respect. Part of him needed to prove that he was better than Fahd, who had no wife, no child. There were two options for surrogacy. He and Sam could use donor sperm to fertilise his sister, then the baby would be a blood relative, which was something. Or Nazia could have an operation that involved her being implanted with Sam's eggs, and inject Bilal's sperm to fertilise them. This relied upon the quality of his sperm and his wife's eggs, neither of which had been proved a propitious match so far, but the doctors said that this technique, called *in vitro* might, nevertheless, work. If it did, the baby would be entirely theirs, should even look like them. Last night, they'd agreed to ask Nazia if she was willing to give it a try. But not if his sister was likely to have the baby in prison.

Bilal parked on the road outside her house in The Park and phoned again. Still engaged. He walked up the drive. Nazia rarely used the double garage because it was tricky to get out of when their other car was parked in front of the house. Today, Omar's BMW and Nazia's Alfa Romeo were on the drive.

He looked around. An intruder could, if they knew what they were up to, access the property from next door's garden by sneaking through gaps in the hedge at the back. He looked through the hedge. No sign of anyone. Except… Bilal passed the parked cars, giving him a clear view of the double garage door. Across it, in bright red, crude capital letters, low enough to have been concealed by the cars, was spray painted the word, 'WHORE!'

He tried the front doorbell. No answer. He got out his phone, thought about dialling three nines but, as he did, a large people carrier pulled up at the bottom of the driveway. Nazia, Tamazur and Ahmad got out, then called goodbyes to the woman in the driver's seat: Sana. Bilal went to help his sister with the shopping she was carrying.

'I hope you haven't been waiting long.'

'I just got here. Send the kids inside. There's something I want to show you.'

Nazia told the children that they could watch TV for an hour. Then Bilal took her to the side of the house.

'Was that there when you left?'

'If it was, I didn't notice. Sana brought the kids back earlier. Surely one of us would have noticed it. We only went shopping an hour ago. How fresh is it?'

'Hard to tell with spray paint, but it looks fresh. I'm not sure it's a good idea for you to stay here. Sam and I think you should all stay with us for a while.'

'That's very kind of you both. Can I think about it?'

'Of course. How did your interview with the police go?'

'OK. I told them about Fahd's behaviour over the years, the

passes he's made, the way he behaved at the funeral. I think they have his measure.'

'I hope you're right. Why don't you let me see if I can get rid of that graffiti before the kids see it?'

'That would be really good of you.'

Removing the single word took a lot of elbow grease and turpentine, but the stain left behind was, at least, illegible. Bilal was still outside, cleaning up, when a police car pulled up in the drive. Three officers – an unusual number – got out.

'Is Nazia Khan home?' the one with sergeant's stripes asked.

'Inside, yes. Why?'

'Would you get her, please? We have a search warrant.'

Sarah did remember Pete Carlson. He was that rare journalist, one who belonged to the Labour Party and wasn't afraid to say so. He didn't only work for left-wing rags. This meant he was probably good. Otherwise the right-wing papers wouldn't touch him. If she were going to be asked about Andrew Saint, better to talk to him than somebody from the Mail, Telegraph or one of the Sunday tabloids. Pete wouldn't be looking to hurt the party in the run up to a General Election. Even so, she wasn't going to tell him much.

'Nice place,' he said, checking out her posters and books. 'Just you?'

'Just me.'

She remembered how, when he had interviewed her before, he'd come on to her: only a little, but enough to let her know he was interested. He was her type, insofar as she had one, and ostensibly single. At the time, however, she'd been in the full flood of her affair with Paul Morris.

'Been asking people how they think you'll do this time round. Most of them reckon your chances are fifty: fifty.'

'I'd take those odds.'

'Meaning you think the true odds are worse.'

She gave a theatrical shrug, which, oddly, appeared to embarrass Pete. She realised that she was wearing a loose T-shirt with no bra. She'd just flashed him. Rather than blush, she forced herself into politician mode.

'I should warn you that I may need to go off the record at some point.'

'Understood.' He got out a notebook rather than a dictaphone. Old fashioned. She liked that. 'How well did you know Andrew Saint?'

'We were at university together. I'm not sure whether Andrew finished his degree. He must have done. He was always into wheeler-dealing, even back then.'

'Drugs?'

'Maybe, but they were never my thing.' Not quite true, though near enough, especially when you compared Sarah's intake to most of her peers. 'Thing is, Andy was more my boyfriend's friend. They used to go the pub, gigs, the usual. He liked to play board games on a Sunday afternoon, I remember that. Anything from *Go* to *Cluedo*. I joined in a few times.'

'My understanding is that Saint was in a business partnership with your then boyfriend, Nick Cane.'

'I don't know anything about that.'

'And that Andrew fled the country back in '92, when Nick Cane was busted for an illicit cannabis factory in the caves below his flat'

Which was only a few hundred yards from here, as Pete doubtless knew, but wasn't tactless enough to mention.

'I didn't live in the city then. I don't know what went on in those years. By the time I came back to Nottingham, Nick was in prison and Andrew was long gone. We're talking ancient history here.'

'Nick Cane is still around.'

'He's served his sentence. He deserves the chance to be rehabilitated.'

'I couldn't agree more, but I'm afraid he won't talk to me.'

'I suppose that's his right.'

'It is.'

Pete left a pregnant pause. Sarah wasn't foolish enough to fill it. If Pete had found out that she and Nick were the people who had found Andrew and Nancy's bodies on Majorca, she'd have to go off the record, plead with him to drop the story. In exchange for… she didn't know what.

'Did you like him?' Pete asked.

'Andrew had a certain… rough charm.'

'Did you know that he cosied up to politicians for a while?'

'Not to me.'

'Particularly a Tory ex-minister, Gill Temperley.'

'You'd better talk to Gill about that, I've no comment to make.'

'You didn't introduce them?'

Had she? Maybe she had. 'I'm not… let's just say "no comment".'

Andrew had given Gill a PR role for his bullshit company, Saint Holdings. Possibly, in hindsight, he'd done this for political cover. At the time, Sarah was convinced that he wanted to get into Gill's knickers. Andrew liked older women. Unfortunately for him, Gill – while in a notoriously open marriage – preferred much younger men. Wisely, she'd bailed on Andrew's company well before his demise, giving her what the Americans called 'plausible deniability.'

'Do you still see Nick Cane?'

'We don't move in the same circles, but our paths cross from time to time.'

'Let me be clear, I'm not after him. I'm after a much bigger story about how drugs crime works in the Twenty-First century. His old friend's murder will be part of that. And his ex-girlfriend, too.'

'Ex?'

'Yes. Nancy Tull, who was killed with Saint, used to go out with Nick, that's what I heard. They were schoolteachers together.'

'I didn't know Nick when he was a teacher.'

Sarah had only briefly met the woman who had been killed alongside Andrew, at Saint's Notting Hill home. Nancy Tull, while strikingly attractive, was clearly in the grip of crack addiction.

'She was also pregnant with Saint's child when she was killed.'

'The poor girl,' Sarah said. This also, she hadn't known. It shook her. She'd pictured Andrew with an escort who'd come along for his money. If Nick used to go out with Nancy, if she used to be a secondary school teacher – all that shouldn't make a difference, but it did. For a few seconds, she couldn't help but picture the scenario. Andrew thought he was safe. He'd landed a beautiful woman, got her clean, and was about to begin a family with her. While they were sleeping, a man kicked in their front door and walked into the bedroom with a gun in his hand…

'Are you all right?'

'Give me a moment, please.'

That day in Majorca, Nick had tried to keep Sarah from seeing the bloated bodies on the bed. But she'd had to look, and the gruesome sight still haunted her. Pregnant. Poor Andrew. Poor Nancy.

Her phone rang and she apologised to Pete before answering it.

'Sarah, it's Brian from *The Post*. I was wondering if you'd be willing to give me a statement re the death of Omar Khan for Monday's paper.'

'He was my dentist. He was a nice man. I don't really have a lot more to say, Brian. I thought you'd covered his death already. What did he die of, a heart attack?'

'That's just it. Omar's younger brother is going round telling people that it was murder. The police have taken the wife in for questioning.'

'Murder? It sounds very unlikely. It also means the subject's *sub judice*. I can't say anything. Sorry. I'm with someone, I've got to go.'

She hung up.

'Murders are like buses,' Pete said. 'You wait ages for one then three turn up at once. Want to tell me about this one?'

Sarah told him the little she knew. 'I'm afraid your time's up, Pete.'

'If you run into Nick Cane, vouch for me, would you? He's a hard man to track down.'

'I will, but there's not much chance of my seeing him,

especially once they've called the election.'

'I thought he was managing your web-site,' Pete said at the door.

This time, Sarah was fairly sure, she did blush. She managed to prevaricate. 'Nick does do web design these days. But you'd have to ask Winston, my agent, about all that. He's the one keen to get me into the age of the world wide web.'

'I may be back in Nottingham again soon. Would it be OK if I tried to take you out for a coffee one day, campaign allowing?'

'I'd like that.'

Pete wouldn't intentionally damage her, she was fairly certain, but he was a pro: he'd take his investigation where it led him. Sarah phoned Winston and told him that, should the question be asked, he must make it clear that she had no involvement in Nick's work on her web-site. Which was true…ish. She considered calling Nick, decided against. Better to be able to deny having spoken to him. For all she knew, Nick wasn't rehabilitated. For all she knew, he could have been deep in business with Andrew but kept it from her. Probably not, but she had learnt not to trust her instincts, particularly where the men she cared for were concerned.

TWELVE

Constituency casework was the biggest part of an MP's job. On Saturday, during the first hour of her surgery at Stoneywood Library, Sarah discussed three social security cases, promised to follow up two immigration issues and counselled a council tenant who was at the end of her tether with noisy neighbours. The last, she was able to pass on to Georgia, the councillor accompanying her. Hugh would handle the other cases from Westminster while she was out campaigning.

She was undecided about how to let things develop when she took him out for dinner on Monday. Pete Carlson's visit was on her mind. Bedding an employee when the Sunday Times were on your case wouldn't be smart. Labour MPs were more heavily scrutinised that Tories. Not that long ago, Foreign Secretary Robin Cook had been forced to choose between his wife and his mistress because of a threatened news story. Moreover, women were more heavily scrutinised than men. Last thing Sarah needed was a scandal during the election. Especially as historical sex with an underage girl had done for her opponent in '97.

Sarah was, however, entitled to a date for Tony's wedding, a week on Saturday. Nick would be there. She couldn't go with him, but ought to take someone. Her research assistant was the perfect cover. That was why Gill Temperley got away with it for all this time, replacing her paramour with a younger model every year or two. Also, if Sarah were with Hugh, she was less likely to succumb to Nick purely because she wanted to have sex this century.

Georgia escorted the couple with noisy neighbours to another room. Sarah took a comfort break. The middle-aged man at the front of the queue when she returned was Asian, with matted hair, starting to grey, sunken eyes and a coarse beard that was greyer than his hair. He was not one of her regular visitors. She offered him her hand. He affected not to see it.

'I'm Sarah.'

'Fahd Khan.'

Alarm bells rang. 'How can I help you?'

'I'm one of your constituents. I want you to look into the case of my brother. He didn't live in your constituency but was, I think, your dentist.'

'He was,' she said. 'And my neighbour. Please accept my condolences. It's very sad when a close relative dies so young.'

'Thank you. But I am not sad. I am angry. You see, his widow murdered him. I want to see her punished. And I want your support.'

Despite the call from *The Post*, she hadn't seen this coming. Still, it wasn't uncommon for constituents to turn up with wild accusations. Grief did strange things to people.

'You should be careful what you say, Mr Khan. There are laws.'

'I'd advise,' Fahd told her, 'that you are careful what *you* say. I know many influential people in my community. If you offend us, we will not vote for you.'

'I suggest you to take a less aggressive tone, Mr Khan,' Sarah said, using her calm but cold voice. 'Would you talk like this to a male MP?'

Fahd ignored the question. 'You know that my sister-in-law has something in common with you.'

'I'm sorry?'

'You used to have a boyfriend called Nick Cane. So did she.'

Sarah was perplexed. 'No, I didn't know that. It seems unlikely.'

'It is true, ask him.'

'I don't see him very often.'

'You know that he is a criminal?'

'I know he had a criminal record, yes. It's publicly documented.'

'Still a criminal, from what I hear. Also, still Nazia's lover.'

Sarah was taken aback. 'You what?'

'He was her lover before she met her husband, when he was her brother Bilal's teacher. Omar knew it. He was very upset when he found out his wife was not a virgin, but he forgave her, because he was a better man than me. But Omar could not forgive her when she started up with him again, in the last few months.'

'You know this *how*?'

'I told him what was going on, advised him to divorce her. She would have lost her children, her home, everything. All for a criminal who lives in the red light zone. That's why she murdered my brother, before it got out and ruined her. This Nick Cane probably helped.'

'I repeat, be very careful what you say,' Sarah told him. 'Nazia's not the only person who can sue for slander.'

'It isn't slander when it's true,' Fahd stood, then added a parting salvo. 'Take the beam from your eyes, embrace the truth. It will save you. Support the murdering whore and you will be defeated long before she is. I will be applying to the coroner's court for my brother's body to be exhumed.'

When Fahd was gone, Sarah found herself fuming. She'd meant to steer clear of the Nazia Khan case. Omar Khan, unlike his brother, did not live in the constituency she represented. Now she needed to talk to Nick.

Georgia returned. 'Did he give you trouble?'

'You can say that again.'

'Who was he?'

'Fahd Khan, the dead dentist's brother. He stood for the council, I believe, before I became an MP. He quoted the bible at me: *take the beam from your eye before you remove the mote from mine.* That is the bible, isn't it?'

'New testament. *Matthew 7:3*, if memory serves.' Georgia belonged to an evangelical church. 'The hyperbole makes it popular with zealots. Everyone's vision is distorted, that's how I read it.'

'Thanks,' Sarah said. 'Please open a file on Fahd. Include a note saying he isn't to be left alone with anyone vulnerable. Including me.'

Bilal parked in the Trinity Square multi-storey, a stone's throw from the shabby Central Police Station where Nazia was being held. He'd taken the kids back to his while the police searched their home. He didn't know what they'd found, only that they had kept his sister in overnight.

Naz had been in custody for over twenty hours. This morning, she looked her age. In the dingy reception area they had a brief hug.

'I don't understand how they could have so many questions,' he said, once they were in his car.

'They didn't. It was the same questions, again and again,' Naz replied.

'Did they have any evidence at all?'

'They took my laptop, my phone, the sheets off my bed. The only so-called evidence is what Fahd claimed to have found. *A needle*. I used to nag Omar about disposing of them. Why one ended up in the wardrobe I have no idea. If it did.'

'The police seem to believe Fahd?'

'They think I'm this Scarlet Woman. I told them, Fahd's a lover spurned. They think he's a pure, religious type. We both know different.'

'Spurned?'

'At the funeral, Fahd took me aside. Which he shouldn't. We shouldn't have been alone together, even for a moment. He told me that, when my *iddah* was up, he wanted to marry me. "It's what Omar would have wanted" he told me, as though he were doing me a favour. As though I haven't seen him look at me with lust in his eyes ever since the very first time Omar introduced us.'

'And you told him to get lost?'

'I don't know what I said. I think I laughed.'

'And you told the police this? It explains a lot.'

'I told them. I don't think they believed me. But I kept telling them: Fahd has it in for me because I made it clear that I wasn't interested in him, at all.'

It wasn't just Fahd who suspected Nazia, it was Uncle, too. Best not to mention this. Did the police have any evidence? No, or they'd have charged her.

They stopped off in The Park to collect some things for her and the kids.

'What the hell's that?' Naz asked, when they pulled up in front of the house.

He'd only been gone an hour, but someone had been at work

with the spray can again. Similar style, but the letters were better formed, and today's graffiti used longer phrases: *MURDERING BITCH! FILTHY WHORE!*

'I'm sorry,' Bilal told her.

'How can people know, so quickly?'

'There was a short piece in today's paper,' Bilal explained, although that didn't account for yesterday's graffiti.

This morning, while they waited to hear that Nazia had been released, Sam had been phoning round to find her a new solicitor. Not easy on a Saturday. It shocked Bilal that her current solicitor – who had also been Omar's lawyer – had not protested when the police kept her in overnight, then resumed questioning her.

It was nearly four before they got back to Wollaton. Sam was sitting on the sofa next to a good-looking white woman about Nazia's age. She had a blonde bob and a crisp, white cotton top with metallic buttons. Naz and Sam embraced, then Sam introduced her guest.

'This is Mary Harris. She'd like to talk to you about taking on your case.'

The he polls still showed Labour firmly ahead. On the train to London, Sarah allowed herself to consider the faint possibility that she might win. Pull off a third win out of three, and she'd have no need to sell up, start a new job. In this unlikely future, she ought to work out what she wanted to accomplish in the next parliament.

'Sarah!' Steve Carter greeted her as they were exiting Westminster Tube for Portcullis House. He used to be her closest friend in the Commons but they'd drifted apart. He'd remained a junior minister while she'd stopped being one, which meant they hardly saw each other these days. 'What are you in for?'

'Clearing my office in case, you know…'

Steve forced a smile. 'You must have a chance, surely?'

'Half a chance. However, when it comes to fate and fortune, I've always been of the glass-half-empty tendency.'

'Why don't I take you for a drink, try and fill that glass up?'

Ten minutes later, they sat on the terrace. The dirty old Thames and the array of buildings that lined it looked magnificent beneath the hazy blue, polluted sky. Sarah told him about the job she had lined up.

'You won't get a view like this from the Police Federation headquarters,' Steve told her. 'Sure about taking that?'

'For the next parliamentary term, anyway. I shook on it.'

'You'll be looking for a safe seat. Any of the Nottingham MPs retiring?'

'Not bloody likely.'

'And if you do get back in, will you be hoping for the front bench?'

'A lot of other people in that queue. Quite a few have managed to jump ahead of me already. Are you expecting a promotion?'

'Not until Gordon takes over.'

Steve, a junior transport minister, had aligned himself with the Chancellor of the Exchequer's party within a party.

'Not sure I was ever cut out to be a minister,' she said. 'Too much paperwork and message discipline.'

'Know what might suit you? The Whip's office. Ever considered that?'

'No.' Whips were essential to government, making sure that MPs voted when and how the leadership needed them to. Labour's whips were all men in late middle age. The last Labour government, which ran from '74-79, had no working majority. At every single division, the whips had to bring in the sick and dying. Eventually, they lost one. Thatcher's Tories got in at the ensuing general election. And stayed there for the next eighteen years.

'Things are changing, and they badly need women. Plenty of power in the whip's office. It can be interesting: you get to find out where the bodies are buried.'

'Think I'm tough enough?'

'To push around your peers? Course you are.'

'I always hated those bossy schoolgirls, the ones who'd have been prefects if we'd had them at my comp. The Tory party's full of women like that.'

'You can tell people what to do without being bossy. Cajole, seduce, threaten if necessary. You're more than capable of that kind of behaviour.'

When Sarah got back to her office, Hugh asked if she could return a call from the *Evening Post*. She corrected him: the *Nottingham Post*. Her local paper had dropped the *Evening* from its name after moving from the city centre to a site by the canal, near the train station, on Castle Wharf. She thought *The Post* would be asking when she expected a General Election announcement. But they weren't.

'Did you see Saturday's paper?' Brian asked.

'Didn't get round to it, sorry. Busy day.'

'This story's on the web-site, if you care to look.'

'*The Post* has a web-site now? Congratulations.'

'We mentioned that Omar Khan was your dentist,' Brian said. 'I know you have nothing to add about him, but wondered if you could talk about his wife.'

'I've never met her. Why?' Sarah had a vague recollection of seeing the dentist's wife once, or at least a photo of her: a stern-faced yet handsome woman.

'The brother-in-law is accusing her of Khan's murder. There're accusations sprayed on her garage doors. The police took her in for questioning.'

'I see.' Sarah thought quickly. She decided not to mention Fahd's accusations, or express interest in the graffiti on the garage doors. She'd meant to talk to Nick about Fahd's accusations, but had been too busy. Or, if she were honest with herself, had put off what was bound to be an awkward conversation.

'I thought you might at least say a few words?'

'I'd rather not be in the story, Brian. You rarely get to know the person who looks after your teeth. It's hardly a social situation. If you need to fill space, I'm happy to write a column on what we're doing with the overseas aid budget.'

'Angling for Clare Short's job after the election?'

'I'd be happy with Chris Mullin's,' she said, referring to Short's deputy, 'but don't quote me on that.'

'Let's meet for a drink now the thing's underway. I'll see if we can help you out a little. I gather you've got an uphill struggle this time.'

'Not helped by the gushing profile you gave my opponent in your Saturday section. You made her sound like a secular saint.'

'Nothing secular about Margaret. She's religious, and she's new. But our coverage will be meticulously balanced now the starting whistle's sounded.'

'I was hoping for rather better than that.'

That afternoon, Sarah got an email from Nick, asking her to call. She'd had more correspondence from Nick during the last fortnight than during the three years they were in a relationship. They'd lived together for most of that time, in a house just off the Derby Road, and had no need to write. They started living apart when she went to Ryton, training to be a police officer. This career misstep, seventeen years ago, had destroyed them as a couple. Nick had written to her while she was at Ryton, but their break-up took place over strained phone calls, during the last one of which she'd admitted to a fling with a fellow trainee. He, tit for tat, told her that he'd slept with one of her oldest friends. Two fleeting affairs in a time before AIDS, when sex could still be casual. How did they let something so meaningless break them up? She'd tortured herself with that question over the years.

She followed the link in Nick's email, then – even though she knew that she ought to keep her distance – returned his call.

'I've been meaning to call you, Nick, but it's awkward. Is this about Pete Carlson?'

'I've been ducking his messages.'

'He's writing about Andrew and Nancy, trying to find out why they died.'

'Good question. Wish I knew who paid the killer. Does he know that we..?'

'Don't think so, but I don't reckon you and I should be meeting, or even talking, now I've brought you up to date. What did you want?'

'The police are harassing this Asian woman who I used to know. She's the older sister of a boy I taught. They're saying she murdered her husband.'

'Nazia Khan?'

'You know her?'

'I know her story. Her husband was my dentist.'

She didn't mention Saturday's visit from Fahd Khan or his allegations.

'Omar died of a heart attack in his sleep. His brother, for whatever reason, has it in for Nazia. He's accused her of murder. I haven't seen this woman since 1989 but the brother also seems to think that she was having an affair with me. It's mad stuff and defamatory, too, but the police seem to be indulging him. They arrested her on Friday evening and kept her in overnight. Could you get involved?'

'It's a very sensitive area.'

'You'd pick up support from Muslim women.'

'But lose most of the men. And Muslim women don't vote in the same numbers as the men. Let me think.'

When they'd first got together, Nick had been her election agent, successfully running Sarah's campaign to become NUS President at Nottingham Uni. Here he was, trying to help her again. Sarah calculated. Muslim women – she had always been led to believe – tended to vote as their family's patriarch told them to. Which nearly always meant Labour. Sarah didn't have much to gain by supporting Nazia. If she alienated Muslim men, she had a lot to lose. But Fahd Khan had put her back up and she'd like to please Nick.

'I'm not at all keen to get involved. However, if you want, I will meet her.'

She finished packing up her office. Tonight was her date with Hugh. Not a date as such, more an unofficial farewell dinner, but she went back to her flat to change, wanting him to see that she'd made an effort. Hugh was from a different generation. She didn't know what – if anything – to expect from him. This might be the last night she spent in the flat but, despite this, she changed the sheets on her bed. Now she'd admitted to herself how the evening might end, she chose her slinkiest black underwear and the red skirt that showed off her hips to best effect.

Hugh had chosen the restaurant, a funky Lebanese place where cheap wine came in a carafe and the pancakes that accompanied her curry were made with chick pea flour. The place was full, but not with people who were going to recognise her. She could relax. Hugh proved adept at carrying his half of a conversation that did not centre on the General Election or party politics. Sarah asked about his childhood and family, which were posh, by Labour standards. He, knowing most of her background, steered talk towards leisure and culture.

'I really don't have enough time to watch films at the cinema. The only time I made it to Nottingham Playhouse recently was to take a look at their new Anish Kapoor installation. Can't remember the last time I went to a play.'

'London's the best city in the world for theatre.' He reeled off a few things he'd seen recently, none of which she'd heard of. 'You ought to come with me.'

'I'd only have time if I lose my seat, and then I wouldn't be here.'

'Stop saying that you're going to lose. I couldn't stand it.'

'You'll find another job easily. I'll give you a brilliant reference.'

'That's not what I meant,' he said, and blushed.

She squeezed his hand across the table. 'I know what you meant.'

That was all it took.

FOURTEEN

And They're off! said the headline in Wednesday's *Post*. The election had been called on the day before, much of which Sarah had spent in bed with Hugh, making up for lost time. She'd come home yesterday evening. Today, she was giving Eric Turnbull the lunch she owed him before getting stuck into her campaign. They were back in the basement of *French Living*. She'd offered to take him somewhere posher, the recently opened *World Service* perhaps, or *Hotel des Clos* in Clifton. She'd heard good things about their new head chef. But Eric preferred a familiar haunt.

'Took a look at your web-site,' Eric said. 'Impressive. You're taking this election very seriously.'

'We're going to put the web address on all of our election literature, so those who have the internet will know to check it out.'

'And those who don't will think *she's so modern with her fancy internet.*'

'Precisely.'

'I wonder whether I ought to have a website for my consultancy work. Perhaps you could introduce me to whoever designed it for you.'

Sarah gave Eric an amused glance. Did he know Nick was behind it?

'You're not a website kind of bloke,' she said. 'You have to keep updating them. Too much hassle for a one-man-firm. Also, I thought your business came from long-standing personal contacts. Would your old police pals be happy about you pimping yourself to the whole world?'

'You have a point.' Eric refreshed her glass, then his. She was canvassing later and had meant to only have one. What the hell. On two glasses, she could still maintain a clear head. Eric, of course, had insisted on buying a nice bottle. A Madiran. Did he have work to do later? Since his retirement, two years ago, the Chief Constable had never been clear about what work he was still doing. She suspected there was little of it. He had a more than healthy pension, albeit with an ex-wife to maintain. His new wife, however, had a good job. They must be minted.

'How's Mary?' she asked.

'She was talking about you before she went to work this morning.'

'Really?' Sarah wondered if wife number two was suspicious of her continuing friendship with Eric. She had no cause to be.

'I told her you were interested in the Nazia Khan affair.'

Sarah explained that Omar had been her dentist.

'Has Mrs Khan been charged?'

Eric shook his head. 'No direct evidence. Police are considering an exhumation application. However, they've yet to approach the coroner's court.'

Sarah wondered why Eric was so well informed about it, but knew better than to ask directly. She always got more out of him by being casual.

'There seems to be more evidence against her than there is against that Freddie Mercury lookalike.'

They spent a few minutes discussing the man accused of murdering Jill Dando. The TV presenter, Sarah's age, had been shot dead outside her home two years before. Dando fronted *Crime Watch* on the BBC. Any number of criminals had a motive to stop an investigation. The evidence against the accused was thin. He had no logical motive. Nevertheless, he'd been put on trial at the Old Bailey.

'The police had to have a result in the Jill Dando killing. Identifying a credible nutter is their most viable option. With Khan, nobody beyond the family cares about the dentist. The brother making the accusation is suspect.'

'Suspect in what way?'

'Always ask the old question, *who benefits?*'

'Nazia benefits. She's free. She inherits money, property, a pension.'

'She had all those things already. Let me play devil's advocate here. Assume the wife was having an affair. Her husband works all hours, so she can have her fun while the children are at school.

Whereas, now he's gone, she won't be able to move freely. If she has been having an affair, she certainly can't marry whoever she's been sleeping with. It'd be a scandal. In Muslim society, widows have less sexual freedom than married women. The family will marry her off to someone who'll accept a widow with kids, meaning a man who wants the money that comes with them. She'd have known all that before deciding whether to kill off hubby.'

'She'd also know what effect his death would have on their children,' Sarah said.

'Domestic killers tend not to worry about the effect on the children. They convince themselves that they're doing it to benefit the kids.'

'If they're happy, the children will be happy.'

'Precisely.'

'Then who else benefits?'

'The lover, maybe, if he wants her all to himself. Or the husband's brother, if Nazia is convicted and he stands to inherit, which is a possibility.'

'For someone who retired two years ago, you've thought a lot about this.'

'True, but I have to be careful what I say.'

'Why?'

'Because my wife's representing her.'

'Have you considered, even for a moment, that Nazia might have done it?' Sam asked Bilal, when they were able to grab a few minutes alone.

'Course I haven't. Why? You don't...'

'I try not to think about it,' Sam said. She'd finished her shift at the Queen's Medical Centre and they had an hour to themselves before he collected Nazia's kids from school. It was a big adjustment, becoming a family of five. 'But...'

'I know.' It was still hard for Bilal, seeing his sister as fallible, impossible to regard Naz as a suspect. When he was younger, she had been his protector, occasionally a rival for their mum's attention. He barely remembered Dad. After they'd lost both parents, she'd become his guardian, more an aunt than a sister.

'How well do we know her, really? She'd cut herself off from you by the time we got together. I tried. I hoped we'd bond, but she always kept her distance.'

'That's just the way Naz is,' Bilal said. 'Except with Tamazur and Ahmad. Even then, she never...' He struggled for words and Sam filled in.

'She never gives fully of herself. Except, you'd hope, to someone she loves. But I never had the sense that she loved Omar. Respect, yes. Affection, probably. But you knew her when she was in love with this Nick guy.'

'Her eyes used to light up when she saw him. You couldn't miss that. I was worried. I liked Nick, he was the only Stoneywood teacher I did like. But I knew there's be hell to pay if it got out. And if they were to marry, Naz would have been out of the family. I'd've had to cut her off or be out of the family too.'

'You understood that at sixteen?'

'I was bad at book learning but I understood people.'

'Do you think they were at it?'

He shook his head. 'I didn't at the time, but I was only fifteen when they started seeing each other, what did I know? Naz was so into him, maybe she would have done. Early on, Nick told me that he'd treat my sister with respect. He knew she needed to be a virgin when she married.'

'Maybe you trusted him too much back then. He was a good-looking guy?'

'A lot of girls in my year fancied him.'

'So Nazia runs into him again. They still fancy each other like mad. He's single. She's in a loveless, sexless marriage. And she's not a virgin any more. All they have to do is be discreet.'

'It's possible.'

'They're not hurting anybody, long as nobody finds out. Not until they decide to murder Omar.'

'Nick's a dope grower, not a killer.'

'The way Omar was killed, if it was murder, that's a woman's way of killing. Nick might not know what she'd done in order to be with him.'

Bilal took a good look at Sam.

'You really think Naz is capable of something like that?'

'I'm not saying she did it, I'm saying it's possible.'

'And where does that get us? Unless she tells us, we'll never know.'

'Fahd's a nasty piece of work, but that doesn't mean he's wrong. There are times I've known Naz be sneaky and secretive, certainly self-centred. But killing her husband is way beyond that. All I'm saying is, keep an open mind and a sharp eye. Don't be distracted by her offering to have a baby for us.'

Her mobile rang and she answered it. 'Bidisha, hi!' A colleague from work. Sam listened for the best part of a minute, her face souring with every second that passed. Then she said, 'thanks for letting me know. I'll do that.'

She hung up and turned to Bilal. 'You'd better go and buy a paper.'

At the end of the first full day of campaign, the team were in the Sir John Borlase Warren on Canning Circus, a busy pub not far from Sarah's flat in The Park. Brian from *The Post* must have remembered that this was where they tended to go after canvassing, for he arrived just after they did.

'Something I wanted to show you,' he said to Sarah, turning to page three of that day's paper. She'd bought one, but not had time to read beyond the front page. There was a photo of Omar Khan, and a six-inch story with the headline *Dentist's brother calls for exhumation.*

'Jesus,' Sarah said. The story didn't spell out that the dentist's wife was having an affair but quoted Fahd Khan as saying that 'only days earlier my brother told me he had concerns that he was being deceived.'

'Any chance of a comment on the proposed exhumation of Omar Khan?'

'None whatsoever,' Sarah told Brian.

'Do you want to defend his wife from the attacks being made on her?'

'No comment means no comment, Brian. I have an election

to fight.'

'Meaning you won't say anything that jeopardises the Muslim vote?'

'Meaning I'll not be drawn into commenting and won't give anybody the opportunity to twist my words. Now, I'm sorry, but I really have to go.'

Winston offered her a lift but he'd hardly started his drink. She insisted the walk would do her good. Sarah still had weight she wanted to lose. The exercise from canvassing was offset by all the inevitable crap food during the campaign. Brian's arrival had, at least, stopped her having another drink. She didn't want to think about Nazia Khan or the dead dentist. She needed an early night, she decided. Tomorrow, the election would start in earnest.

Sarah's walk from pub to flat took about seven minutes. The Park, as usual, was all but deserted. No public transport ran through these wide avenues, and cyclists were few and far between. There were several ways to get into The Park, four accessible by car, the way that most of its monied residents travelled. Sarah took the Derby Road entrance, at the edge of Lenton, where she'd lived as a student. Once she'd passed Walton's Hotel, a little way inside, she had the footpath to herself, which made it easier for her to think.

Hugh, bless him, had offered to come to Nottingham and work in any capacity she chose. Sarah hadn't said no, not exactly. She liked him a lot and the sex had been refreshing. More than refreshing, actually: lovely, especially the second time. And the third. But he was too young for her, and so keen. Best to keep the affair separate from her Nottingham life, especially during an election. They wouldn't be having this fling if Sarah weren't certain she wouldn't be his boss much longer. If Hugh came to Nottingham, she'd have to spend the whole election hiding the fact that the MP was shagging her aide. Though, come to think of it, this was the twenty-first century, and what male MP – especially a single one – would let a thing like that put him off getting his leg over with a willing employee?

Hugh was kind, and clever, and hard working. Moreover, unlike the other candidates she'd interviewed for his job, he'd shown no ambition to become an MP. He was more likely, she reckoned, to end up working for a research institute, or, the party itself. Although, from what she could gather, his politics were well to the left of Labour's current set of apparatchiks. That was OK, he was young.

There was someone lurking in the shadows outside her first floor flat. If they were trying to hide, they were doing a bad job. Her first thought, nevertheless, was of Jill Dando, killed by a single shot to her head the moment she opened her front door. Her second thought was of Fahd Khan, the dentist's creepy brother. Sarah reached into her pocket for her mobile phone. But what should she do with it? She had nobody nearby to call, even if her battery hadn't run out hours ago. Not for the first time, she wondered why she didn't carry a rape alarm.

The figure was sitting, hardly a threatening position. That was something. She'd a small torch on her keychain. She pointed it at the front door.

'Hello,' she called from a distance that gave her time to run. 'Can I help?'

The shaded figure got to his feet and she welled up. 'You came!'

'I had to. Sorry, I tried to call first but your phone was dead.'

She rushed to him. 'Have you been here long?'

'Only half an hour.'

She reached the front door and fell into his arms. They had a long, deep kiss before going inside.

'I know I told you not come,' she said. 'But I'm so, so glad you did.'

'If you're going to lose,' Hugh said, 'I want to go down fighting with you.'

Nazia had been out all day without an explanation. Nor did she offer one when she came in. Bilal certainly wasn't going to ask his sister if she'd been alone with a man.

'We need to talk,' he said. 'Have you seen the paper?'

'Let me say goodnight to Ahmad and Tamazur first. They'll be worried about what's happened to me.'

75

Actually, the kids had been watching TV quite contentedly until Sam sent them to bed. Now she and Bilal only had half an hour before Sam started her shift.

'What are you going to say to her?' Sam asked while Nazia was upstairs.

'What we agreed.'

Bilal did what his wife told him to do. A little before their wedding day, Uncle had advised him that this was the secret of a long, happy marriage. *Do whatever she asks. It's as simple as that.*

'Let's find out what the solicitor said first,' Sam suggested.

By the time Nazia came downstairs, Sam only had five minutes before she had to leave. Bilal asked Nazia for a summary of her meeting with Mary Harris.

'She said there's no rational or legal argument to exhume the body. She's sent a letter to Fahd threatening to sue him if he repeats his allegations in public.'

'That cat's already out of the bag,' Sam said. 'Why not sue him now?'

'You don't take family to court. There's an added complication in that Fahd is Omar's executor. Everything should come to me with money in trust for the children, but Fahd can mess all that up if he chooses to.'

Bilal swore. 'Maybe you should have agreed to marry him.'

'How can you say that?' Sam said.

'Joke.'

'I had the same thought,' Naz said. 'Marry him, then murder him, that'd solve all my problems, yah?'

Bilal faked a laugh. Sam wasn't having it. 'What else did she advise?'

'We need to fight the bad publicity. Not a formal defence group, but a campaign against the stories being spread in the media. Will you help?'

'I'll set up a meeting,' Bilal said. 'You OK with Nick Cane being involved?'

'Nick is a good man,' Nazia said. 'But after the slanders Fahd has spread, and with his prison record, best perhaps if Nick stays in the background.'

'I want to meet this Nick Cane,' Sam said. 'He sounds like an interesting person. Make sure this meeting is at a time when I can come.'

She left for work. Bilal made tea for him and Nazia.

'Does she believe me?' Nazia asked. Bilal didn't immediately reply, so she added, 'I wouldn't blame her if she didn't.'

'She thinks what I think,' Bilal told Nazia, careful with his words. 'That you're not telling us everything. And it's hard to help someone who isn't straight with you. I told her that, when I had you on your own, I'd ask you to tell me the things you've left out – for whatever reason. Then we'll work out how to proceed.'

Nazia was silent for a long time. Bilal sipped his tea.

'I've told you all that's safe for me to tell you,' she said, eventually. 'You'll have to trust me.'

SIXTEEN

The team's lunch break was later than usual: Winston, Georgia, Tony, Sarah and Hugh sat around one of the long wooden tables in *The Orange Tree*. Only Winston had met Hugh before, and then only briefly. Introductions were made, duties discussed. Hugh tried to offset his posh boy appearance by a show of extreme humility, offering to do the most menial tasks.

'Anything from stuffing envelopes to knocking on doors. Only thing I can't do is drive people to the polls. Living in London, I've never had any call to learn.'

'If you're after a place to stay,' Georgia said, 'I know some decent B and Bs.'

'Actually,' Sarah said, 'Hugh's going to have my spare room – initially at least – it makes sense in terms of getting work done.'

'There could be a risk of gossip,' Winston pointed out.

'If anybody stirs the pot,' Hugh offered, 'tell them I bat for the other side.'

This quip was met with what passed for mild amusement, but left Sarah conflicted.

'Why did you say that?' she asked later, when they were alone in the flat.

'I didn't lie, just muddied the water a little. Doesn't bother me if people here think I'm gay. The only woman I'm interested in is you.'

'Are you planning to stay at weekends, too?'

'Of course.'

'The older bloke you met earlier, Tony Bax, is getting married on Saturday. Would you like to come as my guest? You might have to make a pass at one of the waiters, just to bolster your cover story.'

'Love to.' Hugh laughed. 'But I haven't brought a suit.'

'Let me buy you one.'

'You pay me quite well, you know.'

'I know. But I've often wondered what it'd be like to have a toy boy.'

'That's good, because I've spent the last three and a half years wondering what it would be like to be your toy boy.'

Bilal dropped Naz off at the house in The Park. The garage doors, which he'd painted over as thoroughly as he could, had not been graffitied a third time. The security cameras he'd had installed seemed to have done their job. He offered to wait for Nazia while she collected the stuff she needed. His sister said no.

'I've wasted enough of your time. I'll call a cab when I need one and I'll be home before the kids are back from school.'

'OK.' Bilal drove round the corner then did a three-point-turn in the wide road. He parked under a tree, just out of sight of Nazia's driveway, but near enough to observe anyone who went in. After a few minutes, a cab arrived outside. The car turned into Nazia's angled driveway and drove far enough in to be hidden from the road. Bilal hurried out of his car so that he could see how this scene developed. He found a gap in the branches of Nazia's hedge just in time to see a man get out of the cab. Nazia opened the door. She'd changed out of her dull, widow's tunic into tightly cut jeans and a cotton top. The man she invited inside only embraced her fleetingly, but the intimacy of their body language was unmistakeable.

From the back, he looked an awful lot like Nick Cane.

BOOK TWO

Pete

Jerry

Caroline

Sarah

SEVENTEEN

Pete Carlson had a fat folder of clippings about Sarah Bone. She was one of Labour's best looking and, some pundits felt, brightest female MPs. Nobody was surprised when Tony Blair gave her a good job in the previous parliament. Yet she had lasted less than a year as Prisons minister. In the wake of Harriet Harman's more high-profile sacking as both Secretary of State for Social Security and Women's Minister, Sarah's departure from the Home Office was rarely discussed. At the time, however, it had been seen as a bad blow for women in parliament. The story given out was that she had to care for a mortally ill mother. The mother appeared to have fully recovered. Sarah's career hadn't.

Bone held a marginal seat that she was likely to lose, a bar to promoting her. Yet a safe replacement seat could easily be found. Two sources had told him that Sarah had been sounded out about replacing Tony Benn in Chesterfield, her hometown, but turned it down. Bone was left wing enough not to alienate Benn's supporters, but enough of an old school politician to satisfy the right, some of whom had known her cabinet minister grandfather, a former Chesterfield MP.

There must be a black mark against her. Either that, or she wanted to lose. Six years as an MP may have felt like enough. Who could blame her for wanting to move on to a more lucrative job? Her name would enhance the board of a company that needed New Labour links. She would look good on TV. Yet the MP rarely did TV and didn't seem much taken by the trappings of success. She owned a modest flat in The Park and an even more modest one in Westminster. True, she owned a holiday home in Majorca, but she'd inherited that from her late father and, as far as Pete could discover, had not once used the place.

It was pure luck that Pete had worked out Sarah's connection with the villa. He'd been investigating a double murder that had been committed there and decided to establish its ownership. Kevin Bone had left the villa in trust for his daughter, Sarah, who had inherited it after the death of his lover. Interesting that Sarah had a gay dad. She didn't make much play of it. Nor had she kept his sexuality secret. She'd referred to him during a Commons debate about HIV and AIDS, the cause of his death. Andrew Saint, one of the murder victims, had been project managing the villa's restoration for Sarah. That wasn't in itself suspicious. Saint's legit work was in property development, though his main source of income was drug trafficking. Debts from this world were most likely what got him killed.

Did Sarah Bone know anything about that side of Saint's world? Pete hoped not. Pete wanted to like the MP, not least because he'd interviewed Sarah for the *New Statesman* back in 97 or 8. And fancied the pants off her.

Was she currently single? That was a harder nut to crack. She used to have a long-term boyfriend, a social worker called Dan. He'd been referred to in interviews she gave during the 1995 by-election. Dan seemed to have moved in with her at some point, but moved out around the time of the last General Election. Since then, nyet.

Sarah's only other known relationship was with one Nick Cane, whom she'd dated at university. Cane had served five years for cocaine possession and running a cannabis farm in caves under his flat in The Park, a rich part of Nottingham. But they'd split up long before all that, during Sarah's stint in the police. They might be living in the same city again, but nothing indicated that they were still in contact.

Sarah might be single. More likely she was very discreet. If he were to guess, Pete would see Sarah with a married trade union official or, maybe, another Labour MP. She struck him as the sort of woman who wasn't too bothered about conventional morality, more interested in her career than in having a family. Happy to be a mistress, maybe, but on her own terms. Straight, definitely. He remembered the way she sized him up when he interviewed her in the 90s, and her careful rejection when he'd suggested they go for a drink sometime.

'Things are a bit complicated at the mo'. Ask me next time we meet.'

He hadn't followed through because, shortly after that first meeting, he'd had his whirlwind fling with Fatima, which led to their short-lived, disastrous marriage. Pete was out of pocket thanks to the divorce. Hence his move to the *Sunday Times*, which paid a lot better than the *New Statesman*. His new paper needed a scoop on a Labour MP that they could run during the General Election.

Nobody expected a Conservative victory in the General Election, but the Tories might win back some seats. Back in '97, when she'd been expected to lose Nottingham West, Sarah had kept out a popular ex-MP. The Tories were after revenge. Resources would be poured into her seat. In a sense, Pete *was* doing the Conservatives' dirty work, but he hoped – no, *felt* – that, embedded in Nottingham, he'd find a bigger story. Maybe Sarah Bone MP would come out of it badly. Equally, she might emerge as its hero.

Sarah was a pro. She hadn't complained about being door-stepped. She seemed to remember Pete and feel relaxed around him. At one point, while they were talking, Sarah had to lean over for something and gave him a peak that one of the tabloids would pay serious money for a shot of. Not deliberate, probably, but the tantalising flash had given him a little hope in that direction. Especially since, given the lack of male appurtenances in her flat, Sarah did appear to be single.

For the third time, Pete attempted to interview Nick Cane and, for the third time he was rebuffed. At least Cane answered the door, so Pete got a good look at him. Cane was around his age, late thirties. He wore a plain T-shirt and jeans and was well built, with a good jawline, speckled with stubble. He looked like he'd only just got up, despite it being ten in the morning.

'Do I know you?' he asked, when Pete introduced himself.

'We have a mutual friend, Sarah Bone.'

'Friend, eh.' There was a trace of Yorkshire in the way he said this, but the next three words came out BBC English. 'What's this about?'

'I'm writing a story about the death of another friend of yours from university days, Andrew Saint.'

Immediately, the shutters came down. 'I have nothing to say.'

'It's very hard to get anyone to talk about Saint, but people tell me you knew Saint better than anyone. You also knew his partner, Nancy Tull.'

'Yes, I knew Nancy.'

'Perhaps you didn't know that she was pregnant when she died, so, technically, theirs was a triple murder.'

A pained look. He'd hit a nerve. 'No, I... where did you get that?'

'I went to Spain, read the autopsy report. Seems shameful to me that the British press never followed up the story. Just another gangster murdered in Spain was how they saw it, but I think there was more to Saint than that.'

'Calling Andrew a gangster is absurd. He was...' Cane stopped himself. 'Are you recording this?'

'No.' Pete would be making notes the moment Cane shut the door, which he was about to do.

'Andrew was unlucky. I don't know who killed him or why. If you manage to establish those things, I'll look forward to reading your story.'

He began to close the door.

'It would be a lot easier to write if you could find time to answer a few questions,' Pete said. 'For instance, have you got any idea what Andrew and Nancy were doing in Majorca?'

But the door was already closed. Another salient question was who now owned Saint's large, expensive Notting Hill home. Students were living there, a bunch of lively young women. The one he'd spoken to had never heard of Saint.

The Saint side of Sarah Bone's story had serious news potential. The murder of Andrew Saint, Nancy Tull and their unborn child had been a textbook contract killing. The key question was not who had done it, but who had paid them to do it. And why.

Jerry put out the bin. This, along with buying cleaning supplies (a woman came once a week) was her main duty as a landlady. She lived rent-free in Notting Hill with a bunch of second years, four of whom would be staying on for their final year. It was a desirable spot, a big old building in a wide street with a bit of garden at the back. A bit posh, perhaps, but near enough to the multi-ethnic shopping area also known as Notting Hill, with its cool stores and easy-to-find drugs. A friend on her Law degree had his name down for the room that was about to become free.

The lawyer wanted to be more than a friend, but she wasn't interested. Too young. A guy was watching her. Not bad looking, as it goes. Hair a bit too short and twice her age, but that was a plus. Her first lover had been in his thirties. Which probably explained why she was predisposed to associate orgasms with older men. She was only fifteen, so they'd been very careful.

Jerry had learned to love secrecy. None of her housemates had any idea that she'd been brought up in children's homes. People like her didn't get to university. Except when they did.

She'd seen this guy before. He had a proletarian feel about him, with blue jeans and one of those blouson leather jackets that were over, fashion-wise. At least this was an expensive version, she could tell. She liked his look, which was slightly greasy. From a distance, without the glasses she was too vain to wear, he reminded her of Nick Cane. Nick was her platonic ideal, possibly because, during all of the three years that she had known him – he had tutored her through Eng Lit GCSE, then A level – he had been attentive and kind, yet resolutely refused to fuck her.

'Can I help you?' Close up, the guy was slighter than Nick, but still fit.

'Do you live here?' London accent.

'No, I just put out bins for exercise. Haven't I seen you before?'

'My name's Pete. I spoke to some of your housemates.'

'They said. One of them thought you were a copper.'

'Not me.' He handed her a card. *The Sunday Times* 'Insight' team.

'What was it you wanted to know?'

'I'm interested in the guy who used to own this house, Andrew Saint. Did you know him?'

'Never met him. We occasionally get some mail with his name

on. I was told to send it back marked *deceased*.'

'Who told you that?'

Jerry hesitated. 'Can't remember.'

'Anyone ever come looking for him?'

'Not until you.'

'Perhaps you could tell me who owns the building now?'

'Afraid not.'

'Who do you pay the money to, which letting agency?'

'Dunno. It just goes straight into a bank account.' Nick's account.

Pete smiled. He had a nice smile. 'Why do I get the feeling that you're holding something back?'

'My mother told me to be careful with strangers.' This wasn't true: Her mother had been a junkie from before Jerry was born until her death, four years ago. She had never given Jerry any useful advice, or, indeed, much else.

'You're all students, right? What's your course?'

'I'm doing Law at UCL.' Jerry returned to the front door as if she had something urgent to do inside.

'That's a hard course to get onto,' Pete said. 'You must have got good grades. I'm not surprised you're cautious with me. But I'd really appreciate the opportunity to talk further, if you have the time.'

Jerry shook her head. 'I've just started exams. Not a good time.' She looked Pete up and down, decided to make a move. 'But they finish a week on Friday. You can take me out for a drink if you like.'

The journalist hesitated, thrown by this brazenness. Probably he hadn't been thinking of her that way. Maybe he would start now.

'I'd like that, yes. Are you going to tell me your name?'

For him, she decided, she needed to use a different name. Something more grown up. 'I'm Geraldine.'

'Pleased to meet you, Geraldine. You've got my number. Can I have yours?'

'Better I call you. You can come round for me next Friday. Make it seven.'

'Seven it is.'

She returned to her textbooks. Later, she would decide whether she needed to tell Nick about the journalist. Or maybe that would wait until after she'd found out what the guy was after, and what he was like in bed.

EIGHTEEN

'Am I early?'

'No, but Joe's late. Hello, stranger.'

Caroline embraced her brother-in-law. Nick hadn't been round since Christmas. Caroline resented this absence but wasn't surprised by it. The kids were four and a few weeks off two, which meant that the house was often chaotic. Nick and Joe met for drinks, went to the occasional gig together. Nick had ducked two earlier invitations to supper this year. She feared he'd begun to find her boring. She and Joe had decided she wouldn't go back to work until Phoebe started school. As a result, Caroline's world had shrunk, while Nick's had expanded.

Long ago there'd been a time when Nick had hung on her every word, when he'd tried to stop her getting back with his younger brother because he wanted her for himself. A different world. She sometimes wondered how often Nick thought about the late 80s, when she had given herself to him secretly but freely, and often.

This evening, she asked questions about his internet business. Nick replied with the usual evasive generalities.

'Done work for anyone I'll have heard of?'

'A website for the Labour Party. They're starting to get it.'

'Sarah Bone, by any chance?'

'She didn't approach me directly, but yeah.'

Caroline had met Sarah once, when she came to a New Year's Eve party. She'd found her intimidating. The MP had split up with Nick nearly eighteen years ago, but there was still an atmosphere between them.

'Wouldn't it be better for you if she lost this time? After all, if she weren't an MP, the two of you could have another try.'

Nick gave an awkward laugh. 'That ship sailed long ago.'

'I thought you went on holiday together a couple of years back.'

'You got that wrong. Think you had other things on your mind at the time.'

He began to ask about Oliver. She'd been heavily pregnant with him two years before. Classic avoidance tactic. Caroline remembered Nick setting off to Majorca, full of anticipation, and coming back without a tan, or a companion. He'd never specified who he was travelling with. He'd had to return early because of the death of one of his closest friends. Joe remembered Nick visiting the same area with Sarah back in the early 80s. She'd family there. Caroline suspected that they'd attempted a reunion, but it hadn't worked out.

A key turned in the door.

'Sorry, I'm late.'

'Happy birthday, bro'.' The two men shared an awkward embrace.

'Got you something.' Nick handed Joe a wrapped CD, which Joe opened. The new LP by R.E.M., an American band they were both keen on. *Reveal*.

'Still shrink-wrapped,' Joe observed. 'Surprised you didn't copy it.'

Nick now had the equipment to make exact copies of CDs, a concept Caroline found mind-boggling.

'What kept you?' she asked her husband.

'There was something I had to check out for work. But I'm here now.' He turned to his brother. 'Got plans for your big one? Not long now.'

'Trying not to think about it.' Nick's fortieth was only weeks away.

Caroline served ladles of Catalan chicken and rice which they washed down with Rioja. She picked at her food. The men hardly paused while they devoured a leg each. Only when he had cleared most of his plate did Nick start a conversation.

'Remember Nazia, who I went out with in the second half of the 80s?'

'Didn't you bring her along to a couple of matches?' Joe said.

'Several. Only woman I've been out with who genuinely liked football.'

'Then why did you split up with her?' Caroline asked.

'I didn't. She left me, quite suddenly. Married a dentist twenty years older than her. He died last week. It was in the papers.'

Now Caroline knew what he was talking about. 'I saw a story in *The Post*. People are saying she injected him with something?'

'The dentist's brother is stirring the pot. It's nonsense. Horrible for her.'

'Are you still in touch?'

Nick explained how the woman's younger brother, Bilal, whom he used to teach, had come to him for help. He seemed uncomfortable. There was something he wasn't telling them. Joe kept quiet, as though he knew what that something was.

'I think you told me once,' she said, 'that Nazia and Sarah were the big loves of your life.'

Nick gave her a sharp look and she realised that, yes, he had told her this, but in a post-coital haze. He'd been leading up to *third time lucky*. They had only been together for a few weeks, after Joe chucked her. For a while, she'd thought she was falling for him. Nick was, in many respects, a more logical match than his footballer brother. Joe was a lad's lad, constantly tempted by fangirl floozies, while Nick was a teacher, like her. He and his brother, born and brought up in Sheffield, had each ended up in this city: Nick through going to university here, Joe after being transferred from Sheffield Wednesday to Notts County. Nick was more handsome than Joe, and a more considerate lover. One night, they'd been doing that thing young lovers did, where they told each other about everyone they'd ever had a relationship with. Including this Nazia.

Soon afterwards, Joe had a bad injury that ended his career, and decided he wanted Caroline back. Caroline had – wisely, in retrospect – insisted to Nick that he keep their relationship from him. Joe, being the younger, more successful, and, yes, much more arrogant of the brothers, had never suspected a thing. Soon, he proposed, and she accepted. Nick had to pretend to be happy for them.

'I always assumed it was religion that split you two up?' Joe said, breaking an awkward silence. 'Didn't she want you to convert to Islam?'

'I respected her culture,' Nick said, 'but we never discussed religion. Neither of us were religious. I guess that might have changed for Nazia after her marriage.'

'Will you see her?' Caroline asked.

'Maybe. I don't know how I feel about meeting her again,' Nick said. 'But Bilal wants me to help with some kind of publicity campaign.'

'Does she have kids?'

'A couple, I think. Both at Primary school.'

'Those poor children.' Nick, as far as Caroline knew, had been single for more than two years. Before that he'd been being badly burned by a relationship with an undercover policewoman. She could see how a grieving widow might fall for him big time, especially if they had that kind of history. She could also see him stepping in to help bring up her kids. Unlike his brother, Nick had a strong sense of responsibility. One day, the love of a good woman would be the making of him.

The more Pete looked into Nick Cane, the more intriguing he became. The ex-teacher's crimes were from the pre-internet era, so there was bugger all online. A trawl through the *Nottingham Post* archives didn't reveal much of interest, either. The school where he worked until he was arrested said he was a dedicated teacher and they had no comment on his 'unfortunate' behaviour. Until '92 he had been active in the Labour Party (whose records were easy to access, if you were in with the right people) but he had not rejoined the party since his release, four years ago.

The thing about the internet was that it expanded exponentially. New things appeared all the time. Pete had taken to searching for 'Andrew Saint', 'Andy Saint', 'Nicholas Cane' and 'Nick Cane' every day. There was next-to-nothing on Saint either. There'd been pieces in the *Express* and *Telegraph* – neither of them online – papers whose readers loved sleazy crime stories. The *Daily Express* had managed to get an interview with Nancy Tull's mother. She said how mystified she was by her daughter's death. There was also a quote from the dead woman's former boss, a deputy head called Eve Shipton, saying that Nancy was a fine teacher until she developed a tragic drug dependency. The name of the school rang a bell: Stoneywood Comp. Pete checked his notes – it was the one where Nick Cane used to work. It figured that he must have known Nancy before he went inside. Might, indeed, have introduced her to Andrew Saint. The only earlier reference to Saint came from the year before he died. He was listed as one of the men busted for using a brothel in Hyson Green. Could Nancy Tull have become a prostitute after she left school teaching? Not a normal career trajectory for a teacher, but a common one for an addict.

There was another MP he wanted to talk to, one who Saint had persuaded to go on the board of his company, Saint Holdings, which had been wound up after his death. The MP had resigned from the board by then. Interviewing MPs during a General Election wasn't always straight forward. The Tory's seat was as vulnerable as Sarah's. Like Sarah, she would not want to be linked to a scandal.

He did another search on Nick Cane. This time, he found a hotel page which wasn't meant to be searchable: information for wedding guests at Bestwood Manor in Bestwood Country Park, Nottingham. The wedding of Tony Bax and Eve Shipton. Shipton seemed likely to be Nancy Tull's former boss. Bax was a name Pete had come across. He checked his notes: Sarah Bone's constituency chair and her predecessor as Labour candidate for Nottingham West. Also listed was the name of Bax's best man, which was why the page had shown up. Nicholas Cane.

Jerry wasn't sure how to dress for Pete. He wanted to interview her, while she wanted to shag him. Unless he turned out to be a perve. There'd been a couple of times she'd picked up older blokes in bars and it had ended badly. They'd thought she wanted roughing up or, worse, assumed from her willingness that she was on the game. Since then, she'd taken to carrying a rape alarm. A very loud one.

At first, she'd thought the problem she had getting guys was a generational thing: the ones she wanted weren't used to girls who came on strong. Now she suspected that the problem was something women had always had to learn for themselves: the best way to seduce a man was to let him think it was his idea.

She settled for a thin white top and a see-through bra. Older men seemed to find these a turn on. The style wasn't around when they were young.

The journalist was dressed exactly as he had been the week before. Either he was cheap, or he'd decided to stick with a winning formula.

'You're looking good,' he said.

'You don't look so bad yourself.'

He took her to a place on funky Ladbroke Grove, which was walking distance, yet a world away from the smart street she lived on. It did a good goat curry and even better jerk chicken. They talked about films and bands then sat outside over a beer and smoked a spliff, expertly rolled to look like a straight cigarette. It was all going well until Pete started asking direct questions.

'I spoke to one of your housemates. She said you were her landlady.'

'Sort of.'

'I'm interested in the man who used to own your house, Andrew Saint.'

'Like I said before, I never met the guy. He's been dead for years, right?'

'A couple of years. I want to know why he was murdered.'

The word 'murder' made her feel funny, and he seemed to notice this. Or maybe it was just the grass upping her always epic sense of self-consciousness.

'I looked you up,' Pete told her.

'Looked me up how?'

'Land registry. You own a flat in Nottingham.'

'So?'

'Nineteen's kind of young to be owning a flat, that's all.'

'Are you suggesting something?'

'No, no. I thought you might have inherited it.'

'I wasn't on the game if that's what you were thinking.' She regretted that as soon as she blurted it out. She'd already let slip to Pete that she'd been brought up in a children's home. Most of the girls she'd known there had ended up being pimped out. Not her, though. Never her. 'I inherited it.'

This was a lie. Her mum hadn't left her anything and she didn't know who her dad was. She had come into the flat after Paul Morris's death. In a sense, she had inherited it from him.

'Thing is, the address of your flat, it's the same address as one of Andrew Saint's oldest friends, a man called Nick Cane. Do you know him?'

'Do you want another drink?' She needed time to think.

'Let me get them.'

Jerry thought about calling Nick. She wished she weren't so stoned. Pete had let her smoke most of the spliff. By the time he returned, she'd worked out that her best answer was a version of the truth. Nick had made it very clear he didn't want anyone knowing who owned the house she lived in.

'Nick was my English tutor, when I was in the home. If it weren't for him, I wouldn't have got any GCSEs, never mind A levels. He helped me get myself straight. The flat, yeah, it was a kind of inheritance and he pays rent.'

'Sounds like a nice person.'

'I wouldn't have got to university without him. I probably would have become a working girl, like most of the girls I was in the home with.'

'Don't put yourself down. Are you and Nick...?'

At last, the questions were heading in the direction that she wanted.

'I wish,' she said. 'I like older guys, but he prefers women his own age.'

'Like Sarah Bone.'

'I think they used to go out.'

Half an hour later, he walked her back to the flat. She invited him in.

'I'd love to, but can I get a rain check? I have a train to catch.'

She tried not to let her frustration show. 'Going somewhere nice?'

'Nottingham. There's a wedding I need to be at.'

NINETEEN

B estwood Lodge Hotel was on the edge of Bestwood
Country Park, a big wood at the end of a bumpy road
adjoining a large council estate. The former Victorian hunting
lodge had a large car park, regularly policed to prevent walkers
from using it. Walkers' vehicles were meant to use the Country
Park car park, further down the hill. Inside the lodge, nobody
asked for Pete's wedding invitation. The guests hadn't yet arrived
from the church. He bought a coffee in the bar, where he had a
good view of the area sectioned off for the wedding party.

The lodge's demure green upholstery suggested a genteel
event. Tony Bax, a widower, was a former Further Education
lecturer. His bride was twice divorced and had recently been
promoted to the headship of the school where Nick Cane once
taught. It was possible Pete would learn nothing from the guests
today. However, weddings, like funerals, had the ability to loosen
tongues and create interesting situations. Pete lit a Marlboro Red
and watched the guests stream in.

Sarah Bone, hair up, in a scarlet dress, looked better than he'd
ever seen her. The younger man she was with evidently worked
for her. Probably in town to help with the campaign. The bride
was a blonde with a full figure and intelligent eyes. She didn't
resemble any headmistress he'd come across. Whereas the
groom, with grey curly hair grown long at the sides while it
receded at the front, looked every inch the retired college lecturer.
Nick Cane escorted the two young bridesmaids, each in pink.
Nieces of the bride, at a guess, barely past puberty. Nick would
not be exploiting the best man's traditional privilege.

The weather was patchy. As soon as the sun poked out, the
photographer summoned guests outside for photographs, family
first. A woman Pete's age sat down next to him at the bar and
asked if she could share his ashtray. He nodded and gave her a
light.

'Bride or groom?'

'Bride. I don't know her that well but she's my boss.'

'Most bosses wouldn't invite employees to their wedding unless they're mates outside work.'

'I covered for Eve a lot when her last marriage was breaking down.'

'That's a time when you find out who your friends are.' He looked at the finger where he used to wear his wedding ring. She gave him a sympathetic smile, took another drag on her Silk Cut and finished her wine. Then she glanced at the table where the free drinks had been. Empty.

'Can I get you one?'

She accepted and he ordered her a white wine. 'I'm Pete, by the way.'

'Melanie. You're a friend of Tony's, right?'

'No. I'm in the city on business. I had a meeting, but it was cancelled.'

'I'm meant to have a plus one for this, but he stood me up.'

'More fool him.' That explained why she was knocking it back a bit.

She gave a modest shrug. 'If you've got nothing better to do-'

'-would you like me to step into the breach?'

'We could pretend to be having a passionate relationship,' she said, stroking his thigh and giving him an exaggerated stage wink.

'Why pretend?' he said, and winked back.

While Melanie was having her photograph taken, Pete got his stuff from the car and asked for a room with a double bed. He was in luck, the receptionist explained, most of the guests were local. They had vacancies.

'How well did you know this Nazia?' Caroline asked Joe. The football season had ended the week before, meaning that he was at home on a Saturday afternoon. Deep in today's *Post*, she'd found another article about the dead dentist. The new information in it could be boiled down to four words: *police have no comment*.

'Nick introduced us after a match. Bit young for him. Nineteen, twenty maybe. And I told him at the time, dating Pakistani girls was playing with fire.'

'Really?'

'Christ, yes. I remember one of the lads in the team hooked up with a Pakistani fan once. Didn't get her pregnant or owt, but her family still came for him. He got a good beating. They didn't want their girls with white lads. Probably Nick thought Nazia was safe because both her parents were dead, but wider family can be worse. Don't suppose it's so different these days.'

'You'd know, would you?' When Caroline was pregnant with Phoebe, Joe had had an affair with a Pakistani receptionist at the office. She was married to a Pakistani who turned out to be gay, or so Joe claimed. He'd tried to be sympathetic and one thing led to another. It'd never happen again, he'd promised, and Caroline, a new mum with her head all over the place, had no choice but to take his word for it. She'd given him a first and final warning. If you married a bloke who used to put it about a lot, you shouldn't be surprised if he strayed, especially when he wasn't getting any at home. These days, fatherhood had mellowed Joe. There'd been no hint of any further betrayals.

'Do you think that Nick and her...?' She didn't want to spell out what she was suggesting. Her brother-in-law had criminal contacts. If Nick wanted to get shut of an inconvenient husband, it wouldn't be beyond him. He had moved in a world where murders were a commonplace business. Look at Andrew and Nancy.

'I think Nick wants to get back together with Sarah,' Joe said. 'He's hoping that she'll lose the election and it won't matter if she goes out with an ex-con.'

'What makes you so sure of that?'

'The other night, I asked who he was taking to the wedding today. He said nobody. Then he said, far as he knew, Sarah wasn't using her plus one either.'

'What else?'

'What do you mean, what else?'

If this had come up in a conversation between two women, they would have explored all the implications of that statement, but men didn't work that way, especially when they were drinking. If they discussed their emotions at all, it was read-between-the-lines stuff. Good for Nick if he wanted to get back with Sarah. Didn't necessarily rule out rekindling his relationship with the grieving widow. More than one old flame could flicker at the same time.

'What's our how-we-met story?' Pete asked, while they looked for Melanie's designated table.

'Are you in Nottingham often?'

'No, but I've been working on a story here for three weeks.'

He'd told her what he did, without going into details. Safest way.

'Let's say we hooked up at a club. Do you go to clubs?'

'I suppose I might, if I were working on a story that required me to.'

'Make it a bar. I go to this place on Hockley called *Bar Brilliant*. We met there, OK?'

'*Bar Brilliant* worked out brilliantly for us.'

'I didn't invite you to this until the last minute, but you dropped everything.'

'You're worth dropping everything for,' Pete assured her.

They were the first to arrive at their table, which was a fair distance from the top table. It should be a while before Sarah Bone spotted him and wondered what he was doing there. The bride and groom took their seats.

'Good looking woman.' Pete commented, then asked about Eve's marital history, had it confirmed. 'Is she restless or just unlucky?'

'Third time lucky, let's hope. First one cheated on her. The second ex didn't cheat on her as such – depends how you define it. She found out he was a regular at a brothel in Hyson Green.'

Interesting. Andrew Saint had been arrested at a brothel in Hyson Green. Later released without charge, but it appeared to be this that had persuaded the Tory MP on his company's board to quit and give him a wide berth from then on.

'Ouch,' was all Pete said.

'No surprise she's gone for the older, solid type. Tony's a city councillor.'

'Do you know how she met him?

'The best man introduced them. I used to work with him, too. Actually, there's a really interesting story about Nick…'

'Which one's he?' Pete asked. He hoped Nick wouldn't recognise him. They'd only met the once and Nick had looked bleary from having been woken up. Melanie pointed to Cane, who was sitting next to the groom. Melanie gave a fairly accurate account of how Nick Cane had run a cannabis factory while working part-time as an English teacher, then spent five years in prison as a result.

'Eve was Head of English then. They were close. Actually, during Eve's first divorce, I thought she might be having a thing with him. But she was his boss in those days, not to mention being a good fifteen years older than him. If they were up to anything, they kept it hush hush.'

Pete already knew that Nick Cane put it about, though only with one woman at a time, which, by Pete's definition, made him an honourable man.

'You and he never…?'

Melanie gave him a wicked look. 'What do you take me for?'

He guessed that she'd been interested, but he'd knocked her back.

'There was a young teacher had a terrible crush on him, though nothing happened then, far as I know. Actually, she came to a terrible end.'

Melanie regaled him with the sordid details of the death of Nancy Tull, muddied only by her not knowing how Nancy died, or that she had been in bed with a drugs baron (which was how he'd described Andrew Saint to his paper) when she was shot to death. Nor that she was pregnant.

'Crack cocaine, that was her downfall. The way I heard it, she'd gone on the game, but then she met some rich bloke and moved abroad. They were both killed in a burglary. Horrible way to go.'

'Horrible,' Pete agreed. Interesting to discover that Nancy had had a crush on Nick. It was Nick who'd reported the killings to the Majorcan police. What Pete didn't know was what Nick had been doing in Majorca, or who with.

The other guests arrived at the table. The waiting staff began to pour wine. They switched to safer topics of conversation.

An hour later, Nick Cane gave his best man's speech. He was nervous, but warmed up as he went along, and got quite emotional toward the end.

'As some of you know, I've had troubles in recent years. That's when you find out who your true friends are. People who'll stick with you when it'd be convenient not to. Tony and Eve have been two of my strongest and dearest supporters. They helped me rebuild my life. It's wonderful to see them rebuilding their own lives, giving such strong support to each other. They're two of the finest people it's been my privilege to know and they truly deserve each other. I want you to join me now in raising your glasses to wish them a long and happy life together.'

People stood, then drank. Melanie wiped a tear from her eye. A few more minutes and it was all over. People began to talk about the party in the evening.

'Want to come up to my room for a rest before the evening do starts?'

'I was going to invite you back to mine,' Melanie said. 'The evening party's at the Labour Club in Arnold, not here. My flat's near there.'

He needn't have forked out for a room. Oh well, it was on expenses, and he'd have somewhere to escape later, if he and Melanie got tired of each other, or anything else came up. Still, he'd better do his duty now.

'I'll need to sleep off some of this wine before I drive anywhere.'

Melanie narrowed her eyes. 'You're pushing your luck, aren't you?'

He smirked. 'It is a wedding.'

She giggled. 'Only teasing. Come on, then, show me to your bedchamber.'

She took his hand. Sarah Bone did a double take when Pete passed her table. He affected not to notice her. Life was full of coincidences. But it was also full of deceptions. The trick was to figure out which were which.

TWENTY

'Know that woman over there?' Sarah asked Nick, pointing at a forty-something bottle blonde in a green dress that displayed deep cleavage.

'Melanie Carter. She works at Stoneywood with Eve.'

'What about her boyfriend?'

'Didn't notice him. Melanie used to get through blokes more often than I replaced my razor blades. Doubt she's changed.'

'It was Pete Carlson, the reporter. He's writing a story about Andrew.'

'He's the fucker who doorstepped me when I didn't return his calls. I told him to get lost. Want me to steer clear of you for the rest of the evening?'

'Don't be daft. Everybody knows we're old friends. I suggest we hit the dancefloor together.'

On Arnold Labour Club's makeshift dancefloor, bride and groom were having their first dance to Whitney Houston's version of 'I Will Always Love You'. That was OK, Sarah thought. A slow dance with Nick would put people off the scent of her and Hugh, who she'd spent the last two hours in bed with.

It was a long time since she'd been in Nick's arms. The moment he placed a firm hand on her back did something funny to her. It felt like coming home.

The song ended and the room applauded the happy couple. The DJ segued, unimaginatively, into Houston's 'I Wanna Dance (with somebody who loves me)' and the floor filled.

'Did you bring anybody?' Sarah asked.

'Too much, asking a casual date to sit at the top table. Who's your toy boy?'

'My parliamentary assistant, Hugh. He's over for the election and it's a good way for him to get to know people.'

'Don't get many "Hugh"s these days. His parents fans of your grandad?'

'One's a Methodist minister and the other's a Sociology lecturer, so doubtful.'

103

Nick gave her a slightly odd look. Sarah realised she'd messed up: bosses never knew what their employees' parents did. He could still read her. The song ended. Time to get away.

'I'm going to find out what Pete's doing here. Thanks for the dance.'

Nick looked disappointed. Did he still…? But it was too late for them, even if she weren't with Hugh. Soon, she'd be in Leatherhead.

Pete Carlson had changed his shirt since she noticed him this afternoon. That meant he'd been somewhere to get changed. He was sat on his own while his partner chatted with friends at the bar. Sarah joined him.

'Small world,' she said.

'Was that Nick Cane you were dancing with?'

'You know it was. What are you doing here, Pete?'

'My girlfriend invited me. Had no idea you knew the happy couple.'

'Tony was the Labour candidate before me in Nottingham West.'

'It's the new wife that Melanie knows. How are you, anyway?'

'I'll be glad when this is over, for better or worse.'

'Not one of those MPs who like elections, then?'

She shook her head. He leant forward conspiratorially, a move which allowed him to fleetingly check out her boobs. Again.

'You'd be missed at Westminster. A lot of people respect you.'

'Thanks. Now try to convince me you're not here working on that story.'

He had a cheeky, attractive glint in his eyes. 'I'm always working, can't help it. So are you, I surmise. But I promise not to grill you. Would you like to dance?'

At that moment, the Jackson Five came on, 'I Want You Back', a song that Sarah had loved since childhood.

'Sure,' she said. 'Why not?'

Pete danced well. His girlfriend glanced at them proprietorially.

'Please say it's OK for me to call you,' Pete said, as they parted. 'It's not you I'm interested in doing over, I assure you.'

'I can't stop you calling me, Pete.'

It was an hour before she judged it safe for her to dance with Hugh. It would, she decided, look odd if she didn't. The music wasn't from his era, but he moved well to 'Use It Up and Wear It Out'.

'Enjoying yourself?' her secret boyfriend asked.

'Bit of a busman's holiday. People keep asking about my chances in the election. We can get away in half an hour or so if you like.'

'Best if I leave first and you follow when you're ready. We don't want tongues wagging.'

'You've done this kind of thing before, have you?'

Hugh used his debonair smile. 'I want to keep doing *this kind of thing* for as long as possible. While *you* want half the people here to knock themselves out for you over the next two and a half weeks. Take as long as you need.'

'I remember who you are.' Nick had gone outside for a smoke, so Pete had followed him.

'I gather that you still don't want to talk about Andrew Saint.'

'You gather correctly.'

Pete lit a spliff. He'd bought some grass to share with Geraldine the night before, hoping it would open her up. It had. The stuff might work equally well on Nick.

'I was at your friend's old house this week, talking to a girl there.'

That got Nick's attention. 'Why?'

'Trying to figure out who owns it. I thought knowing that might give me some clue as to why your friend got killed.'

'Blind alley,' Nick said. He stubbed out his cigarette and turned to go.

'Wait. The girl's called Geraldine. She owns your flat.'

Cane's eyes flared. 'Jerry's a kid. She didn't know Andy. Leave her out of this.'

'I want to. But I'll need a bit of help from you. Do you still indulge?'

Nick took a quick look to his left and right before accepting the joint.

'Look,' he said, after two pulls, 'I don't know who killed Andrew and Nancy. I wasn't involved in what Andy was involved in. All I know is that he left the country because he owed someone a lot of money. They tracked him down. Does it matter who they were? It's the way that world works.'

'It wasn't the first time that Andrew had run when he got into trouble. He scarpered to the States around the time you were arrested, didn't he?'

'Ancient history.'

'You can learn a lot from history. Give me something I can use.'

Nick took one more pull on the spliff and handed it back.

'Andrew was a crook. I never have been. Once, I saw the opportunity to make a decent wedge by growing weed and, yes, Andrew did help me sort out the distribution. Yes, he put some distance between us when I got arrested, as anybody in their right mind would have done. No, I don't know who killed him. End of.'

'I want to believe that. But there are people who think that there was a much bigger figure behind Andrew Saint. Behind a large proportion of the drugs in Nottingham, and beyond. That's who my story's really about.'

'You mean this isn't about fucking up Sarah's chances of re-election?'

Their dilated eyes met. Pete got the impression that Nick was still into the MP. Useful. Or was it more than that? He tried to clarify.

'I've no interest in hurting Sarah unless she's involved. When drug trafficking gets to that scale, politicians do tend to have their noses in the trough.'

'Dream on.'

'Andrew's wasn't the first murder in this. There was also Paul Morris.'

That was a guess. The former county councillor's murder remained unsolved. One of Pete's Insight colleagues had briefed him. The reporter suspected, but couldn't prove, that Morris' death was connected to the drug trade. Cane was silent. The

Morris comment had clearly thrown him. Pete pressed his advantage.

'Morris was quite a powerful local politician before he went to the Home Office. Any idea why he was killed?'

'You're asking the wrong man. I was inside for half the 90s, remember.'

More people came out to smoke. Pete stubbed out the joint, which, while it might not have loosened Cane's tongue, had certainly thrown him off balance.

'Labour county councillor. Left town for a job as a Home Office Drugs policy advisor, knifed to death a few weeks later. Unsolved case.'

'I remember the news story. Maybe he used to be your *Mr Big*, but if he was, he'll have been immediately replaced by someone else. That wasn't Andrew.'

I know that, Pete thought but didn't say. *Question is, was it you?*

TWENTY-ONE

Nazia Khan was the kind of woman whom other women described as 'handsome': full figured, with a striking face that was a little too square-jawed to be conventionally beautiful. She wore a plain salwar kameez that made her appear older than her thirty-six years. Beside Nazia on her brother's living room sofa was Eric Turnbull's wife, elegant solicitor Mary Harris.

'Good of you to come,' Mary said, 'especially during an election.'

Sarah wondered if Mary knew that her new husband had assiduously pursued Sarah for a good two years before settling on her. Probably not.

'My presence is off the record,' Sarah said. 'I trust that's understood.'

'It's a very difficult situation,' Mary agreed.

'Your brother-in-law came to my surgery,' Sarah told Nazia. 'I found him quite intimidating.'

'Me too,' Nazia said, voice softer than her stern demeanour suggested. 'What did he tell you?'

'That he was sure you'd killed your husband. Did you?'

'I did not.' She didn't sound affronted by the question, more resigned to it.

'He also told me we both used to go out with the same man. Nick Cane. Is that right? Nick was my boyfriend when I was an undergraduate.'

Nazia smiled affectionately. 'Nick was my first boyfriend. I was nineteen when I met him.'

'So was I,' Sarah said, with a smile. 'As was he.'

'This would have been a few years later. He was my younger brother's teacher. He treated me very... respectfully.'

Their eyes met and Sarah gave the smallest of nods to indicate that she understood what Nazia meant by this.

'Of course, we could never marry because of cultural differences. My family suspected what was going on and hurried me into marrying Omar.'

'Did you stay in touch with Nick?'

She shook her head. 'I was sorry to hear about his trouble, later. You?'

'I see him from time to time. He's doing well.'

'I'm glad to hear that.'

'In fact, he urged me to see you, after Bilal went to see him.'

'I didn't know that Bilal had been in touch with Nick.'

'But I don't know how I can help.'

Nazia leant forward. 'You used to be in the police, yes?'

'For a short while, a long time ago.'

'Can you find out if they are investigating me? And if they aren't, can you get them to release a statement saying so?'

'I've told Nazia that this isn't how the police work,' Mary said.

'It isn't. And my current contacts are limited,' Sarah told them. Her police links were about to become a lot stronger, but that was confidential, and Sarah didn't want to do anything out of line before she started her new job. In the old days, she would have talked to Mary's husband.

'Can Eric help?' she asked the solicitor.

'I'm afraid that there is nobody as ex as an ex-chief constable. Eric's removed himself from the loop completely. Says it's the only way. His perspective, which I share, is that Mrs Khan should keep her head down but make sure that influential people are willing to speak on her behalf.'

Sarah smiled. 'And what should these influential people be saying?'

'That the police have to do their job but these vicious rumours don't help a grieving widow with two young children. Perhaps add that the accusations are fuelled by racism and private resentments.'

'One Muslim attacking another is hardly racist.'

'Agreed. But Fahd's attack gives racists the ammunition they need to harass a strong Muslim woman. Fahd's accusations are caused by private resentments.'

Sarah turned to Nazia. 'I understand your position is that Fahd has concocted all this, may have even planted the hypodermic needle himself. If what you're telling me is right, why did the police get a search warrant?'

Mary answered for her, which irritated Sarah. 'Fahd has powerful friends, and the "hidden needle" gave the police sufficient cause. They found nothing else.'

'That works in your favour. Is it worth considering that Fahd might have murdered Omar? Say he was jealous of his brother and wanted Nazia for himself.'

She glanced at the woman who was at the centre of this passion and tried, once more, to imagine her with Nick. But she could not picture them as a couple.

'It is true that Fahd made a clumsy proposition to me,' Nazia said, carefully, 'but I don't see how he would have had the opportunity to hurt my husband.'

That was good. She hadn't clutched the straw that Sarah had offered – as a test, of sorts. Sarah wasn't sure if she liked Nazia. But she thought she believed her.

Nobody would talk to Pete about the death of Paul Morris. His widow had remarried and wanted, naturally enough, to put the past behind her. Morris had not worked at the Home Office long enough to have left much of an impression. The main thing people there remembered about him was how he died.

One executive officer mentioned that Morris used to flirt a lot.

'Good looking bloke, bit of a stud. I've always been a sucker for the Denzil Washington type, but he was way too fond of himself. Plus he had a photo of his wife and kids on his desk when he was acting lascivious, which I found creepy.'

Some of the Nottingham people Pete spoke to also hinted that Morris screwed around. None suggested that he was into the drugs trade. That could be a blind alley. A jealous lover was the most likely murderer. His wife had a solid alibi. Morris was in London, near King's Cross, when he was knifed in the shower. At the same time his wife was dropping two of their three kids off at school.

Pete had managed to track down one of the officers who handled the initial investigation, but the DS was ducking his calls. When Pete did succeed in catching Rob Walker on the phone, he wasn't forthcoming.

'Sorry, mate, been a busy time. Anyway, there's nothing I can tell you about Morris or how he died.'

'Let me buy you a drink, help me get the general background.'

'New baby at home, I'm off the booze. The case is open, but I'm not on it any more. Suggest you try the press office.'

'Wait, please. I know there's something that didn't come out. Tell me, off the record, was Morris dodgy?'

'Quite possibly, but we couldn't prove it. That's not why…'

'Not what?'

'Gotta go. Like I said, try the press office.'

He hung up. Pete tried to figure out where the unfinished sentence had been going. *That's not why we think he was murdered?* Or *that's not why I'm being very careful about what I say to you?* He'd have to speak to Rob Walker again, but best leave it a while. Next, he needed to establish whether there was any connection between Morris and Andrew Saint. That would take him back to Nottingham, which he didn't mind at all. He and Melanie were having fun. Before seeing her again, he had a nineteen-year-old to hook up with. He boarded a bus to Notting Hill.

'You took your time,' Geraldine told him when he showed up at her door, having phoned half an hour earlier.

'No rest for the wicked. Wondered if I could come in.'

'I thought you'd never ask.'

He'd come for a look round Saint's former home while the other students weren't there. This was now a posh area for a student house, but it wasn't so long ago that Notting Hill was awash with squats. Saint had probably bought cheap, using drug money, then started doing it up, but never finished.

Pete went for a pee. The bathroom was high spec, as was the kitchen where Geraldine made him a brew. Chrome everywhere. Other parts of the house were run-down, in need of new carpet and a lick of paint.

The rest of the students had gone home for the summer. Geraldine, however, didn't have another home to go to. Nick Cane lived in the flat she owned.

'You could make good money renting out these rooms to

tourists over the summer months,' he told her.

'The others pay a retainer. Also, it's too much hassle.'

Geraldine was wearing a little make-up and a thin blouse with no bra. A blatant come-on. Pete wasn't prudish. He'd been known to sleep with a woman to get a story, but never one so young. Moreover, although this wasn't a strict rule, he tended to sleep with one woman at a time. He prepared a friendly lie for later.

'Would you mind if I took a look around?'

'Be my guest. What are you looking for?'

'I'll know when I find it.'

The bedrooms had locks and Pete didn't see much point in asking if Geraldine had spare keys. The house had a first-floor fire escape, useful for a quick getaway. Access to the loft was padlocked, which intrigued him.

'Know what's up there?' he asked.

'No idea.'

'Got a key?'

'For emergencies, yeah.'

'Think we could create an emergency?'

Geraldine looked him straight in the eye. He saw that she was wiser than her years and not in the least embarrassed by her desires.

'You scratch my back…' she said.

'Think anyone suspects?' Hugh asked.

'Do I look as if I care?' Sarah was in the bath with him, face to face. She couldn't remember the last time she'd found time to take a bath, never mind shared one.

'What will you do,' he asked, 'if you don't win?'

She'd been waiting for him to ask this but wasn't going to answer. No point bursting their bubble until the election was over.

'We're not allowed to talk about losing,' she said. 'Be positive.'

'I am positive. Never been more positive. OK, assume you win. Are we going to carry on, in secret? Or are we allowed to go public?'

'I haven't really thought about it,' Sarah said, truthfully.

'Think about it now.'

'OK, I'm thinking.' Sarah played with his penis until it hardened. This was one advantage of a twenty-something lover, that he could be aroused again so quickly. Satisfied by the sight, she leant forward to kiss its tip, then sat back.

'I've thought. I don't want to get a reputation, but if one of us were to take another job, we've nothing to hide, then we'll see how we flourish in the open.'

'Are you telling me to get another job?'

'I'm not telling you to do anything, I'm telling you what I want. Now, tell me what you want.'

'I want you to suck my cock.'

The phone rang. Sarah heard the voice leaving a message on the machine and stopped what she was doing.

'I have to take this.'

The person on the line was Rebecca Allen. Rebecca had been at Ryton with Sarah when both were training to be coppers. Sarah wasn't suited to the job. She'd lasted little over a year. Rebecca, meanwhile, had been promoted, married a cop, got divorced, and not dropped off the greasy pole. She'd transferred to Nottingham a few months ago. That was when she'd sent Sarah an email, suggesting a drink. Sarah felt a little guilty that it had taken the Omar Khan case to prompt her reply, but, then, Sarah had always been bad at maintaining female friendships. Since leaving uni, her relationships had all revolved around work.

'…my hours are pretty crazy but I expect yours are too, so-'

'-Becky!' Sarah interrupted the message. 'Thanks for calling me back so quickly. I'm sorry I took so long to call you. My life's been mad.'

'I know the feeling. I prefer Rebecca these days, Becky makes me feel like a teenager. What's this about? Your email was ambiguous.'

'It's a bit complicated. When can you meet for a drink?'

'I'm going away for the weekend. It'd either have to be tonight or next week.'

'I'll have finished canvassing by nine, I hope.'

'I'm in the city centre. Matlock Court. New development at

the bottom of North Sherwood Street. Know it?'

Sarah knew it: a short walk from the Central Police station and several of the city's best pubs. Rebecca told her the number. 'Come when it suits. We'll go for a drink. Or, if there's something confidential you want to discuss, bring a bottle.'

TWENTY-TWO

'There is a light in the loft but we might need a torch as well,' Jerry said.

Pete pulled down the loft ladder. 'Do you possess a torch?'

'No, but I think there's one up there.' Last autumn, the day before the others moved in, she and Nick had moved the crap they hadn't had time to sort. She had to keep reminding herself not to mention Nick's name to Pete. Difficult, when her head was woozy after sex. She hadn't had an orgasm with a bloke since he-whose-name-must-not-be-mentioned years ago and it was doing funny things to her head. Nice things. She wanted to please Pete. She didn't want today to be a one off.

Pete found the light switch on one of the rafters. A dusty fluorescent strip flickered into life, casting good light on the central section of the boarded loft, but leaving the eaves shrouded in shadow. She and Nick had shoved numerous plastic bags up there. It was easier than sorting out Andrew's things for the charity shop.

'Did your landlord put it all up here or was that Andrew Saint?'

'Dunno,' Jerry lied. When she and Nick went up to the loft, there'd only been a couple of boxes left by Saint – or one of his predecessors, she had no means of knowing.

'The bags look fresh but the boxes are dusty. Let's check them out first.' He opened one. 'Books. Belonged to Saint's father, by the looks of them. Funny what people keep.' He opened another. 'Board games. Anyone still play board games?'

'I like Monopoly.'

'Let's try the bags.'

The plastic bags, as she knew, held letters and documents, mostly. A few gig tickets and a Glastonbury Festival programme. One graduation photo. Most of the stuff could safely have been thrown away. There were some legal letters about Andrew's mother's estate and a receipt for putting in a damp course. Boring. No love letters. Nothing incriminating.

'It might be better if we take the bags downstairs, look at them properly,' Jerry suggested.

'You're right.'

'But we'll have to put them back exactly the way we found them. I don't want my landlord to know I've been up here.'

'What did you say your landlord's name was, again?'

'I didn't.'

Pete took the hint and didn't repeat the question. They began to carry bags down to the landing. The work was dirty and, later, they would shower together.

'Ever regret leaving the force?' Rebecca asked, while Sarah poured Viognier. They were in her two-bedroom maisonette, which was smart but small, half the ground floor being taken up by her parking place.

'Never. The culture back then…'

'It's not much better now. But… slow change is still change. And if you want to see change, you've got to be part of the change you want to see.'

'I'm with you on that. Figured I could make more difference as an MP, though it's unlikely I'll have that job much longer.' She explained how marginal her seat was.

'This thing you want to talk about in confidence, will it swing the election?'

'Not as such, but you might be able to stop me embarrassing myself in public, which could certainly lose me the election.' She described the situation with Fahd and Nazia Khan, concluding: 'It's created a lot of publicity but, from where I'm sitting, looks less like a police case than a family feud, complicated by desire and – maybe – money. That said, I know I'm biased in favour of the woman. Maybe she really did murder him.'

'I asked around about the case after you mentioned it on the phone. Insulin poisoning is very hard to prove without a confession.'

'You're saying she can get away with it?'

'I'm saying it will be very hard to prove. Let's assume the brother's right: she was having an affair and decided to do in her husband. We'd have to exhume his body, find a puncture mark, then somehow prove that she injected him with sufficient insulin to induce death. That's a tough call.'

'But not impossible.'

'Our people *are* investigating her, so I wouldn't go public with your support for the widow if I were you. Was that everything you needed to know?'

'Yes, it was. Thanks.'

They drank the rest of the bottle of wine before returning to the subject. It was nearly eleven and Sarah was about to leave. Her feet were tired from trudging door to door, canvassing votes. She would treat herself to a cab on Mansfield Road, save herself the twenty-minute walk home.

'Do you know who it is Nazia's supposed to be having the affair with?' she asked, at the door. 'Just me being nosy. Now I've met her, I'm curious. She doesn't look the type to take big risks.'

'Sex scrambles the brain sometimes. Certainly scrambled mine.' They had spent much of the last half hour discussing Rebecca's marriage to a former colleague, the end of which had caused her move to Nottingham. 'Actually I do recall the bloke's name, mainly because I keep seeing it on the side of cabs. According to a neighbour, she was seeing someone called Cane.'

Under close inspection, Pete saw that the papers they'd brought down were, if anything, even less promising than they'd appeared in the loft. Some were connected with the purchase of the house. There were solicitor's letters about the death of Saint's mother. Saint and his sister, Pauline, had split the inheritance. Presumably the sister had inherited this place, though how she'd come to rent it to Geraldine confused Pete.

But suppose Pauline didn't know of the house's existence, and Nick Cane had set Geraldine up here, told her to keep quiet about its ownership? Cane, Pete decided, was the bloke who'd given the teenager her taste for older men. Which meant that Pete was two degrees of sexual separation away from Sarah Bone, who had once been Nick's lover.

After they'd showered, and been to bed again, Pete left Geraldine sleeping. He went through more documents. She'd told him not to take anything away, but what she didn't see didn't count.

He started taking the boxes and plastic bags back up to the loft, where he had another look round in case they'd missed anything. Most of the clothes, Geraldine had told him earlier, they'd thrown out. There were a couple of boxes of LPs. An eclectic mix. Talking Heads. Blondie. Fleetwood Mac. R.E.M.. Gong. Kevin Ayers. Everyone he knew had put their LPs in the attic, if they had one, or given them away. What used to feel so valuable had become outmoded, but the covers were still cool, and some people found the objects hard to part with.

Best to be methodical. He looked in the sleeve of each one, came up with nothing more interesting than lyric sheets. Geraldine had brought down the box of board games. Hadn't Sarah said something about Saint liking them? That must be why he'd hung onto these childhood relics. Pete thought about returning it to the loft, then remembered Geraldine wanted the Monopoly set. When he removed the rectangular box, he noticed something at the bottom of the box. It was dark grey with a small touch of bright, crayon-like red. He reached into the box and pulled out what looked like a Walkman.

The device's rubric read *Sony TCH-353V Cassette-corder*. He hadn't seen one of these in years. Some journalists used to have them, though most preferred the quality and size of the slim dictation machines that took tiny cassettes. Just another useless object whose owner couldn't bring himself to throw things away. There was a cassette inside. He tried to play it but the cassette-corder's batteries were dead.

He took the cassette out. It was labelled *1996* on one side and *Chestnuts* on the other. What did that mean? Pete prayed that it was evidence – of what, he'd no idea. He put the machine in his bag.

Returning to the bedroom, he found Geraldine up and dressed.

'You look like you're about to leave.'

'I have to be back in Nottingham by the morning.'

'I haven't been there for a while. Want me to come with you?'

'Best not. It's work.'

'You've got a woman there, haven't you?'

Never lie unless you need to. 'Only a casual thing, but, yes.'

He watched her weigh up how to deal with this information and decide on dignity. 'You can come and see me again if you like. No strings.'

'No strings,' he agreed. 'You're quite something, Geraldine.'

'My friends call me Jerry,' she told him.

'I prefer Geraldine.' He kissed her softly on the lips. 'Gotta go.'

He liked her, he realised on the bus home. She was wiser than her years. Being brought up in care would do that. But she was damaged, and he had learnt to steer clear of damaged women, no matter how great they were in bed. Melanie was more his speed. Before going underground, he phoned her mobile to let her know which train he'd be on.

TWENTY-THREE

'Y ou've got my vote, duck. All Labour here. We like that John Prescott, too!'

The election, so dull for so long, had sprung into life. The Deputy Prime Minister was on repeat on every news channel, endlessly punching the thug who'd thrown an egg at him. From close quarters. In Rhyl. John's instinctive reaction wasn't a disaster. If anything, it was boosting Prescott's popularity.

Sarah went through the motions. The more she talked to people, the more she wanted to win. Fighting to win was in her DNA. She'd been campaigning in General Elections for nearly twenty years, since she and Nick helped Ken Coates' bid to take the new seat of Nottingham South. And lost. This time, the polls were holding up for Labour, but that hardly helped Sarah. Thanks to a scandal, she'd had a larger than average swing in '97. Wouldn't happen again.

Until Eve and Martin's wedding, Sarah hadn't seen Nick for two years. She'd kept her distance because of the murders at her Majorca villa. Sarah owed Nick a lot. She wanted to think well of him, despite what Rebecca had told her. Nick never used to be the sort of man who pursued married women. That said, Nick had history with Nazia Khan. Maybe that made a difference. Suppose Nazia had killed her husband in order to be with Nick? That was within the bounds of the possible. Impossible for Sarah to believe that Nick would have knowingly helped her.

Mary Harris wanted another meeting about the case. She was after a public statement. Sarah responded that she was too busy until after the election. If she lost, the dead dentist would become someone else's problem.

'Where to next?' Hugh asked. They'd reached the last house on the street.

'Ask Winston.' She still hadn't told Hugh about the Police Federation job. She didn't know if she wanted him to come with her. The way she saw it, they could try a long distance relationship. If that went well, they might make a go of things in

Leatherhead. One day, though, she might want to be back in Parliament. Hugh, she suspected, now she knew him better, also meant to end up there. Many office staff had parliamentary ambitions and Hugh was better qualified than most.

There was a call on her mobile. Few people had the number. Sarah rarely ducked calls. This one, though, she was tempted to ignore.

'Mary, hi. Sorry, but I'm really, really…'

'Something I thought you ought to know. I've heard a rumour the police have made an application to exhume Omar Khan's body. New evidence has come to light. They're now treating it as a potential murder enquiry.'

'I'll see what I can find out and get back to you.'

Pete had time to buy batteries and cheap headphones at WH Smith in St Pancras before boarding the Nottingham train. He preferred a table seat, allowing him to spread out his stuff. The train being quiet, he hoped to have all four seats to himself. Fat chance. An older woman sat opposite him just before they pulled out. She soon tucked into her Ken Follett. Pete pressed 'play' with no idea of what, if anything, he was about to hear.

The conversation was muffled, as though recorded from inside a bag or a pocket, which it probably was: we weren't talking high-technology surveillance equipment. The first voice was regionless, BBC English. The second had a slight Northern twang.

'This is the one and only time that we'll meet.'

'Then how will I know whether people who claim to be your representatives speak for you?'

'Anybody who mentions my name is suspect. Should it happen, you must call via (*unclear*).

'Our retiring friend you're asking for fifteen percent. That's high.'

'Not when you consider who has to be kept sweet. The price may rise.'

'For that kind of money, I need reassurance you can deliver.'

'Read the papers next week. You'll see that I've been promoted.'

'I already knew that,' said the man who must be Saint. 'Otherwise we wouldn't be talking. I need to promote someone on my side. Any thoughts?'

'I have one or two candidates in mind. Now that we're partners, I'm open to suggestion. They need to be on the way up, but with an ear to the ground.'

'I have someone in mind. He's just gone on the County Council.'

'I know who you mean. One of yours, is he?'

'He's his own man, but I gave him his start.'

'OK, then. Use the same money channel as before. We're done now, I think. We won't be meeting again.'

The tape ran on for thirty seconds before the recorder was turned off. The rest of the side was blank. Pete could infer who was being referenced at the end of the conversation: Paul Morris had been elected to the County Council in 1996.

The key question, though, was the identity of the second man, the one who wanted fifteen per cent of Saint's turnover. This was the man who Saint had taken the risk of recording, giving himself leverage should anything go wrong. For that kind of percentage, the man was offering serious protection. He must be police. Senior, and about to be promoted. Pete needed to play the tape to one of his police contacts. He'd have to be careful who he asked. The police looked after their own.

The rest of the cassette was blank. He put the other side on and pressed *play*. Music. He fast forwarded, got another song, so fast forwarded again. Sounded like the same group. It was only three songs in that he recognised a song, one that Fatima used to like. *That's me in the spotlight*. No, hang on, the title came later in the chorus: *Losing My Religion*. It was a home-made mix-tape, the best of R.E.M..

TWENTY-FOUR

I n the morning, Sarah rang Rebecca at work, told her the rumour she'd heard from Brian the evening before.

'Your source is correct. We'll be making an official statement the day before it happens: you can't do this sort of thing on the quiet.'

'And when will that be?'

'Soon. But there isn't a team in place yet.'

'Presumably there's some new evidence?'

Rebecca lowered her voice. 'If so, nobody's told me what it is. Political pressure is what I'm hearing.'

'Do you know what they're hoping to find?'

'Needle marks in unusual places, I expect. Bear in mind, there was no post mortem. Nobody anticipated any controversy, then family members kicked off. So the force is covering itself. The chances remain that the results will be inconclusive.'

Sarah thanked her and called Mary Harris back.

'That's worrying, but thanks for letting me know. I'll phone Nazia.'

'Tell her not to panic. They're unlikely to get a clear-cut result.'

'That's the problem. A clear-cut result is what Nazia needs.'

Caroline and Joe had long planned to move from Sherwood to a place in The Park. There, or one of the villages between Nottingham and Newark. Unless.

Unless things fell apart. In business, bankruptcy was always a risk. Conditions changed. You couldn't always predict how people would behave. Joe's name was a fading asset. It was over a decade since he'd played for Notts County and the taxi world was dog eat dog. DG Cabs were challenging Yellow Cars for the top spot in the city, while Nottingham Taxis were closing in on Cane Cars for third place. Joe, distracted by two young children, needed to keep his eye on the ball.

The state of their marriage, too, was far from perfect. Caroline had made the effort, got her figure back after Oliver, though it took the best part of a year. By the time she could fit into her old clothes and her libido returned, the sex had fallen right off. They'd slipped from twice weekly full service pre-pregnancy to fortnightly fumbles. Call her paranoid, call her insecure, but lately she'd started worrying that Joe was, once again, getting it elsewhere.

Caroline was still a full-time mum, but Phoebe had started nursery and she'd begun leaving Oliver with a child-minder two afternoons a week. Unbeknown to Joe, she'd recently upped that to three afternoons a week. Wednesday, she had gathered from a couple of 'no message, I'll get him on his mobile' calls, was an afternoon when her husband rarely showed up in HQ. At breakfast, when she'd asked about the day ahead, he'd mention paperwork, seeing corporate clients.

But that was not what he was up to this afternoon. This afternoon, he was visiting a private house in The Park.

The house had its own drive, slanting uphill off Park Valley, the wide road at the bottom of the Park Steps, which were carved into the sandstone cliff the city rested on. Climb to the top of them, you were at Hart's restaurant on the old General Hospital site. From there you could walk down Park Row, cross Maid Marion Way, and be in the city centre in five minutes. On Park Valley, by contrast, you were in a different world, utterly unlike the former council estate where she and Joe lived. Its streets were lined with old, dignified houses and, occasionally, architect designed new builds. Like this one, hidden from the road.

Joe had parked their Peugeot on Park Valley. Caroline stood behind it, peering up the slope. If Joe came back, she'd have time to duck behind another car before he saw her. He didn't come out, so she ventured a little up the hill. The Park was the sort of place where people left a note on your car if it didn't display a permit. She'd be very visible, walking up that drive.

The house Joe was visiting had a long, flat-roofed, single storey structure. Possibly a garden hidden behind the building. Above and beyond, on a ledge with wooden steps leading to it, was another structure, the size of a shipping container, with large windows. The sun reflected off the glass. She couldn't see inside.

A study, possibly, or a children's play room. Or a specially designed area for the woman of the house to shag her taxi driver bit of rough.

There was an Alfa Romeo parked in the drive and room for another car or two. If Caroline drew close enough, she could crouch behind the Alfa, get a closer look at what was going on. But suppose somebody was watching from the extension on the hill? She already looked suspicious, standing on the drive. Nobody had climbed the steps to the extension so, whoever Joe was visiting, they probably weren't up there. It would be a hubby at work with bored wife at home situation, Joe her back-door man. Except this house didn't have a back door.

A cough. Caroline glanced behind her to see an old bloke in a cardigan, standing at the bottom of the drive, arms folded. He wore slippers. A neighbour, or an Alzheimer's case. Possibly both. Caroline got out her phone and pretended to be checking an address. She shook her head in a stagey manner and, ignoring the man in slippers, returned to her Maestro. It was parked tightly between two other cars, where Joe was unlikely to notice it. The pensioner crossed the road and disappeared behind a large tree. His point had been made. He could be calling the police, alerting them that a woman burglar in sweat pants who was casing a nearby joint, but this seemed unlikely, so she stayed put.

An hour later, her husband sauntered down the drive and, without looking round, got into their car. He'd timed his departure nicely to collect Phoebe from nursery. Caroline watched him go, then headed to the child-minder's.

She'd been home two minutes when Joe turned up, all smiles.

'Good day?' she asked.

'Still got a ton of receipts to go through but, yeah, OK. I met a potential corporate client.'

'Who was that?'

'Jatinder Singh. Went to his place in The Park. He has a chain of restaurants, so could put a lot of work our way: staff and customers.'

'Great.' Caroline broke out her widest smile, relieved to find that her paranoia had been misplaced. 'Maybe he'll invite us for a meal next time.'

'I don't mind his mint tea, but you know how I feel about curry.'

'It said in *The Times* that it's become our national dish.'

'That's as may be. Give me fish and chips any day.'

'I was thinking', Caroline said, 'why don't we rent a DVD and I chill a bottle of Chardonnay while you pop to Captain Cod, save me cooking? Quiet night in.'

'I'd love to, babe, but I'm meeting a couple of people for a drink. Potential new business. I need to spend more time cultivating contacts.'

'Of course you do.' Caroline kissed him lightly on the lips. 'But don't get too rat-arsed. I might have a use for you when you get in.'

They both knew that this was for show. When Joe did get home, whenever that turned out to be, she would already be spark out, having been on the go since six in the morning. She was mad to worry about Joe sneaking off for illicit liaisons in the afternoon. For, after ten at night, he could go anywhere he liked. She wouldn't have a fucking clue.

'Nice of you to come,' Sarah told her old friend at the International Community Centre. She was about to debate with the other candidates for Nottingham West.

'This isn't an act of loyalty,' Rebecca told Sarah. 'I wanted a word. CID need fresh eyes. I've been put on the Omar Khan case.'

'And I'll bet you're still not going to tell me what new information prompted the exhumation.'

'The exhumation's still not been scheduled.' She took a breath. 'Nick Cane.'

'What about him?'

'According to Fahd Khan, Cane was having an affair with his sister-in-law. Fahd's also saying that Cane may have been involved in Omar's death but that he's protected because he's a friend of yours.'

'That's ridiculous. He was my boyfriend, but we split up eighteen years ago, around the time I first knew you. I've only seen him twice in the last two years.'

'That's about to change.'

'What do you mean?' Sarah asked, as the organiser signalled that it was time for her to go out. The other candidates were already in their seats.

'He's in the audience. Sixth row. I've saved myself the chair next to his.'

The debate went about as well as Sarah had expected. The government's record was solid. They could and should be criticised for not doing enough, but had been careful to manage expectations. Moreover, Sarah was able to throw the last Tory government's record back at her main opponent. The Liberal, while he had no chance, was trickier to deal with. For a start, he was in favour of unilateral nuclear disarmament. Sarah couldn't say what she actually thought: that Britain's nukes were an expensive form of cock waving and there were no circumstances under which they'd be used. Their main purpose was to keep Britain at the top table of world security. But unilateral disarmament was no longer party policy, so she had to find a formula by which she embraced multilateralism without outright fibbing.

'I very much hope that a situation will emerge whereby we can, as a country, divest ourselves of all nuclear warheads. Unfortunately, the government and the voting public aren't ready for that yet, so I must reluctantly disagree.'

She couldn't help but look at Nick to check his reaction. They'd each joined the Labour Party when unilateral nuclear disarmament was the burning issue. They'd had to watch the then leader, Michael Foot, twist himself in knots trying to defend that policy. Nick caught Sarah's eye and gave a reassuring nod. Rebecca, next to him, was poker faced. Her politics – insofar as Sarah knew them – were old school Tory, like most police, laced with a profound cynicism about all politicians.

Public events like this one had little tangible effect on the constituency vote. Hustings were a throwback to pre-TV days, a duty rather than a necessity. Tony Blair's charm, backed up by

John Prescott's common touch and Gordon Brown's reputation for financial rectitude, all counted for far more. Sarah wished that Labour had a woman in that senior mix, but there were few to choose from. Didn't help that, often, capable women were stuck in marginal seats like Sarah's. According to those in cabinet, the real decisions were no longer taken there. Tony Blair ran the government as though it were a Law firm, relying on close advisors and confidantes.

The Tory tied herself in knots defending their manifesto policy of making every criminal serve their full sentence. Sarah surveyed the audience. A hundred and fifty people. Looking at Rebecca with Nick, Sarah felt like she'd time travelled back to the first half of the '80s. It made her feel old. She hoped that Rebecca wouldn't use this opportunity to interrogate Nick. He would be blindsided.

What if it were true? What if Nick had conspired with his mistress to murder her husband in a manner that was almost impossible to detect? What if he planned, after a suitable interlude, to get together with her? The Nick she met nearly twenty years ago was not the Nick of now. People changed, not always for the better.

'Sarah?'

She realised that she was being asked a question and had zoned out. She smiled at the moderator, a local vicar, who took mercy on her.

'Anything to add on sentencing?'

Silently thanking him for the prompt, Sarah answered on autopilot. The Conservative manifesto, she told the crowd, was called *Time for Common Sense*, but there was little sense in what they were proposing.

'You have to believe in rehabilitation,' Sarah said, using her compassionate voice. 'And the parole service has to have the flexibility to allow early release for good behaviour. Our Justice system isn't only about punishment. It's about making society safer. That means turning criminals into productive members of society. It's not easy, but the Tories' one size fits all punishment policy is a failed policy.'

There was a smattering of applause, including from Nick, though, not, she noticed, Rebecca. The debate ended a few minutes later. Sarah shook hands and took congratulations, trying to get to Nick before he left. He smiled in her direction. Then she was button-holed by a colleague she couldn't avoid and, by the time she could escape, he had gone. As had Rebecca.

TWENTY-FIVE

J erry was glad to get out of London. When the city heated up it got too clammy for her. Jerry's first year exam results were a week away. She'd a summer job lined up, temping in the office of a Law firm.

She'd phoned Pete a couple of times, a booty call. He was out of town. Work, he said, but she knew he was staying with his Nottingham piece. Melanie. Or Mel, as she wrote at the end of her texts, which Jerry had read while Pete was showering. Only people over thirty signed their texts. Mel sounded keen, but not super keen. Maybe theirs was primarily a booty call type relationship, too.

Mel appeared to be a recent thing, much as she and Pete were. Jerry understood that the journalist might require company nearer his own age. And variety. She could relate to that. Although if she ever committed to a bloke, she would expect complete fidelity, no matter how handsome or horny he was.

Her train pulled into Nottingham. It had taken ages to find out how old Nick was. She'd sneaked a look at his passport when he stopped in Notting Hill on the way back from a holiday. This year, she knew, a card wasn't enough. Forty. Hard to work out what to get a guy so ancient. She'd settled on a Boss shirt. Purple, with silver buttons. Smart. If he played smart, it wouldn't be his only present from her.

Jerry had one of those wheelie cases made for carrying on aeroplanes (not that she had ever been on a plane). She walked from the station to Waverley Street, which, even at a fast clip, took a good half hour. She arrived in time to see a woman leaving Nick's house. Not necessarily visiting Nick. There were two other flats in the building, although both were owned by people with proper jobs. They wouldn't be home at this time in the afternoon. And Jerry recognised this woman. Hard not to, when she was on the front page of the evening paper she'd seen at every news stand on her walk across town. Nazia Khan.

Instead of walking up to Nick's, Jerry turned into the

Arboretum. The public park ran along the other side of Waverley Street. From there, she got a good view. Nazia's Alfa Romeo was parked round the corner on Burns Street. She got into it but seemed in no hurry to leave. Looked like she was on the phone. Jerry's suspicions were confirmed when she saw Nick leave the house, his head down. He got into the passenger seat. The two of them drove off in the direction of Alfreton Road.

Plan B. Jerry let herself into the flat and deposited her bag behind the sofa, where Nick wouldn't see it. Then she freshened up before calling Pete.

'I found some more stuff about Saint that I think you'll want to see.'

'Great. Want to describe it to me? I won't be back in town for a bit.'

'No need. I'm in Nottingham. Want to get together?'

He hesitated, confirming that he was staying at Melanie's, wherever she lived. But his other woman should still be at work, presuming she had a job.

'There's a pub just up the road from where I am. The Vernon. Know it?'

'I know it. Give me twenty minutes.'

Jerry didn't have much to show Pete, but she liked to make him jump. She would find a way to entice him back to this flat. And if Nick were to come home, catch them *in flagrante delicto* (you learnt a little Latin in the Law), well – sauce for the goose… she needed her mentor to know she was a woman, no longer a vulnerable girl he ought to take care of. At least, not in the old way.

The Vernon had seen better days. Geraldine kept Pete waiting for ten minutes. She'd had her hair done since he saw her last and wore a bob with straight edges. The new cut made her appear more like a model than a student. She was becoming a beautiful woman. Pete remained wary of her. Geraldine was volatile. Inevitable, given her age and what he had gleaned of her background. She didn't spot him in the corner, so he joined her at the bar.

'What are you having?'

'Gin and tonic.'

He bought her a single measure. 'You said you'd found something out. Did you come all the way to Nottingham to show me?'

'I came because it's Nick's fortieth birthday tomorrow and he's my friend.'

'Just a friend, eh?'

'If he was more than a friend, I might not be here with you.'

'It's near here, isn't it, your flat?'

'Very near,' she said, with a quiver of the eyebrow.

Pete would like a look inside that flat.

'Is he home?'

'Not at the moment. Are you thinking what I'm thinking?'

Ten minutes later, they were in Nick's top floor flat. It had a box room that doubled as a spare bedroom. No sheets on the single bed. Plenty of boxes to open, should Pete get some time alone.

Geraldine kissed him. She took it more slowly than before. Her hand did not hurry to his flies. He kissed her softly, letting his hand run down her back, listening to her breath deepen. He felt a tang of guilt about Melanie. She'd be getting home from work around now. But Melanie had made it clear that they were not exclusive and Geraldine knew about her. There was no need for him to be overly fastidious.

'I think I might smoke a spliff,' Geraldine said, and he realised that she had been very stoned when they had sex before. She must need that.

'I don't have any with me.'

'I've got some in my bag,' she told him. 'Give me five minutes.'

He pulled out his mobile. 'Fine. I've got some messages to return.'

He'd left a note for Melanie, telling her that something had come up and he didn't know when he'd be back. She'd texted to ask if he wanted to eat. He texted back. 'Prob but don't wait if ur hungry.' Then, as quietly as possible, he began to sift the cardboard boxes lined along the wall. Various instruction books.

Receipts. Print-outs about coding. There was a box file for all sorts of material that Nick had to put on the web. This was more neatly filed than the rest. Pete heard footsteps and stopped. Geraldine returned, a neat joint in her mouth. She lit it.

'Find anything interesting?'

He gave a sheepish grin.

'I know you're interested in Nick, but he'd gone straight before I met him. I wanted to prove that to you.'

She offered him the joint. He shook his head. 'It's Andrew Saint I'm interested in, and whoever he was working with before he was murdered. If that's not Nick Cane, I'll try not to bring him into it.'

'Very noble of you.' She sucked some more of the joint and gave him a lazy, sexy smile. 'Now, why don't you...' She stopped speaking. A moment later, he heard what she'd heard. Footsteps on the stairs.

'I don't think it's a good idea if he finds me here with you,' he told her.

'Have it your own way.'

Had she planned this to happen? He remembered her comment in the pub, implying that he was second choice after Nick. She wanted him to find them at it. A key turned in the lock. Geraldine stubbed out the joint and left the room, closing the door behind her.

'Surprise!' he heard her say.

'Jerry! This really is a surprise,' Nick replied. 'Why didn't you...?'

'Then it wouldn't have been a surprise, would it?'

They couple remained in the hallway, talking. Nick Cane came over more like a school teacher than a lover. He asked about Geraldine's course, when her results were due. He called her *Jerry*. Pete couldn't leave until they were out of the hall, so used the time to look under the bed. He could roll under there should Cane come into the room. Not that there was much space. He pulled out a box of dusty cassette tapes. The writing on the cases was familiar. The same as on the music compilation he'd found on one side of that cassette in Andrew Saint's loft. There was also one of those metal boxes people used to store important documents in case of fire. Pete slipped it out, hoping that the box wouldn't be locked.

It wasn't. He sifted through the files inside until he found what he was after. He made notes, then put the papers back and returned the box whence it came. The hall had gone quiet, so he risked opening the door. He could hear Geraldine and Nick in the living room, mid-conversation, their voices raised. Geraldine was, Pete assumed, provoking a loud conversation to give him cover to leave. She would expect him to have gone by now. The two of them might come out any minute, so he'd better get his skates on. Nevertheless, he couldn't resist a brief listen.

'…don't give me that. A married woman doesn't sneak around to yours in the middle of the day unless-'

'-unless she's under suspicion of murder so can't meet at her own home or anywhere public. Jerry, you don't know anything about this.'

'What I'm curious about is, what have you got to do with her?'

'We're old friends.'

'What kind of friend?' Geraldine sounded like a jealous wife.

'I knew her before she was married. I used to teach her brother.'

'Where did you go to in the car with her?'

'If you really must know, I took her to my brother's in Sherwood. Naz needed somewhere to stay that the press don't connect with her, somewhere she could take her kids. She can't use her own house, or her brother's. Joe and Caroline have a big place. Joe knows Naz from way back and Caroline said it was OK for her to stay with them until this exhumation business is over.'

'A family affair. You're too nice for your own good, you know that?'

Nick seemed to have convinced Geraldine, but Pete wasn't buying what he was selling. There was more to him and Nazia Khan. Useful, anyway, to know where the woman was hiding. It gave him leverage. Pete let himself out with the minimum of noise and texted Melanie to say that he'd be back in time for dinner.

TWENTY-SIX

T amazur played *Snap!* with Phoebe while Caroline nursed Oliver. Ahmad kept himself to himself, watching lots of television. Nazia said he took after his father, who had the same punched-in nose and twinkling eyes. The same shyness too.

'Omar was a kind man,' she'd told Caroline over a mug of strong tea. 'But his brother, Fahd, is not. This entire thing, this accusation, is because I refused to marry Fahd. He's lusted after me for years. The idea of sleeping with him repels me. He can see that on my face. It drives him crazy.'

Caroline was surprised by her frankness, this stern-faced woman who wore chunky jewellery and matronly Asian mourning dress. Nick had once fallen for Nazia, so she must have had plenty about her. When he'd asked Caroline if it was OK for Nazia to stay, she'd said yes without consulting Joe. It was only for two or three days, until the exhumation was done with.

'Who are those kids in the front room?' her husband asked when he got in. Seven. Early for him. Caroline explained. Joe's eyes narrowed.

'Where is she?'

'Having a bath.'

'Which room is she sleeping in?'

'Tamazur's sharing with Phoebe. Ahmad's in the spare bedroom. I've given Nazia my office.' This was the room where Caroline used to use to do her marking and preparation, but she hadn't gone back to work since Oliver was born. The office had a single bed for guests.

'You should have asked me first.'

'It's you who used to know her, not me.'

'In the 80s!' He lowered his voice. 'And she's being accused of... you know. If word gets out, it could hurt business.'

'Then we'll change the name, like I suggested last week,' Caroline snapped. Cane Cars was a good name when Joe started the business – nearly a decade ago. But these days his footballing career was a distant memory and the name made the firm less attractive to anyone who might want to buy it. Caroline had suggested that they change the name to ABC. There wasn't one of those in Nottingham. Joe said he wasn't going to name his company after a band he'd never liked.

'I'm going for a shower,' Joe grumped. Their bedroom had an en-suite, one of the first things Caroline had insisted on when they moved into this house.

'We'll be eating with Nazia in half an hour,' she told him.

Part of her, she admitted to herself, was excited about having a murder suspect in the house. When this was over, and Nazia had left, it would give her something to tell the other mums. Once a week a gang of them had lunch after yoga.

'I feel better for that. Anything I can do to help?' Nazia wore jeans and a loose top. She had a good figure, Caroline observed, fuller than hers, but not heavy. Her jeans were pale blue and expensive, with ornate silver studs. Prada, if Caroline wasn't mistaken.

'It's in the oven. I hope you like lasagne. Don't worry, I bought halal beef.'

'That's very thoughtful of you.'

'Not at all. How about a glass of red?'

To her relief, Nazia did drink alcohol. They made small talk about their children. Once they were halfway down a large glass of Valpolicella, Caroline asked the question that she'd been working up to.

'Has it been weird for you, reconnecting with Nick after all these years? I know that you and he were… close once.'

'Not at all', Nazia told her. 'Back then, you know, Nick was a perfect gentleman. He was a friend to Bilal and to me. We had a… thing, but we both knew that it wasn't going to go anywhere. I'm sorry he never married.'

'He has time. Your husband was in his 40s when you married, wasn't he?'

'True. Omar had been working all hours, building up a career. He didn't want to get married until he could be a very good provider.'

And the better off he became the higher quality wife he could attract.

'It must have been hard, losing him so suddenly.'

'These accusations have made it even harder. I hope this will be over soon.'

'And then?'

'And then I will decide what to do next. Move, maybe. Sell the house and use some of the proceeds to start a business.'

'What kind of business do you have in mind?'

'I was thinking maybe... taxis?' Nazia had kept a straight face. It took Caroline a second or two to realise that she was joking. She laughed politely before returning to the subject that interested her most.

'How does Nick seem after all this time? Has he changed much?'

'So much interest in Nick.'

Caroline blushed. Was it obvious that she and Nick...

'Sorry, that was rude of me. I am accused of having an affair with Nick, did you know that?'

'No, I didn't,' Caroline lied.

'That is why I'm sensitive about him. But I'm no longer his type. I think he likes bony women, the way I was when I met him, barely out of my teens. As for me, I've only just been widowed. I'm not looking at men that way. It's friends I need, not a lover. I hope that you and I can be friends.'

'Me too,' Caroline said, as Joe returned from his shower. He brazenly checked out Nazia's behind. It wasn't Nick she needed to keep an eye on.

'Darling,' she said, 'do you remember Nazia?'

Joe put on his twinkly, footballer's smile. 'Naz! It's been a long time.'

'Who's that?' Hugh asked Sarah when they pulled up outside her flat, where Pete Carlson was leaning against the wall, looking at his phone.

'He's a journalist. Sunday Times.'

'Think they're onto us?'

She shook her head. 'He's chasing another story. Andrew Saint.'

Hugh knew as much as he needed to know about Saint. She'd had no choice but to tell him. Hugh couldn't manipulate the facts if he didn't know what needed to be concealed. He was aware that Sarah had been at her Majorcan villa when Andrew and Nancy's bodies were discovered, and that this had been kept out of the press. He knew how Nick and Eric had kept her involvement quiet. He didn't know, any more than she did, who had had the couple murdered. Or why.

'Does he know you were there?' Hugh asked Sarah.

'He may have worked it out. I think he thinks I know why they were killed.'

'Why don't you drive round the block a couple of times, leave this to me?'

She gave him a fond look. Was he being chivalrous? Or did he have a plan?

'Sure?'

'Quite sure. If you want, I'll text you when he's gone.'

'There is something else I need to do.'

Hugh got out. He waved at Pete, who was leaning against her wall. Sarah drove off. This shouldn't take long. Nick was only five minutes away. Odd, that his home was so close by, yet, until today, she hadn't visited him there.

She parked on Burns Street, between Forest Road and The Arboretum. The new tram line made it impossible to park outside Nick's flat. She rang the bell. There was a light on the top floor landing. It took two or three minutes for him to answer the bell. Nick wore a plain grey T-shirt and faded Levis, slightly torn at the knee. Wear, she figured, rather than following youth fashion. He looked startled.

'Sarah, what can I do for you?'

'I need a private word. It won't take long.'

'You'd better come up, then. I should warn you, I have company, but it's not what it looks like.'

'I didn't mean to snoop into your private life. I can come back if…'

'It's a girl called Jerry. She owns the flat. Long story. I used to be her tutor and I still keep an eye on her. She'll stay out of the way.'

'OK.'

After climbing two flights of stairs, Sarah got her first look at his flat. Big landing, slightly shabby but clean. A skinny girl with a blonde bob darted into a back bedroom with barely a glance in Sarah's direction. She looked about twenty. Was Nick sleeping with her? None of her business. Hugh was only a few years older than this kid. Pot. Kettle. Black.

'Jerry's the one who persuaded you to do a computer course?'

'You have a good memory.'

'When you said you had someone here, I thought it might be Nazia Khan.'

'Nazia and her kids are staying at my brother Joe's for a couple of nights. The press won't find her there.'

'That's good of them.' Sarah refused a drink and perched on a sofa opposite Nick, who had taken the armchair. 'Actually, the reason I'm here… it's about the press. The Sunday Times journalist you met, he keeps pestering me. He wants to know why Andrew and Nancy were murdered.'

'He's not the only one.'

'I've never understood what happened back then. You must have some idea.'

'Some,' Nick admitted. 'But I doubt it'll help much. Where shall I start?'

'I don't know any more than I did the night Andrew left the UK.' That had been at Andrew's house in Notting Hill. 'Andrew told a story about how he'd been ripped off and couldn't pay money he owed.'

'Neither of us believed him, as I recall.'

'I didn't know what to believe,' Sarah said.

'Andrew was too good a businessman to get ripped off in a huge deal. I think he got to a point where he'd been given extensive credit and decided to do a runner. But he didn't have time to sort out the documentation and accounts he needed, so he and Nancy hid out in Majorca until he was ready.'

'Things must have become complicated when he found out that Nancy was pregnant, too.'

'I've thought about that a lot since Pete Carlson mentioned it,' Nick said. 'Poor Nancy. You know, Andrew always fancied being a dad. I wonder how it would have…' His words trailed off, then he collected himself. 'Has Carlson interviewed Terence Tailor in prison?'

Tailor was a drug dealer and brothel keeper, currently serving time for rape.

'He hasn't mentioned it.'

'From what I know, the person who Andy ripped off must have been Tailor's ultimate boss. And I don't know who that was. I don't even know if Andrew knew who that was. Not much help, sorry.'

'It wasn't you?'

Nick gave her the strangest look. She didn't like it.

'Sorry,' she said. 'I had to ask.'

A wry smile. 'Ask your friend, the former chief constable. He'll have a better idea than I do. My best guess, given Tailor's involvement, is that, ultimately, the killing was a Yardie operation.'

'The other thing that's been hinted at is that Paul Morris was part of this.'

'Paul was killed long before all the stuff with Andrew happened.'

'But his killing was never solved. And people have started saying that he was involved in the drugs trade.'

Nick hesitated, which made her paranoid. Maybe he knew that she and Paul had had an affair. But how the hell could he know that? Intuition?

'Don't hold back to spare my feelings,' she said.

Nick lowered his voice as though someone might be listening. 'Paul used to work for Andrew. As far as I know, he'd gone straight before he took that home office advisor job. Even so, his death could have been dealing related. Someone could have thought he'd grassed them up. The other thing about Paul is that he was a ladies' man, always putting it about. A jealous husband or a spurned lover – take your pick.'

'You're sure – I mean, that he worked for Andrew?'

'He used to collect big bags of grass from me, Sarah. I'm dead sure.'

'Thanks.' Her phone pinged and she checked the text.

He's gone.

'I'd better leave,' she looked around the room for the first time. Nice rug, comfy sofa, an awfully dated Grateful Dead poster, framed. Decent hi-fi. Not many books, for a former English teacher.

'I nearly forgot,' she said. 'Happy birthday on Sunday. Big day!'

'Don't remind me. Middle age.'

'Forty isn't middle-aged these days,' she assured him. 'Not unless you choose it to be.'

He saw her down to the front door. She kissed him on the cheek, like a relative. Had she learnt anything? Only that one of her ex-lovers was a crook, as well as an adulterer. And that she still had feelings for a reformed dope farmer.

TWENTY-SEVEN

P ete showed up at the flat on Saturday lunchtime.
'Is he here?'

'No. Nick's having lunch with friends. You're safe to come in.'

From the look on his face, she could tell it was Nick he'd come for. Pete followed her upstairs anyway.

'What did you find out last time you were here?' Jerry asked, once they were in the flat. 'You went rooting under the bed.'

'I found out that he owns the house you live in.'

'You must have worked that out weeks ago.'

'I did, but it was only a guess until I confirmed it. Must have cost a few bob. Has he always owned the place, even when Saint lived there?'

'How would I know?'

'Any idea where he keeps his bank account statements?'

She did but wasn't going to tell him. Not unless Pete made it worth her while. And not before she'd checked there was nothing incriminating.

'I can try and find out. I'm pretty good at getting things out of Nick.'

Pete smiled. 'He's where you got your taste for older men, is he?'

'That was somebody else, before I met Nick.'

She wasn't going to tell Pete about Paul Morris, who'd been her first lover, when she was barely fifteen. He'd given her the love she'd been deprived of for ten long years, stuck in children's homes. It was Paul who first paid for Nick to tutor her. And Paul who, in the end, had paid the price of not loving her enough.

Pete seemed edgy. She considered offering him a drink, or a spliff. She could tell he wasn't in the mood to fuck. He'd probably already done it today, paying for his board in kind. But if he wanted help from Jerry, he'd have to give her something in return. She put her hand on his belt buckle and used her little girl voice.

'Please take me to bed. I wanted you so much last night.'

It wasn't working, so she went for broke, talking quickly as she unzipped his flies, trying to turn him on.

'Last night I lay in bed, touching myself, thinking about you...'
She kept talking, but he stepped away.

'I can't do this, Geraldine. You're too young.'

'You didn't say that when you were fucking me a fortnight ago.'

Pete zipped himself up. 'I wanted something from you. I gave you sex in exchange. It's the oldest transaction in the world. Don't say you've never done it.'

She slapped his face.

'What am I supposed to do? Go to bed with you because I want your landlord's bank details?'

'You can go now.'

Pete began to leave then stopped at the top of the stairs. 'How come you own this flat, if you don't mind me asking? It used to belong to a dealer who comes up in the story I'm working on. Frank Davis. Mean anything to you?'

'No.'

'Frank used to run the Crack Action Team. Then he turned out to be a big league drug dealer himself. Got sent down a few years ago.'

'Before my time.'

'So how come you own his old flat? Did Nick put it in your name as some kind of cover?'

'Why have you got it in for Nick?' Jerry asked. 'He's been better to me than any other bloke I know. And he's never used me for anything illegal.'

'Just asking,' Pete said. 'Take care of yourself, Geraldine.'

'I always do.' She was glad she'd never let him call her Jerry. Geraldine was the name on her birth certificate, on the property deeds. Jerry was who she was – the resourceful mouse who kept bouncing back and running rings round the tom cats trying to crush her.

A call on her mobile. Nick.

'Sorry, I won't be able to have that drink with you later. Joe got me a surprise birthday present. Motorhead are playing Rock City. Tonight.'

143

'What kind of music's that?' Jerry asked. 'Maybe I'd like it.'

'Speed metal. Doubt it's your kind of thing. Not mine, especially, but with a few drinks and the rest, it can take you out of yourself. Anyway, I couldn't say no. Forgive me? We can do lunch before you go tomorrow.'

'It's fine,' Jerry told him. '"There's an old mate I want to see, anyway.'

She texted Shaz, told her she was in town. Shaz always had good weed, and, if she wasn't working, they'd have a laugh. Pete had been wasting his time with that metal box under the spare bed. Nick didn't keep anything important in here. Jerry knew where he kept his bank statements and other financial stuff. A little combination safe in the kitchen. It was in a cupboard below the sink. A bunch of pots and pans acted as camouflage. You'd need to be a diligent burglar to find the safe behind them. For a while, Nick had kept the combination written down on his desk. Hopefully, he hadn't changed it.

He hadn't. There was cash in there, and the deeds to the London house, along with the deeds to this flat, which he looked after for her. An emergency credit card. Visa. His passport and a sheet with various passwords written down. Also, his bank statements, council tax and an Inland Revenue self-certification form. She looked through the statements. Nick was well off by her standards, with a few thousand in the bank. But the money came and went, and there was no deposit account, no stocks and shares, no secret stash in Switzerland or an offshore account. Nothing to interest Pete or persuade him to start sleeping with her again. Unless, just for the hell of it, she made something up.

'Did you get what you were after?' Mel asked when Pete got back to hers for lunch.

'Sort of.' Mel knew a little about what he was working on, just enough to stop her asking difficult questions. Pete's primary purpose in visiting Geraldine one last time had been to get her to confirm that the London house was Nick's. By pretending to have found something, he'd caught her out. Cane's ownership of the house in Notting Hill was most likely indirect, via a company registered abroad that used to be in Saint's name. In due course, Pete would like a proper word with Mr Cane. But not until he had more questions ready to put to him.

'Your story, does it link up with the one about the Pakistani woman whose husband's being exhumed?'

'Have they said that they're digging up the body?'

'It was on the lunchtime news. Early tomorrow morning.'

'What time?' He ought to cover the exhumation for the paper. It might turn into a big item, one which could buy him extra time to work on the Saint story.

'All they said was *early*.'

'Just after sunrise, it'll be. I'd better get there by half five.'

'Lucky you're already in Nottingham, eh?'

'I seem to be a lucky man these days.' He squeezed her hand.

'Just try not to wake me when you leave. I love my Sunday lie-ins.'

'You're safe with us, duck.' It was the same message on most council estate doorsteps, even the smarter sections that were mostly privately owned. The council had been forced to sell them – heavily discounted – to tenants, then not allowed to replace them. Sarah thanked her elderly constituent, put a tick on the canvas card and continued next door.

'Done that one already,' Winston called. 'We're finished.'

They had an army of volunteers out, not all of them party members. Sarah's was the most marginal seat in Nottinghamshire, so it was all hands to the pumps. If hard work was what it took to win elections, she'd have the seat sewn up. But organisation and local campaigning accounted for, at most, 5% of the vote. The national polls were holding up well for Labour, yet still showed Sarah losing. At some point, she'd have to tell Hugh what she planned to do next.

Her secret boyfriend had to head back to London later. Tomorrow was his mum's fiftieth. Sarah was nearer her age than his. She decided not to mention that his mum's birthday was the same as Nick's. Astrology was bunkum: we took the cards we were dealt and played out our own fate with them. Sarah wanted

145

to use her hand in a way that changed the way the world worked. Most people, including the ones who would be voting for her, didn't think that change was possible. They voted for their tribe, but were, when pressed, cynical about politicians. Maybe not the one standing in front of them. Confronted with a real person, voters could recognise a candidate as well meaning and potentially useful. But politicians as a class they viewed with contempt.

She managed to duck out of a lunchtime drink with the canvassers, pleading urgent commitments, and walked back to the flat with Hugh.

'What will you do tomorrow, without me?' he asked.

'There's an open day in The Park. A few stalls: homegrown veg, that kind of thing. I'll trundle along there after canvassing, then drive to Chesterfield for Sunday lunch with my mum. Not seen her since the election started.'

'I'd like to meet your mum.'

'No, you wouldn't. She an irascible old dragon and she wouldn't approve of you. Too young. And don't tell *your* mum about me, please. She'll say I'm too old for you and she'll be right. Let's keep this between us.'

'You'd get on with my mum,' Hugh said. 'She's open minded. You're only twelve years older than I am, it's not that much these days.'

'Your mum will want grandchildren, and she won't want you stuck with a woman who's married to her career.' Sarah stopped herself. 'How did we get onto this? We're having fun, Hugh. Let's keep things as they are.'

'Sure.' He looked crestfallen. Why had she raised the spectre of children? She hadn't even had a lunchtime drink to loosen her tongue.

There were two messages waiting on the machine. *The Post* wanted a comment about the exhumation of Omar Khan, which was evidently taking place tomorrow. Tony wanted her to know that he and Eve were back from their honeymoon and he was available to help in any way whatsoever.

'Only feels like five minutes since they left,' Sarah said. 'I'd still like to know how Pete Carlson wriggled his way into the wedding party.'

'I think he picked up his girlfriend at the bar in the hotel,' Hugh said.

'I wonder who Pete was watching that day: me or Nick? Did you find out anything else when you talked to him yesterday?'

'Only that Pete's curious about the murder of a guy called Paul Morris, which he thinks might be linked to Andrew Saint's death. He thinks you know more than you do, but he doesn't seem to have worked out that you were having an affair with Morris.'

This stopped Sarah in her tracks. 'When did you work that out?'

'When the police took you in for questioning just after his death.'

'Only the Home Secretary was supposed to know about that.'

'They contacted me first to find out where they could find you that day. I'd picked up the clues before, but it was none of my business. Still isn't, unless there's anything you think I need to know to protect you from the press.'

'I don't make a habit of it, you know, sleeping with married men.'

'I don't need to know. All I need to know for my own wellbeing is whether – whatever we are – I'm the only person you're with right now.'

'Course you are,' Sarah said, then felt bad because she was thinking about going to see Nick on his birthday.

BOOK THREE

Nick

Jerry

Bilal

Sarah

Caroline

Pete

TWENTY-EIGHT

Nick's appetites had changed. In the old days, he and his brother would have snorted a line of coke before going to see Motorhead. The show would have passed in a flash, an intense, exhilarating experience. Tonight they'd settled for a couple of pints in Lily Langtry's and still had a good time. In Rock City, they washed down cigarettes with bottles of Newcastle Brown.

'Want to go clubbing?' Joe asked, once they'd made their way out of the crowded venue.

'I'm a bit sweaty, to be honest. Could do with a shower. Not sure I feel like dancing and trying to pull in this state. Do you?'

'Not in the slightest, mate. But it's your birthday.'

'And it's been a good one. Happy to call it a night if you are. Or you could come back to mine. Have a few smokes and listen to some sounds.'

Joe scratched his chin. 'Tempted, but… you know what, I probably ought to go home and do my marital duties.'

'Didn't you complain earlier that Caroline was always asleep by ten?'

'I can wake her up, can't I?'

Nick left his brother on Talbot Street. His flat was only five minutes' walk up the hill. When he got in, he would have a shower, then maybe share a spliff or two with Jerry, if she was back. He felt bad about leaving her alone, but she was a big girl. Jerry still had a few friends in Nottingham, both from her college days and, before that, the children's home.

There was no light on in the hall upstairs. Jerry must still be out. Nick drank half a pint of water then undressed in the bathroom, throwing his sweaty clothes straight into the laundry basket. A cool shower sobered him. It might be past midnight, but he felt alert and ready for anything. Today he turned forty.

He put his towel over the immersion heater tank to dry off then went into the bedroom, where he was surprised to find he'd left the bedside lamp turned on.

'Happy birthday!' Jerry sat up in bed, naked. Her breasts were surprisingly full. 'I think we've waited long enough, don't you?'

Nick, like her, was naked. Not half bad… for his age. He gawped for a moment and she was glad. He needed to see that she was no longer a girl. Jerry flung the duvet aside so that he could get a good look. He was hesitating, which she'd expected. She had made a pass at him once before, when he was her new tutor and she was still underage. But now she was a woman and he was a bloke who'd had a few beers. He'd have to be superhuman to resist.

Nick reached for the dressing gown that hung from a hook on the bedroom door. He threw it at her.

'Put this on, please,' he said in his teacher's voice. She did as he asked. By the time she was out of bed, he'd already put on a pair of jeans and was getting a T-shirt out of a drawer.

'Sorry,' she said, and it came out in a little girl voice. 'I just…'

'You wanted to give me something nice for my birthday,' he said. 'But I'm old enough to be your dad.'

'You're the nearest I've ever had to a dad,' Jerry said. 'Doesn't mean you are my dad. It doesn't mean we can't…'

He stopped her with a finger to the lips. She wanted to hold him. They did hug from time to time. But she knew better than to try that now.

'You don't have to thank me with sex,' he said, softly. 'That might be how the world works in some places, but it's not the way it ought to work.'

'I wasn't thanking you,' Jerry insisted. 'I was trying to fuck you. I've wanted to be with you since I was fifteen.'

His eyes followed the trail of flesh she'd left on show by not tying the gown. She retained a sliver of hope that he might relent.

'Nineteen might feel adult,' he said. 'It isn't. You need to have a relationship with someone nearer your own age, someone who's an equal.'

'I don't like boys my own age, Nick. The only men I've enjoyed being with were both your age. We don't choose what turns us on.'

'Paul Morris groomed you when you were fourteen. You thought he was your knight in shining armour, but he was your abuser.'

'Now you sound like a therapist.'

More than once Nick had encouraged her to get counselling. She'd brushed the suggestion aside. Too many confidentiality issues, for a start. Only Nick knew the bad things she was capable of. He stuck by her regardless. She loved him for it. Always would, whatever he said.

'You're right,' Nick laughed awkwardly, then changed tone. 'Why don't you get dressed while I roll us a spliff? I fancy a bit of a session... if you're up for it.'

'I'm up for it. But not your crap music. A movie, maybe. Could we watch *Chinatown* again?'

'It's my birthday, so I get to choose, OK?'

'Anything you say... Daddio.'

Bilal got to Wilford Hill at five. It was one of the city's more modern cemeteries, a vast, well-tended space designed to make death seem commonplace, which it was, and politely bland, which it could never be. In the half-light of early morning, the pale hill was eerily calm.

He'd been told that the exhumation team would start work at sunrise. This was only partly for religious reasons. Exhumations always took place early in the morning, in order to keep them as private as possible. However, there were already too many people for this operation to feel private. Still less, personal. Three cordon control officers blocked the paths that ran toward the grave area. Bilal stood with his imam, who had been summoned to ensure the religious proprieties. The imam kept his thoughts to himself, muttering prayers throughout.

Omar's gravestone had not yet been carved, so there was no need to move it. The coroner was already there and introduced herself. She identified the people as they turned up: the Scene of Crime officer, an Exhibits officer, a pathologist and a toxicologist. The cemetery superintendent watched from a distance, accompanied by two tall gravediggers. A representative of the undertakers who had buried Omar was last to arrive. He would need to formally identify the casket when it was raised. The tent went up before the digging began. The imam went inside, as did the gravediggers, the Scene of Crime officer, and an accompanying PC.

For an hour, there was nothing to see. Bilal listened to the scrape of spade on hard earth. The casket had only been in the ground for three weeks: it shouldn't take terribly long to dig it up. Bilal found himself remembering Omar, in ways he hadn't been able to at the funeral, when everybody who cared was still in shock.

Nazia's husband was a quiet man, a stubborn professional who did not eat adventurously or go on holiday, beyond an annual visit to family in Pakistan. Omar worked long hours and, when home, spent more time with his children than with his wife. The times they were happiest in each other's company, he'd heard Nazia tell Sam, were when they were looking after the children together.

Once both kids had started school, Nazia had begged Omar to allow her to resume her social work degree. Omar had refused. He was worried, Nazia told Sam, who later told Bilal, about her meeting other men. Yet, eventually, she had met another man. And she had strayed. With her heart, certainly. Possibly with her body, too.

Only when the gravediggers left did Bilal notice Fahd, uphill of the exhumation site, beyond the officer guarding the highest footpath. Fahd stepped aside to let the sturdy men get by. If he saw Bilal, he made no gesture of greeting.

They brought the casket out half an hour later, having done whatever tests they needed to do on site. The imam accompanied it to the mortuary. Family members were not allowed. As the van was leaving, a TV crew pulled up. They were too late, yet got their equipment out to film anyway.

By half seven, the police were packing up. The hole in the ground was covered by a well-secured tarpaulin. Bilal looked for Fahd, but he'd slipped away as quietly as he had come. Bilal was able to start work early, which would make up for some of the hours he'd lost lately. This time of day it was mostly taking old ladies to church. Before logging on, he made time to phone both Nazia and Uncle. Each listened without comment. The date of the inquest was yet to be announced, but the coroner had told them that it wouldn't be for at least a week. Probably longer.

Finally, he rang Sam, who was on a six to two shift. He wanted to hear her voice. He told her about the exhumation. Omar's body was being taken to the mortuary at Queen's, where she worked. Sam began to whisper.

'I had the oddest conversation with Nazia this morning, just after you'd gone out. She rang, saying she couldn't sleep, and knew I'd be up. Then she started going on about the surrogacy thing, did we still want to do it. I said we were definitely very interested but hadn't wanted to explore it while all this was going on. Then, do you know what she said? *You wouldn't mind, would you, if we used my eggs, not yours. The baby would still be related to you and look like it was yours.'*

'I don't understand,' Bilal said. 'I can't impregnate my own sister.'

'She didn't mean that,' Sam told him, her voice quiet, yet far from calm. 'She said something else: *I don't want anything from you, but you might need to tell lies. Ask Bilal not to discuss this with anyone else, nobody at all.* What do you make of that?'

'I don't know what to make of it.'

'You know what I think? I think she's pregnant.'

'That's ridiculous. She more or less told me that she and Omar no longer…' he stopped himself when he heard what he was saying.

'Exactly.' Sam left a few moments for what she was saying to sink in. 'My guess is that she's going to ask me to pretend that I donated my eggs, and that's why the baby she's carrying is mixed race. Question is, who's the father?'

'It has to be Nick, doesn't it?'

'If it is, what do we do about it?'

TWENTY-NINE

Something felt different. Sarah got out of bed, put the kettle on and checked her messages. It was only then she worked out what it was. This was the first time since the campaign began that she had woken up alone. She quite liked it. While waiting for the kettle to boil, she wrote the card she'd bought for Nick's birthday. There was a bottle of champagne in the cupboard for her to take round. Tattinger, a gift from a Women's Institute she'd given a speech to. She had no idea whether it was a good one. Would it be cheeky to chill the champagne so that, if he felt like it, they could share a glass? Or two. She considered phoning Nick to arrange meeting later, but he'd always liked to sleep in on a Sunday. She didn't want to wake him.

Before she could visit Nick, anyway, there was canvassing to be done. She watched the local TV news over breakfast. Omar Khan had been exhumed. There was video, though you couldn't see anything beyond the tent covering his grave.

At the Maynard Estate, Tony Bax was back from honeymoon, tanned and raring to join in. He was full of what he and Eve had been up to in Cuba.

'The country's starting to turn itself round after a terrible nineties. It's such a beautiful place. Fantastic beaches. And there's music everywhere.'

It was still a police state, though. Sarah resisted mentioning this. She enjoyed the Buena Vista Social Club CD but didn't think Cuba a wise place for a Labour MP to holiday. Or, for that matter, the Police Federation's General Secretary.

'One day', she said, wistfully. 'Have you spoken to Nick since you got back?'

'He's coming round for dinner tonight. It's his fortieth today, did you know?'

'I knew,' Sarah said.

'Perhaps you'd like to join us. The two of you go back a long way, after all.'

'That's...' Sarah considered. It could be awkward, or it could be nice. And it would be a way to find out how she and Nick got on in civilised company, the sort of company they would be bound to keep were she and he to begin again.

'Or do you still have that young man staying with you?'

She knew Tony well enough to read him, and he her. He knew. Or suspected. She hoped that she wasn't blushing.

'I do give Hugh the weekend off,' she told him. 'He's not back until tomorrow afternoon.'

He half smiled, so she risked a question.

'People aren't… talking, are they?'

'People will always talk,' Tony told her, not meeting her eye. 'But it's none of their business. Or mine.'

Sarah nearly said something about it being a waste of time and money putting Hugh in a hotel, then stopped herself. No need to mislead Tony, who would never pry. Winston was strolling towards them. She leant in.

'I'd love to come, if you're sure that Nick would like it and Eve's alright with an extra guest. Just between us though, for obvious reasons.'

Tony nodded.

'Ready for the off?' Winston asked.

Nick had a lie-in until ten, then waited around for Jerry to get up. They'd stayed up talking until gone two, putting the awkwardness of Jerry's attempted seduction behind them. Teenagers could do that, he realised, act like embarrassing mishaps were just that, mishaps. Over and done with. If a similar thing had happened with a woman his age, they'd avoid each other for at least a year.

He'd bought sausages from Beedham's Butchers in Sherwood and fried them, hoping the smell would wake Jerry. When it didn't, he knocked on her door.

'Breakfast in five minutes. Fried eggs or scrambled?'

Jerry sat up. 'It's your birthday. I should be making breakfast for you.'

'Too late.'

Five minutes later, she'd washed and joined him at the table, still wearing the old Ramones T-shirt he'd given her, half

157

covering her skimpy grey knickers. Her legs, so skinny when he first knew her, had become womanly. He stopped himself looking. They talked about the legal internship she was about to begin.

'And they give you money?' Nick asked. 'It's not slave labour?'

'They call it expenses, so there's no tax, but there should be a bit left over after buying lunch and paying for transport. I won't lose out.'

Tony Bax rang at half twelve, wishing him a happy birthday.

'Still on for tonight?'

'Looking forward to it.'

'I've just been out canvassing with Sarah. I invited her along too. Thought you'd enjoy catching up with her, away from the public eye. Said I'd check with you before confirming the invitation. Neither of us wanted to blindside you…'

'No, that'd be… great. I'd love to see her.'

'That's what I hoped. Eightish. OK?'

Jerry had her bag packed, ready to leave. It was a glorious, sunny day so he walked across town with her. At the ticket barrier, they hugged. Anyone watching would take him for a father seeing off his daughter on her way back to university.

Nick crossed the road in front of the station and took the steps down to the canal below. He fancied a stroll. Maybe he'd pick up a Sunday paper and have a quiet pint at the Fellows, Morton, Clayton or The Navigation. It felt like the sort of thing a forty-year-old might do. His mobile rang. Caroline.

'Happy big birthday, brother-in-law! Are you joining us for Sunday dinner? Joe was supposed to ask but can't remember if he did.'

'He didn't, and I've just accepted another offer, from Tony and Eve. Sorry.'

Caroline's tone changed. 'I could do with you around today, Nick. Nazia's hard work to talk to. Joe's not much help with our kids, never mind hers.'

'How about I come over now? I don't have anything on for hours.'

'That'd be lovely. You're a saint.'

'I'm no saint. But I am family. Give me half an hour or so.'

So much for the rest of his stroll. If he forked out six quid for a taxi, he'd be there in fifteen minutes, but that went against the grain. Were he at home, he'd bike it. That was how he'd get to Tony's later. He decided to stride across town, then catch a bus up the Mansfield Road.

He'd meant to do some work when he got home, but it could wait. Since inheriting Andrew's house, he'd had less need to work hard. The Notting Hill rent, transferred once a month by Jerry, covered his walking around money and then some. Website development jobs paid the rest of the bills. More people were coming into the field, but not as quickly as demand was rising. Nick kept putting up his rates and still got offered more work than he could take on.

How long would the internet bubble last? The thing had felt brand new when he got out of prison, four years ago. There were fortunes to be made, but he'd never been motivated by greed. That was Andrew's bag. Nick's weakness, insofar as he had one, was easy money. That was why, ten years ago, he'd started selling weed grown in the caves below his flat. He'd meant to do it for five years, tops. But before he could get out, he'd been arrested.

That was the trouble with easy money. It usually involved skating over thin ice, legally. And Nick had no intention of going back to prison. He used to con himself that he was honest. He'd never cheated anyone. But he'd still been caught. The nearest he'd come to breaking the law since (unless you counted smoking dope) was when he helped Jerry with her bit of trouble. That, too, was well in the past. She never talked about it, so neither did he.

When he reached Lower Parliament Street, Nick took a bus that went up Hucknall Road and got out at the stop before Perry Road. He passed Nottingham prison, which stood on a high hill, making it visible from miles away, a warning to all. He'd been incarcerated there at the start of his sentence, but the sight no longer spooked him. He turned left and weaved his way down the hill, through the tangled estate with its cul-de-sacs and cut throughs.

His brother's taxi was parked outside their big former council house. This meant Joe was home. At the door, Caroline gave him a half embrace.

'Good of you to come.'

He kissed her on the cheek, a gesture she accepted grudgingly. It was over a decade since they had been, briefly, lovers. These days Nick only felt the occasional smidgen of desire for Caroline: nothing compared to what seeing Sarah did to him. Or the effect of seeing Nazia descend the stairs.

Caroline watched Nick watching Nazia. Hard to picture the two of them together – what? – twelve years ago. The squeeze he'd just given her, the affectionate kiss on the cheek, reminded her of what they'd once had. If she'd stayed with Nick, rather than taking Joe back, he'd never have done the stupid stuff that landed him in prison. They'd be a two kid, two teacher family, living in West Bridgford or Beeston. Whereas Joe would always be a chancer, the sort of hubby you needed to keep a close eye on, with little time for the kids and less for her.

Nick and Nazia's conversation was strained. Caroline retreated to the kitchen to make tea, giving them the illusion of privacy, though she could still hear every word. They sounded like former colleagues with little left in common.

'When do you think I'll be able to move home?' Nazia asked, as though Nick had any way of knowing. 'I've been here two days. I think that's long enough.'

'Getting on OK with Joe and Caroline?'

'Your brother I've hardly seen. She's very nice, but…'

The rising rumble from the kettle drowned what came next. By the time Caroline brought the tea through, Nick was in the living room, organising a game of *Let's Go Fishing* with three of the kids. Nazia was reading the copy of *The Observer* that he'd brought with him. Hearing the noise, Joe came down.

'Can I join in?' he asked.

'There are only four rods,' Tamazur explained.

'Daddy, play with me!' Phoebe called, and Joe did as his daughter asked. After a while, Nick gave Joe his rod and told

Caroline he was going outside for a smoke. Smoking wasn't allowed in the house, though this rule was sometimes relaxed after the kids had gone to bed. She said she'd join him.

'How are you getting on with Nazia?' Nick asked.

'She's pleasant enough but doesn't give much away.'

She took a drag of his roll-up.

'It's hard to know what she should do,' Nick said. 'If I were her, regardless of the post mortem results, I'd get out of Nottingham.'

'How close are you two?' Caroline asked.

'I knew her well once. Some people hardly change from their teenage years to their thirties. Andrew was always the same Andy I met in our first week at uni. But Nazia's closed down on me. I don't know who she is any more.'

'What about me?' Caroline handed the cigarette back. 'Have I changed in in the ten years you've known me? Apart from putting on a couple of stone, that is.'

'The extra weight suits you,' he said, ever the diplomat. 'No, you're always really straight forward, even when you're pissed off with me. Or with Joe. Make that especially when you're pissed off with one of us. Most people don't change, I think, but people do learn to hide their personality. Even from themselves.'

Caroline decided to ask the question that kept preying on her mind. 'Was the Nazia you knew capable of poisoning her husband?'

A wry smile. 'No more nor less than you.'

N o news from the post mortem. The police wouldn't even confirm that it was taking place today. Could be they would keep Omar's body chilled until Monday, when overtime rates didn't apply. Nevertheless, Pete hung around near the Central Police Station, hoping to catch one of the officers who was working on the case. This kind of old-fashioned legwork could pay dividends. Also, there was a limit to how much time Pete wanted to spend cooped up in Melanie's small terrace. He'd left her with a big pile of marking. At least three hours' worth, she said.

The early start at Wilford Hill had taken it out of him. Pete yawned, then had a good stretch. He was only interested in Omar Khan insofar as his death overlapped with the Nick Cane/Andrew Saint/Sarah Bone triangle. Nothing so far suggested that it did. Even so, fascinating case, and the wife was a tasty suspect. Were he to get an exclusive, his brownie points would accrue. Which could, in turn, buy him more time to work on the Saint story.

He recognised the officer coming out of the station, who used to be in the Met. She wore the standard, sexless, black trousers of senior, plain clothes females. Rebecca Allen, a DI who used to work Fraud. She must have been transferred here. Time to waylay her.

'Rebecca! Remember me?'

She smiled. A pretty woman, late thirties and recently divorced, if the white line on her ring finger meant anything at all.

'Pete! What brings you to Nottingham?'

'I'm with *The Sunday Times* these days, working for the *Insight* team. Got time for a drink?'

She looked at her watch the way people do when they know perfectly well that they have nothing on but are trying to decide whether to tell you this.

'I'm not much of a daytime drinker,' she said, 'and I need to get changed.'

'Do you live far away?'

She pointed up the hill. 'About two minutes up the road. You can come back to mine and have a brew if you promise to behave yourself.'

Had he tried it on when he was pursuing that money laundering story? Flattery loosened tongues, so there were occasions when it seemed impolite not to make a pass, though he tended not to come on too strong with married women.

'Best behaviour,' he said, 'Scout's honour'. Rebecca had the grace to look a little disappointed.

Five minutes later, she was in jeans and a *Nottingham Panthers* sweatshirt, pouring boiling water onto Tesco teabags.

'Go on, then. What are you working on?'

'Funny thing is, my story's started to intersect with a case you're working on.'

'How do you know what I'm working on?'

'I saw you at the cemetery early this morning.'

'Did you now? And what does Omar Khan's death have to do with you?'

'The figure that connects the two is a local MP, Sarah Bone.'

Rebecca's expression changed. 'What's Sarah's connection to your story?'

'It's about a murdered drugs baron, someone she was at university with. Andrew Saint. Mean anything?'

'I was at Ryton with Sarah but I never met her Nottingham friends.'

'He was in London by then. Saint was murdered in Sarah's house on Majorca. To be precise, in a house that she had inherited from her father. Her connection with the place was kept quiet. I only managed to confirm it recently.'

'What was this Saint doing there?'

'Hiding from the people who tracked him down and killed him.'

'I see.' The detective looked thoughtful. They drank tea in a silence that was not companionable, but not uncomfortable either.

'Husband not moved here with you?' he asked, after a while.

'Divorce is nearly final.'

'Sorry to hear that.'

'Really? I remember having to tell you more than once that I was married. You said you'd never come across a male copper who let that stand in his way.'

'Sounds like the sort of thing I say when I want to get my wicked way.'

'In the case of my ex-, you were pretty spot on.'

Pete saw where this was heading and didn't want to go there. 'Last question before I go: if insulin poisoning's so hard to prove, why did they exhume the body?'

'Off the record? Political pressure. We need to be seen to be doing everything possible, not giving the Muslim community a raw deal because they aren't white and hyper-connected through the usual establishment channels. Also, there's some evidence corroborating what the brother-in-law was telling us.'

'Evidence indicating that Nazia Khan was having an affair?'

'I've told you enough already.' She nodded slowly while she said this.

'Any chance of a heads up when you have the new post mortem results?'

'Not a hope in hell. You'll find out what we want you to know at the same time as we tell the rest of the media.'

'You've got rather more out of me this afternoon than I have out of you.'

'You scratch my back, I'll scratch yours.' Rebecca smiled. 'Maybe I'm better at my job than you are. Now, are you going to make another pass at me, or am I going to kick you out so that I can have a nice, long bath?'

'The other reason I'm in Nottingham is that I have a girlfriend here.'

Rebecca smiled wistfully. 'Good for you. But don't expect a repeat invitation when you next happen to be single. I'm not normally such a pushover.'

'Understood.' Pete gave her his best, grown-up smile. 'We're mates, right? I can call you again and we can do some sharing when it's mutually convenient.'

She gave a half nod. He considered kissing her on the cheek, thought better of it and shook her hand instead. A moment later he came up with a convincing lie he could tell Melanie, an excuse that would allow him to spend the evening with Rebecca. Too late. It offended his sense of himself, but he had become a one-woman-man. Or, at least, one who knew on which side his bread was buttered.

Nick was halfway down a gin and tonic when Sarah arrived. He kissed her on the cheek and gave her waist a little squeeze.

'It's not much, but...' She handed him the present she'd picked out at Jessop & Son the day before: an Italian wallet in black leather.

'How did you know...?' He pulled out a tatty brown leather wallet, the same one he'd had on their ill-fated holiday, two years before, when it was already the worse for wear. She'd always had a good memory. He transferred the wallet's contents to the new one. While he was doing this, Eve came down, looking rather glamorous in a spangled, low-cut, silk top over tight jeans. She had good legs. Both Tony and Nick gave her admiring looks. Sarah hoped she'd still be getting looks like that in her fifties. She complimented the dress and handed Eve the bottle of champagne.

The early part of the conversation was taken up by an account of the honeymoon in Cuba.

'Don't worry,' Tony said. 'We're not gauche enough to show you photos.'

'By which he means they aren't back from *Prontaprint* yet,' Eve added.

Only after the first course, a fish chowder, did they start to discuss the interminable election. Ten days of campaigning remained. Tony ventured that the Tory campaign had been so weak, Labour might even increase its majority.

'I appreciate your optimism,' Sarah said, 'but, in West at least, the Tory vote can only go up.'

'It might not go up by the two thousand they'd need in order to overtake you,' Nick said.

Tony opened a bottle of Chablis. Sarah accepted her third glass of wine. She needed to keep count.

'Even so,' Nick went on, when she didn't reply, 'it's as well to have a contingency plan. What will you do if you don't get in?'

Sarah hated having to avoid direct questions. It was a key political skill but not one she liked to deploy when talking to two of her oldest and closest friends. She settled for vagueness.

'I've had one or two offers.'

Tony raised an eyebrow. 'Do tell.'

'I can't,' Sarah said. 'Confidentiality agreement. If I get back in as an MP they don't want whoever gets the job to think they were second choice.'

This was an exaggeration, but the table seemed to buy it.

'Can't you give us a clue?' Nick asked.

Their eyes met and she saw something that hadn't been there the last few times she looked. Tony and Eve had set them up, she realised. They thought that she and Nick ought to get back together, or at least give it a go. If someone as old and wise as Tony thought she might be best off with Nick, maybe he was right. She remembered that Eve, a long time ago, had been Nick's boss. Presumably she, too, thought he might be good for her. But Sarah – *déjà vu* – was on the verge of taking a job that Nick would hate her doing, one that would take her away from him. She decided to let him down with the lesser of two evils.

'It's better paid than what I do now, but it would involve moving south.'

'The majority of better paid jobs do,' Tony said, distracting both women from Nick's look of disappointment. 'You know what I'd like to see in the next Labour term? Close down the Palace of Westminster to be refurbished for the Twenty-First century and move the Commons to Birmingham. Or Manchester. Somewhere nearer the middle of the country. Then maybe forget to move back.'

'What about the Lords?' Sarah asked.

'Abolish it altogether.'

'Or move it to Derry and see how many of them turn up,' Nick suggested. 'Let them effectively abolish themselves. None of it will happen though, because the Labour Party is even more London-centric than the Tories. Islington socialism, that's what we've got now.'

'I won't argue with you on that,' Sarah said.

Over the main course, a beef cobbler with new potatoes and spinach, conversation turned to the Omar Khan exhumation. Eve and Tony hadn't been aware of Nick and Sarah's connections to Omar and his wife.

Eve swore. 'I'm sorry if I put my foot in it, but now you mention it, I do remember teaching Nazia's brother. Didn't we call him *Billy*?'

'That's right,' Nick said. 'I met Nazia at a couple of parents evenings and she contacted me for advice. Then we started seeing each other.'

There was something odd going on in this conversation, some subtext that Sarah was missing. Eve seemed almost disapproving, but what was wrong with a teacher dating the older sister of one of his students?

'Do you think Nazia's capable of what she's being accused of?' Eve asked.

'I can't be certain,' Nick said. 'People do crazy things. She says she didn't and I believe her.'

'But you don't really know her in the same way that you used to?'

He shook his head. Eve didn't press it further. Between the lines, she had been asking if he was having an affair with Nazia. How definitive was that denial? Nick shifted the subject.

'Did you ever come across Omar Khan's brother, Fahd?' he asked Tony.

'A long time ago. He was active in the party for a couple of years. There wasn't a lot of dialogue between the Pakistani party members and the rest of us in those days. There's still nowhere near enough, if you ask me.'

'Didn't he stand in the council elections?' Sarah asked.

'Yes. He lost narrowly. If he'd won the seat, we'd have tied the election but, as it was, the Tories got in by one. Fahd blamed racism and Labour members not working for him. There may have been something in his claim. After that, he tried to orchestrate a takeover of his own ward, turned up at the AGM with about fifty members nobody had ever seen before, and a big stick shoved inside his jacket. "In case there was any trouble", that was how he put it. But people saw the stick and they saw a lot of strangers with party cards and they took umbrage. There were tons of complaints and the ward was closed down for a few months.'

'I vaguely recall all that,' Nick said. 'but I'd forgotten Fahd's name. The whole business was ugly. Set race relations in the party back years.'

'There was an enquiry. Even before he was expelled, the Asian councillors distanced themselves from Fahd. You could argue that he got a raw deal. After all, the way he worked was the way politics worked back home. Some cultural differences can take decades to sort themselves out, but, compared to many cities, Nottingham's always been pragmatic about race. The St Ann's riots aside.'

'Which riots are you talking about?' Eve asked.

'Summer '58. I was home from my first year at university.'

'Before I was born,' Nick pointed out.

'The riots here probably sparked off the riots in Notting Hill a week later. They're the ones people remember. It was West Indians, as we called them then, who were in the thick of it, but things like that are never just about race.'

'I remember the riots in summer '81,' Nick said. 'I was living in Hyson Green, a student shared house. It wasn't safe to go outside.'

After five more minutes on riots and deprivation, Eve said she needed to prepare the dessert. Nick got out his tobacco tin.

'Mind if I go outside for a smoke between courses?'

'I'll join you if I may,' Sarah said, ignoring the amused look on Eve's face.

There was a small garden. Nick produced a spliff from his tin.

'Oh, good,' Sarah said. 'I hoped you had one of those.'

'Your lot have practically legalised it.'

'Let's just say we're very relaxed about soft drugs.'

He lit the spliff and passed it to her. 'Please tell me you're not moving away.'

'That's in the hands of the electors.' She took a couple of hits then tried to hand the tightly rolled tube back. He wouldn't take it.

'Let me say this first, while I'm just drunk enough to get it out and not stoned enough to make a mess of what I say. A large part of me was... is hoping you'll lose this time, because I figure you and me, we ought to give it another go.'

Sarah smiled and kissed him softly on the lips, in what she hoped was a loving but non-sexual way. She took another drag on the joint before speaking.

'We very nearly got it together the night of the last election, didn't we?'

Nick laughed. This time, he accepted the smoke back. 'If you hadn't got so drunk that you passed out.'

'I wasn't paralytic, I was exhausted!'

'Then you got the job as Prisons Minister, so you could hardly date a bloke who'd just got out of prison.'

'I couldn't.'

'But I've been out more than four years. I'm not on license any longer. I've kept my nose clean, even done some work for the Labour Party. Maybe we'd be all right to see each other even if you do get back in. But not if you move away.'

'Maybe we would,' Sarah said. 'Only...'

'Is there someone else?'

'It's not that.' Sarah realised she hadn't thought about Hugh for a moment during this conversation, which she'd anticipated so many times. 'It's just...'

'What?'

'People do change. I've changed. You've changed. Right now, I want you, but maybe that's down to nostalgia for the person I used to be, what we used to be.'

'Maybe it is,' Nick said. 'But there's only one way to find out.'

This time, their kiss was deep and lingering, leaving her in no doubt. They might be a little drunk but there was still strong desire on both sides. 'We'd better go back in,' she said, when they broke apart. 'They'll think we're being rude.'

'They won't mind at all,' Nick assured her, big grin on his face. He took a puff on the joint but it had gone out, so he put it on the window ledge. 'For later.'

They had sticky toffee pudding with ice cream and brandies, which Sarah refused. She needed a clear head tomorrow. Also, if – as she now suspected it would – the evening ended with her going back to Nick's and their screwing each others' brains out, she wanted to remember it well. Her phone sounded an alert.

'Sorry,' she said. 'I thought I had it on *silent*.'

She checked the text. Hugh.

Came back early to surprise you but nobody in. Pubs have closed. Where are you? Xx

She considered ignoring it, sighed, then texted back. *Tony's for a meal. About to call taxi. xx*

He replied. *Don't bother. I'll come and collect you. On my way.*

Hugh was rescuing her from herself. Going to bed with Nick would have been a stupid idea. Her life was complicated enough. She needed to leave soon, before this went any further. Hugh would come more quickly than a taxi.

'I'm afraid my minder's back in town and insists on coming to collect me', she told her hosts.

Tony and Eve exchanged glances. Each clearly suspected what was going on between her and Hugh. Nick looked crushed. At least he wasn't aware that Hugh was about to benefit from the passion that he had stirred up in her tonight. A few minutes later, when the car drew up outside, she gave the birthday boy another gentle kiss on the lips, and heard herself whisper, 'to be continued.'

The rueful smile he gave in reply would stay with her for a long time.

THIRTY-ONE

F ahd and Uncle sat opposite Bilal in the cramped family room of the Central Police Station. This was where people were given bad news, where victims could be kept away from perpetrators, a space where people could cry in private. Uncle, in an embroidered *kurta* and white *dhoti*, looking every one of his sixty-eight years, wore a severe expression. It reminded Bilal of the time he'd had to tell him that he was marrying a white, non-Muslim woman. Nazia had already guaranteed their bloodline would continue, bearing good Muslim children. Uncle had given him a hard time nevertheless. He gave everyone a hard time.

Fahd still had that characteristic snarl imprinted on his face. Bilal couldn't remember once having seen Fahd give a genuine smile, not unless you counted the smug grin he used when things went his way.

The officer who came to see them looked more like a young business executive than a detective.

'I'm DI Rebecca Allen, acting as family liaison today.'

Uncle leant forward. Fahd sat up straighter, maintaining his snarl. Bilal tried to give a neutral but encouraging smile.

'Investigations like this are very difficult indeed.'

She talked patiently and attempted to answer their questions. There were marks between two of Omar's toes, but these could not be definitively attributed to insulin injections. The condition of Omar's heart was such that a coronary was by far the most likely cause of death. That said, insulin shock could not be ruled out. She understood why they wouldn't be satisfied by what she was able to tell them.

'Insulin shock could not be ruled out?' Fahd pressed her.

'Not definitively, no.'

'These marks between his toes,' Fahd said, 'were they the same?'

'They are very similar.'

'There was no sign that he regularly injected himself between the toes?'

'No.'

'What would the presence of two marks mean, that he was poisoned twice?'

Rebecca shook her head. 'Nobody can say with any degree of certainty that these were injection marks. If they were, the presence of two marks would suggest two injections, which seems unlikely. One would be adequate for most purposes.'

'Maybe she injected him once but he didn't die so she did it again.'

'That's far-fetched. To repeat, we can't ascertain that these were marks left by injections. What we can say is there's no conclusive evidence your brother was murdered. Nothing to warrant further investigation, never mind criminal charges.'

'She murdered him,' Fahd said. 'You know she murdered him and we know she murdered him, but you're going to let her get away with it. Has my sister-in-law been interrogated about these marks between the toes?'

'Mrs Khan has spoken to us extensively,' the DI replied in a quiet voice.

Uncle put a calming hand on Fahd's upper arm. 'We will deal with this as a family. Thank you for your time, Inspector.'

The pair of them left without looking at Bilal. He lingered to have a word with the DI.

'They won't leave this alone,' he told her.

'They should. We've done everything we can.'

'Have you told Nazia what you just told us?'

'I spoke to her on her mobile before I came here, yes.'

'Did you tell her it was safe for her to go home?'

'That's Nazia's call,' Rebecca told him. 'All I can tell you is that our evidence to the inquest will be that there is no evidence a crime was committed.'

'But the pin pricks between his toes, surely they suggest…'

She stopped him. 'It could suggest that he got a thorn in his shoe, or had injected himself there once or twice because he thought it would be more effective. It proves nothing. But I can't convince people who want to be convinced of the opposite. Do you think your brother-in-law will do anything foolish?'

'Fahd's a law unto himself.'

An hour later, Bilal collected Nazia from Caroline and Joe's house in Sherwood. He explained what the police had told them.

'Fahd didn't take it well. You know, I'm worried about you and the kids being in the house on your own. You're always welcome at our place.'

Nazia raised her head, proud as of old. 'No. It's over. It has to be over. I'm going to rebury my husband then start a new life.'

'What do you mean, *a new life*?'

'I need to talk to you and Sam properly. When does she finish her shift?'

'She's off today. Early shift tomorrow.'

'Then let's go and see her after we've dropped these things off, collect the rest of my stuff, and talk before I have to collect the kids from school.'

When they got to Nazia's home in The Park, he called Sam.

'There's no need for Nazia to come here,' his wife said. 'I'll bring her stuff over. How are things at the house?'

'I didn't see any new graffiti. The police did search the place again but this time they seem to have left everything tidy. There's not much in the fridge.'

'I'll pick up some bits and bobs. Think she wants to talk to us about surrogacy?'

'Can't see what else it would be.'

Back in The Park, Bilal helped his sister sort out clean sheets for her and the children's beds. In the living room, he watched her return an ornately framed photograph of a smiling Omar to its central position above the fireplace.

'He was good to you, wasn't he?' he said to his sister.

'Except when he wasn't.' She didn't look at him when she said this. 'He was always good to the kids. Even Tamazur.'

'What do you mean "e…"' Bilal stopped himself. Nazia meant because Tamazur was a girl, and not a beauty like her mother, more of a gangly, tomboyish type. Her name meant 'brilliant'. Bilal liked her more than he did her brother, who was lazy and more than a little spoilt. Naturally Omar had taken more pleasure in Ahmad. Girls cost money. Boys were your legacy.

By the time Sam arrived they had the house sorted out. There was over an hour to spare before Nazia had to collect the kids from school. The three of them sat in the lounge, below the gaze of the departed patriarch, sipping tea.

'You wanted to talk to both of us together?' Sam said, carefully.

'What I tell you doesn't go beyond this room. Ever.'

Sam and he exchanged glances, then murmured agreement. Bilal's mind was racing ahead. Were Nazia to act as their surrogate it would be impossible to conceal. Maybe if she moved to Pakistan… yet, even then, how was Sam supposed to fake a pregnancy? Impossible for a nurse.

'I'm pregnant,' Nazia said.

'How far gone?' Sam asked.

'Not far at all, but I know.'

'It could be Omar's?'

Slowly, Nazia shook her head. 'We haven't… this year.'

'Is it Nick Cane's?' Bilal asked.

'Who the father is is not important, except for one thing.'

They waited for her to explain but Nazia couldn't get the words out. After a few seconds, Sam said them for her.

'Is he white?'

'Yes.'

'You want us to take the baby from you and pretend that you used my eggs, that you're acting as our surrogate?'

Nazia looked up for the first time, her beseeching eyes red and watering. She looked more vulnerable than Bilal had ever seen her before.

'You'd have to sort out the documentation. Could you make it work?'

Sam glanced at him. She'd figured all this out days ago, and she was ready. He nodded. Sam raised her chin and looked her sister-in-law firmly in the eye.

'Oh yes,' she said.

THIRTY-TWO

Victor and Patrick was one of London's oldest law practices but its offices in Holborn were airy and hi-tech. They felt modern, in every sense but one. On her first day, when it was sunny out, Jerry had made the mistake of wearing a skirt. She wasn't expecting to get her bum pinched in a Law firm. It happened twice that day. Once, in the lift on her way up, when she couldn't see who was responsible. Later, when she happened to find herself in the office of a senior partner (married, photos of wife and kids on his desk), whose two fingers squeezed rather than pinched, then moved quickly along her arse before she could pull away. She'd used the line she'd worked out for the next time it happened: *do that again and I'll report you for assault.*

The look on his face told her that he saw this as a gross over-reaction. She's been nice as pie with him since. The perve wasn't bad looking, as it went, but if she were going to do a co-worker, it'd be the managing partner, who was fiftyish, with silver at the edge of his closely trimmed hair, beautiful suits and the most perfect skin. Only she was 99% sure he was gay.

Pete was back in town. Jerry knew this because she sometimes stalked his flat. Pete lived alone and worked unsocial hours. He never called. She told herself she was keeping an eye on Pete because of the risk he presented to Nick. But deep down she knew it was also because she hated being rejected. Nick had rejected her both times she'd offered. That hurt most. But everyone's allowed to say "no". You had to respect their choices. The way it felt with Pete, though, was like he'd fucked her then chucked her, and she hated that. Especially since he was such a good fuck.

Nick had principles. His reluctance was to do with her age and his having been in some kind of position of responsibility for her. This kindness on his behalf only made her want him more. She could wait. A year. Longer maybe, until she saw him look her way with unmistakeable lust in his eyes. Third time lucky.

Tonight she found herself outside Pete's flat in Clapham, with only half an hour before the last tube. He'd just come in, probably from the pub. If she were to make a move, it had to be now. Pete had a girlfriend in Nottingham. OK. Jerry was content to be Pete's London piece, his dirty little secret. That was how she'd started out, as somebody's dirty little secret, and the feeling turned her on.

She got out her phone.

Got something to tell you. Are you home? she texted.

A minute later, he phoned. 'What is it, Jerry?'

'I need to see you, to talk in person. I'm near yours. Are you in?'

'I am. But I've got an early start.'

'Me too. I'm working now, remember?' She could sense the hesitation in his silence, so added a breathy 'I've missed you,' just so the message was clear.

'How far away are you?'

She got up at six the next morning, Pete still sleeping heavily by her side. The night before, she'd fed him a few insignificant snippets about Nick, who he still seemed to think was dodgy. Then he'd asked the question that she knew was on his mind.

'Do you and him… you know?'

She stroked his thigh. 'Nick's like family. You're the only man I do this with, the only one I want to do this with. Is that all right with you?'

Flattery worked on most men. He took some persuading, then swore it was the last time, but their eventual satisfaction was mutual. And extended.

Jerry opened Pete's computer and went straight to the documents folder. She'd bought a pricey new USB stick that held 500 megabytes of information, enough for every file in Pete's 'active' folder. There was a spare pair of knickers and a fresh top in her bag. She got the top out and hung it over the door to his small shower room. While the files were transferring, she turned the shower on, hot as it got, then checked to make sure the memory stick had finished loading.

In the shower, she brought herself off by remembering the

night before. She often found the memory of sex more exciting than the act itself, which could be awkward and unpredictable. Was that weird? Every girl who grew up in the home with her was weird about sex. That was something Shaz had said the other night, after two spliffs and a couple of lines. Shaz said she never felt like sex was really happening to her, which was why she was able to treat it as work.

'What about you?' she'd asked.

'I'm no weirder than anybody else,' Jerry insisted, without going into details.

'I sometimes pretend I'm with Brad Pitt or Wesley Snipes when I'm getting myself off,' Shaz told her. 'But never when I'm with a punter. That'd be pathetic.'

'When I get myself off,' Jerry admitted, 'I have to pretend I'm with a guy I've really been with, so I can remember what he felt like on me, inside me.'

'Even the one who died?'

'Especially him. How did you know about Paul? I never told you.'

'I had eyes, girl. He was always turning up at odd times. I even saw him come out of your room once. He was well known, wasn't he? Had to keep it quiet.'

'And I was under-age. He was my first.'

'You waited until you were fifteen? Respect.'

She finished herself off by remembering her first orgasm. That night, on the floor of that seedy single room in Alexandra Park, Paul fucked her from behind while fingering her clit. It was only the third time they'd done it. The pleasure was so unexpected, so intense, she'd nearly wet herself.

When she got out of the shower, the steam has made the creases fall out of her work top. She was able to set off bright and early, get to the city before the lifts were packed with predators. Meanwhile, back in Clapham, Pete slept on, unaware of what has been taken from him.

Jerry waited until she'd been given a load of printing to do then put the USB stick into a computer. She knew better than to transfer the files off the tiny stick onto a work computer, but the office system allowed her to print directly from USB without storing the files on the computer desktop first. There would be no record.

She took her lunch break at the new Starbuck's, where she didn't like the coffee but could get a table to herself. The manager was her age and unlikely to hassle her for lingering over a latte and millionaire shortbread. The caramel and the caffeine give her a buzz, enough to carry her through Pete's work in progress.

It was a chunky story, spanning two decades. Pete had left her out of it. Result. Seducing Pete had prevented Jerry from being a salacious bit on the side of his story: the teenage mistress of Nottingham's Mr Big, Nicholas Cane, mass purveyor of weed and much more besides.

In Pete's account, Nick Cane and Andrew Saint had begun their empire at university. Andrew started a property firm while Nick got a job as a schoolteacher – each covering up their real business. Then Nick bought a flat with access to a network of caves dry enough to grow weed in. Eventually, he got caught. It wasn't clear how. Pete was unable to say who had dobbed him in, or what stroke of luck had led the police to catch him.

While Nick was inside, Andrew carried on building his business. Once Nick got out of prison, Pete reckoned, they picked up where they'd left off. After Andrew's death, Nick became the new Kingpin of Nottingham's drugs scene. He had maintained a veneer of respectability, aided by his friendship with Sarah Bone, MP. Recently, Jerry had seen the 'honourable' lady when she visited Nick's flat. Nothing special, not unless the only women you compared her with were other MPs. Nick could do better. But maybe Pete was right and Nick was using Sarah. Like Jerry was using Pete. Maybe Paul Morris had been using Sarah, too, sleeping with her for her connections. Pete mentioned rumours that the two of them had had an affair but didn't indicate whether there was any evidence to support them.

Jerry knew what she had to do and she had enough lunch hour left to do it in. The long draft went into a big, old fashioned legal envelope she'd filched from the stationery cupboard. She pulled down the small metal wings that sealed the documents inside. She considered sending the memory stick too, but it had been costly and she might need to use it again. She'd already typed Nick's name and address on the envelope. All she had to do was queue up at the post office.

Nick needed to see this stuff, to protect himself. If he *was* some kind of Mr Big, Nick needed to be aware that somebody was onto him. If, as Jerry thought, Nick was innocent of anything worse than misguided loyalty to old friends, he needed to know that Pete was after him. Either way, he'd have to take evasive action.

She could phone Nick. Better, maybe, to leave it until tomorrow, check that the anonymous envelope had arrived. How would she explain where she'd obtained the documents? She didn't want him to think of her as a slag. Maybe he already did, after the stunt she'd pulled: waiting for him, naked, in his bed.

Push came to shove, didn't matter if Nick thought she'd whored herself to save his arse. What she needed him to know was that she was watching his back. And that somebody was about to stab him there.

THIRTY-THREE

There were nine days to go until the election and Nick was finding it hard to concentrate on his paid work. He'd rather be campaigning for Sarah. If she won, he still had a chance of getting back with her. But if she moved away, could he follow? Only if she encouraged him to.

He'd had plenty of flings in the long years since he was with Sarah, but only four real relationships: Eve, Nancy, Nazia and Caroline. Eve, he'd had a casual arrangement with when her marriage – correction, both of her marriages – were on the rocks. Nick didn't know whether Tony was aware that they used to have a thing and he didn't want to know. Nancy had been a disaster. He refused to count Chantelle, the secret policewoman who'd dated him because of a case. He'd had strong feelings for her, but what they'd had wasn't real. Nazia and Caroline were the only women since Sarah that he might have settled down with, if either of them had wanted him enough. But both had chosen other men.

Lately, he'd become more and more convinced that he wanted Sarah back. It would have happened two years ago, he was sure. But then Andrew and Nancy got themselves murdered in the villa where he and Sarah were about to have a romantic getaway. It had been weird, this last week, seeing both Caroline and Nazia in the same room, realising that he had romantic feelings for neither of them. Whereas, every time he saw Sarah, it felt like they had unfinished business.

Nick hadn't been entirely celibate for the two years since Majorca. It was harder for a bloke his age to pull on a drunken night out than it used to be. But not impossible. Occasionally, friends tried to set him up, as Tony had on Sunday night. With a similar degree of success. He'd yet to have sex this year, the longest drought since he got out of prison. This as probably why he kept picturing Jerry, naked in his bed, begging for it. Remembering that night fed his fantasies. Yet, when it was happening, he hadn't felt remotely tempted. Funny old world.

On Tuesday morning he cycled over to the council estate

where the Nottingham West canvassing schedule kicked off. This was an area where plenty of potential voters were home during the day. Promises could be firmed up and leaflets pushed through the doors that didn't open.

The estate was quiet. Few cars about: these streets weren't a cut-through to anywhere. Plenty of red posters in windows, hardly any blue or yellow. No green whatsoever. Nick spotted Sarah's car parking up just ahead of him. She wasn't driving it, though. The driver was tall and thin, with foppish hair and a slightly pointed, aristocratic chin. Sarah got out of the passenger seat. Nick was about to call out a hello, then stopped himself and freewheeled instead.

When you were on a bicycle, people tended not to hear you coming. Something about the body language of these two made him wary. Sarah joined the bloke – presumably her secretary, Hugh, who she'd last night referred to as her 'minder' – and squeezed his arm. Turning the corner, the couple adjusted their stride until they were a comradely distance apart.

Nick had a rival.

Ninety minutes later, when the team were on the final stretch, Nick found himself alongside Tracey, secretary of the ward they were canvassing. He'd known Tracey since he was a teacher. Back then, always with an eye for older women, he'd fancied her. They used to talk from time to time, even flirted a little, but she was married and unobtainable. Since then, he'd heard, she'd divorced, taken early retirement, moved into the area where she used to teach and now ran the ward for Labour. Which made her that rarity, a socialist who practised what she preached.

A horn sounded. Sarah was back in her car, which pulled up at the end of the road. Sarah wound down her side window, leant her head out and called.

'Got to go and speak at the WI. Thanks so much for coming out today. I really appreciate it.'

'We're getting there,' Tracey called, while Nick gave an obliging smile.

'What's the story with those two?' he asked, when their car was gone.

Tracey gave a sly smile. 'Nothing to tell, according to her. He lets on that he's gay but I've known a lot of gay men and I don't get that vibe off him. I do know he stays in her flat. What they get up to is their business, don't you think?'

'Sure.'

'You look a little miffed. Don't tell me that you had designs in that direction. She's out of your league, Nick.'

'Suppose you're right.' Humiliated, he turned on the twinkle that had served him well as a younger man. 'Whose league would you say I'm in these days?'

Tracey gave him a wicked look. 'I could have you promoted to my division.'

He hadn't been thinking of Tracey that way, not today. But she followed the offer with a cheeky, more than endearing grin.

'How near's your place?' he asked, returning her grin.

'Your bike's locked up at the end of my road.'

Before leaving Tracey's, Nick turned his Nokia back on. A missed call from Jerry. She never rang unless it was something important. The call would have been made during her lunch hour. He made a mental note to phone back in the evening.

'Better get on my way.'

'Not a word, you hear? I don't want the gossip Sarah gets.'

'Anyone saw me coming in, we had a spot of lunch and talked politics.'

'What conclusion did we come to?'

'A mutually satisfying one,' Nick said. 'I'd best be on my way.'

'So you said.' She had changed when they got out of bed and was wearing a thin grey cardigan over a T-shirt. There was no attempt on Tracey's part to be alluring. She'd already had what she wanted. Nick took in her double chin, the loosening of the skin around her cheeks. She was nearer sixty than fifty, but that didn't bother him. There was something he found particularly attractive, erotic even, when he looked at a woman who was on the verge of losing her beauty, of becoming – there ought to be a word for it, that murky territory between middle-age and old-age – post-sexual.

182

There hadn't been an older woman in his life since he broke things off with Eve. More of Tracey might do him good. At her door, he was about to kiss her lightly on the lips. She saw the kiss coming and took a step back.

'This was a one-off,' she said. 'Don't go expecting a repeat performance.'

Nick spent the afternoon visiting a client in Basford, using his new digital camera to take images for their furniture sales website. Then he stopped off at Russell Press, the publishing arm of the old philosopher's Peace Foundation, whose internet business he was pitching for. Tony, the boss, hadn't made up his mind, but Nick left with a couple of freebies. He stopped in The Old Pear Tree, opposite, for a pre-dinner pint. He'd meant to read a pamphlet by Kurt Vonnegut, but there was a copy of that day's *Post*. He skimmed it for news on the exhumation of Nazia's husband. Then his phone rang, drawing irritated looks from the old regulars in the snug. This was not a mobile-free pub. There weren't enough phone users to make such an edict necessary. Even so, he kept his voice down when he answered. Jerry.

'I saw I missed your call,' he said. 'Sorry I didn't phone you back.'

'I need to know if you got a big, brown envelope in the mail today.'

'The post hadn't come when I left this morning.'

'You'll know who it's by when you open it. And why I sent it anonymously. Thing is, I looked through Pete's email too. The first part of the story is due in on Friday, for publication on Sunday. If I were you, I'd go home and read it.'

Nick finished his pint, then did as he'd been told. The large brown envelope was in his mail box. He waited until he'd had a shower before opening it. There were at least thirty sides of A4, double spaced. He saw Sarah's name, early on, and Andrew's. He also saw his own name, a lot. How had Jerry got hold of this? He took the manuscript through to the living room and began to read.

After two minutes, he knew that he'd have to see Sarah. He

texted her. She replied that she was canvassing until half eight. She'd come to his flat at nine. He had time to reread the long piece and make a few notes. Then he rang Jerry. He needed to ascertain how she'd acquired the article.

'I hope you didn't have to sleep with him to get hold of this,' he told her.

'I didn't have to do anything I wasn't already going to do,' Jerry told him. 'Getting that draft for you was a bonus. Want to know what else I found?'

'Sure you don't want me to come in with you?' Hugh asked, dropping her off on Waverley Street.

'Nick will be more frank if it's just the two of us.'

'I know you two used to… I haven't anything to worry about, have I?'

'Only my losing this election.'

Hugh, as his last question indicated, was becoming more confident about their relationship. Inviting your squeeze to move in with you, even when it was purely a matter of convenience, would have that effect. If Sarah were re-elected, Hugh might want to make their relationship public. But victory was less and less likely. On the phone Nick had indicated that the information he'd been sent, should it get out, would be toxic to her campaign.

Nick was freshly shaved, wearing a new looking blue linen shirt, probably a birthday present. It suited him. She noticed a fat wad of paper on the sofa.

'Do I get offered a drink?' she asked.

'When you've finished reading. Coffee first. You'll need a sharp mind.'

Something between them had changed since Sunday night. The neediness she'd sensed then was no longer apparent. The main vibe Nick gave out was one of determination. She began to read, pausing only to take occasional sips of black coffee. There was a lot to take in. She could hear Nick in his little office off the hall, tapping away on his computer keyboard. When she was done, she called his name. He came in a minute later with a bottle of claret and two glasses.

'Figured you'd need this.'

'You figured right.' She put the sheaf of papers down. 'This is Pete Carlson?'

'Word is he's due to send the first part to the Sunday Times by end of play tomorrow, with a view to it being in this weekend's paper.'

Sarah swore. 'That doesn't give us much time. Why did he send it you? What does he want?'

'He didn't. A friend of mine got hold of it.'

'Useful friend.' Sarah waited to see if Nick would volunteer more. 'Does she have any leverage with him?'

'No, and she'd have even less if he knew she'd given us this.'

'It's bad for me, but it's worse for you. Nottingham's *Mr Big*.' She lowered her voice. 'There isn't anything to it, is there?'

Nick lit a roll-up. 'He's got some dirt on Andy I wasn't aware of. Criminal links beyond anything I ever suspected. Until recently, Nancy's being pregnant was news to me, but I doubt it had anything to do with Andy going on the run. That was to get away from the people who killed him.'

'The article suggests that you might be back in business with the people who murdered Andrew.'

'*Might* being the operative word. Pete always stops short of anything outright libellous. If he publishes, I may have grounds to sue, but I'm a convicted drug dealer. It's hard to libel someone with no reputation to lose. Whereas you...'

'Everything he says about me is true. Even the innuendos. I *did* have an affair with Paul Morris. I *was* the last person to see him before his murderer.'

'Pete still hasn't got a story,' Nick said. 'He's missing the key element, which is who was behind Andrew. The police took Terence Tailor down, but there were at least two rungs above him.'

'Surely Andrew was one of those?'

'Andy was one level higher than Tailor. But there was someone beyond him, someone who ordered Andy's murder. At least Pete stops short of saying it was me. From what I learnt in prison, we're either talking about a long-established crime family or a senior policeman with a network of corrupt officers to draw on.'

'How senior?'

'Anything from Deputy Superintendent to Assistant Chief Constable.'

Sarah decided it was time to bring up Eric. 'I know the former Chief Constable. He might be able to throw some light on potential suspects.'

'If Eric Turnbull was willing and able, he'd have dealt with whoever we're talking about while he was in the job. I don't think we've time to chase shadows. We need to put Pete off for a week so that he doesn't interfere with the election.'

'By threatening to sue?' Sarah didn't like the idea of using lawyers.

'Wouldn't work. He's got an early deadline so that the paper's lawyers have time to make sure everything in the piece is watertight.'

'Give me a minute.' Sarah knew what she had to do but didn't know how to do it. 'There's only one, time-honoured way to stop him,' she said, 'tell him if he holds the story back for a week, I'll give him something better.'

'Could work.'

'Only if I have a good enough story to give him. Don't suppose you're sitting on any secrets?'

Nick hesitated. 'Nothing I can tell without causing a lot of pain. You?'

'The one that springs to mind is how I helped to get a double murderer freed on appeal only for him to confess to me that he'd committed one of the killings.'

'That'd be worse for your election prospects than your connection to Andy.'

'Agreed. Is there anything we can give them about Omar Khan?'

'I'm not sure that's much of a story outside Nottingham.'

Sarah drank some more wine. 'We're being straight with each other, right?

Nick spoke softly. 'I'll tell you anything that I'm free to tell.'

'Other people's secrets are a bugger, aren't they? You know that the police think you've been having an affair with Nazia.'

'When I saw Naz at Bilal's house, it was the first time in over a decade. And, in case you were wondering, there was no... feeling there, on either side.'

But there was feeling here.

'Actually, there is something we could use,' Nick went on. 'Pete would most likely buy it. But I doubt very much that you'd be comfortable with the story coming out.'

'I'm curious. What?'

'It wouldn't hurt your election prospects. It might even help you.'

'What?!'

'Your big family secret. Trouble is, with your mum still alive...'

'What *big family secret*?' Sarah had no idea what he was talking about. Nick looked away from her, embarrassed.

'I thought you'd have worked it out,' he muttered.

'Worked *what* out?'

'Look, I'm not sure.'

'You'd better explain what you mean.'

'It was one of those late night conversations on Majorca when we were both pissed and very stoned. The next day, I tried to push it away and I don't think Kevin remembered telling me, he'd been so out of his skull the night before.'

'My dad? What could my dad have told you that's such a big story?'

'That he wasn't your dad.'

H alf an hour later, they were on their second bottle of wine. Sarah wanted to know how Nick came to know more about her paternity than she did. Seemed he'd only processed the information after the visit to Majorca when they found Andrew and Nancy's bodies. If Sarah hadn't been so close to the story, she'd have worked it out when she was young. Nick, for his part, assumed she knew, or half knew, but had chosen not to take the situation on board. Maybe there was some truth in that.

The man she'd always thought was her father, Kevin Bone, was a feckless, self-centred egotist who'd never had a heterosexual impulse in his life. In 1960, gay sex was illegal and Kevin needed cover. So why would Mum have married him – unless she were pregnant? Her real father, Sir Hugh – she had to stop thinking of him as Grandad – was still a married man. Grandma was severely disabled but wouldn't die for several years. Easy to see why he would start an affair with his secretary, but Sir Hugh was a senior Labour Party figure, twenty-odd years Mum's senior, with cabinet ambitions. He needed to cover up Sarah's paternity.

Her phone buzzed. A text from Hugh. *Crisis sorted out? Want me to come for you?*

She texted back. *No. Walking. Need time to think. Back soon.*

'I'd better go,' she told Nick. 'I'll phone you when I've sorted things out.'

'I'll walk you home.'

'No. I'll be fine. I need the time to think.'

'I'll walk a couple of paces behind you all the way. Or you can call a taxi. But these streets…'

He was right. She could usually risk The Park, because its roads were so quiet and there were few places for potential attackers to hide, but it was late and her route home from Nick's flat took her along the edge of the city's red light zone.

'OK,' she said. 'Thanks.'

Nick, as promised, stayed a pace behind her. She really did

need time to let her thoughts settle. How would Mum take this? Would she deny it?

Sarah spoke to her mother most weeks, but their last conversation had been before the election was called. No offence would be taken. Mum knew how distracting elections were.

She'd fully recovered from her op two years before. Sarah had given that crisis as the reason for her stepping down as Prisons minister. Her real motive had been murkier: there'd been a strong risk that Sarah's relationship with Paul Morris would come out. If the press discovered that Sarah had left Paul's flat only a few minutes before he was murdered, they'd have had a field day. Moreover, until the police found the CCTV footage that cleared Sarah, she'd been the prime suspect.

Mum knew Sarah had used her ill health as political cover. She was fine with that. Mum used to be a cabinet minister's secretary, knew all about the necessity of subterfuge, even thrived on it. Had she ever had ambitions in that direction, she'd have made a good MP herself. Several women from Mum's generation – Clare Short, Mo Mowlam, Margaret Beckett – sat at the top table now.

At least, while Mum was recuperating, Sarah had been there for her. She'd had no choice but to become the dutiful daughter she puported to be. The pair had, briefly, through choice rather than necessity, become closer. Yet each remained a loner, happy in their own company, not relying on men for fulfilment. Neither of them, truth be told, was cut out to be a mother. Too many better things to do.

Mum's political life had been all about supporting Sarah's grandad, Sir Hugh Bone, a cabinet minister under Harold Wilson. Marrying Hugh's son was, Sarah had assumed until now, another aspect of Mum wanting to stay close to Hugh: *OK, you have this troublesome gay son. Let me take him off your hands.* Turned out it was the other way round. Kevin had been helping his own father.

Sarah would have to fib to Mum and say that the reporter already had the story, this was how to play it. She could add that Mum might even make some money. One of the tabloids would surely pay serious money for a one-to-one confessional. If Mum

190

could bring herself to do it.

Could Sarah lie to Mum like that? Why not, when Mum had been lying to Sarah her entire life? But Sarah couldn't lie to Nick. He was her oldest, truest friend. They crossed Alfreton Road at busy Canning Circus, its two pubs full, turned onto Derby Road, then cut through the semi-secret passage that only Park dwellers knew about. The Park tunnel was big enough to take a coach and horses. It had been open to cars for part of the last century but, these days, was little used.

She waited until they were inside the tunnel, away from the city noise, in between each of their worlds, before she told him.

'You know Hugh, who's staying with me? We're sleeping together.'

'I'd figured that one out, too. How serious is it?'

'Quite, on his part. As for me, it's flattering, being worshipped by a twenty-eight-year-old. But I only let it happen because I was sure I'd be out next week.'

'Yet here you are, fighting to keep your job.'

'I have to. I'm good at it. There are days when I feel jaded but there are others when I feel I've hardly started.'

At the bottom of the hill they turned and walked towards her flat.

'I'm here for you,' he told her. 'Lover, friend, or both. You can count on me.'

'I know I can.' The flat was in sight. Hugh would probably be looking out for her from the window. She didn't want him to see Nick. 'I'll be all right from here.'

THIRTY-SIX

'**A**re you an honourable man?' the MP asked Pete over the phone.

'Is that *honour* as in *honourable member* or as in *honour among thieves?*'

'The latter, I suppose. I want to make a deal with you, but I need to be sure that you'll keep it.'

'If I didn't, I wouldn't have a career. You know how this business works.'

'I'm going to offer you a big story. You'll need to delay sending in your *Insight* piece, but the paper will be very happy when they see what you've got.'

'How do you know what's in the *Insight* piece?' Pete adopted a wary tone. 'Are you trying to delay the story until after the election? It won't work. If I miss the *Sunday Times* deadline, there are three days to get it into *The Times* daily edition.'

'I'm well aware of that. And I have a reputation too. I'm not asking you to kill all of your story, just delay it. As a bonus, I'll help you make it more accurate.'

'And how would you know that it isn't accurate to begin with?'

'Let's just say I know. Also, there are some things in the piece, things that might be described as "informed speculation", which I'd like you to lose.'

'Those being?'

'That I had an affair with a man who turned out to be a big-league drug dealer, and a strong suggestion that a former boyfriend of mine is some kind of drugs kingpin. Which I can assure you he's not.'

'Prove it.'

'Hard to prove a negative. But I'll give you a sexier story, one that'll delight your bosses.'

'A crime story?'

'No. Personal.'

'How personal?'

'Personal as it gets. But you'll need to come to me.'

'That's OK. I always welcome an excuse to visit Nottingham.'

'I'm not talking about Nottingham. We have to meet in Chesterfield.'

'Long way.'

'This afternoon, if you're in a hurry.'

'It's almost as though you know my deadlines.'

'I'm taking time out from a tight election, Pete. Do we have a deal or not?'

Pete thought for a moment. He had been trying to get proof positive of Nick Cane's role so that the paper could splash the story before next week's General Election, but he wasn't there yet. A week's delay and an even juicier story suited him down to the ground. It might even get him kudos from his new employers. But he made Sarah sweat for close to a minute before replying.

'Tell me where to meet you,' he said.

The M1 traffic was heavier than usual on Friday afternoons and the drive to Chesterfield took longer. Never mind. Sarah needed more time to think. How to play this? The story of her life that she told to herself had changed. While her new history made more sense than the old one, it still took some getting used to. Grandad had always been her political hero. Dad was a counter-example, an embarrassment. She'd loved him but had been determined not to emulate him.

Grandad had always been far more affectionate with her than Kevin had, which made all the more sense now that Sarah knew what she knew. Grandma's physical incapacity (she was partially paralysed after a stroke) must be what had driven Grandad into the arms of his secretary. Sarah reminded herself that Grandma was not grandma. Sarah's real paternal grandmother had died of tuberculosis during the Second World War. Her real paternal grandfather had been shot dead during the battle of the Somme in the First.

After half an hour's crawl along the motorway, she turned onto the A61, where she concentrated on her speed. Regional police procedures were not to prosecute speeding cars if they didn't exceed ten percent over the speed limit, plus three miles per hour to allow for speedometer discrepancies. If Sarah kept to 77mph, she'd avoid a ticket.

The modest, three-bedroom semi on Chatsworth Road was where Sarah had grown up. There had also been frequent visits to Bone mansion, as they called Sir Hugh's large pile at the edge of the Peak District. A stark contrast that she'd hardly questioned. Grandad was a knight after all. Knights lived in castles.

Mum's car was parked outside. She was in good form last time they spoke, but their phone calls had dwindled to weekly, then fortnightly, then never less than once a month. Today, Mum knew that Sarah was coming, but not why.

'I made lunch. Hope you still like pea soup.'

Felicity Bone, in a flowered pinny over shapeless jeans and a pink jumper, had aged since her operation. Not that 63 was old these days. Her mind remained sharp. As did her tongue.

'Must be important for you to interrupt an election and visit me for the first time this year.'

'Is it really that long? I'm sorry. I need your help with something delicate.'

'I'm intrigued.'

'It can wait until after lunch.' They'd talked over the usual stuff about neighbours, old work colleagues and the things that needed doing on the house. Sarah worked up the courage to tell Mum about her affair with Paul Morris.

'He was married, you say?'

'I know it was bad of me, but it was only sex, and it was very good sex. It wouldn't be a story – man cheats on wife for umpteenth time – but for two things. One, he was murdered.'

'Ah,' Mum said. 'That's why I remember the name.'

'Two, a journalist is about to reveal that he wasn't just a politician and a Home Office Drugs advisor, he was also tied to one of the city's biggest drugs traffickers. In fact, he used to deal himself.'

'And when is this story going to be all over the news?'

'On Sunday, unless I can bargain my name out of it by giving them something bigger.'

'I see. And you've come to see me because…?'

'I think you might be able to guess what I have in mind.'

'I have no idea.'

'A tell-all about my grandfather really being my father.'

Mum stared at her in incomprehension. For a second or two, Sarah thought she must have got it wrong. Then Mum's face went red and Sarah worried that she might be having a heart attack. Abruptly, Mum got up from the table, went to the sink, and poured herself a glass of water.

'How long have you known?' Mum asked, after drinking half the water.

'For 24 hours. Nick worked it out, not me. I tried to tell myself that I always knew, subconsciously, but, really, I had no idea. I just thought Dad was in denial when he married you and you married Dad because he was his father's son.'

'Some truth in that last bit, anyway.'

'I remember bringing Nick to visit once, during the Falklands war, and he asked whether you and Grandad were… you know. I shut him down so heavily that he didn't bring it up again for eighteen years.'

'You should have stuck with him,' Mum said. 'He understood you.'

'Don't change the subject. Is there anything else you want to tell me?'

'Hugh was the love of my life. What more is there to say? But when I fell pregnant with you, people would have guessed. It could have been the end of Hugh's political career. Kevin was willing.'

'And you got away with it.'

'Round here we did. Harold Wilson worked it out, or so Hugh always thought. That was why he took so long to promote him.'

Sarah left a long pause before asking the crucial question.

'Will you speak to this journalist?'

'Why do you need me to do that?'

'To confirm the story. You don't have to give many details. In fact, I'd hold back as much as you can if I were you. The tabloids will come in with big offers.'

Mum gave her a hard, calculating look. 'I'll give him the bare minimum. And I won't kiss and tell. What would people think of me? I'm all right for money.'

'I know you are. If you don't talk, though, they'll just tell lies about you.'

'All right, but I won't talk to any tabloid apart from the Mirror.'

That was her mum, Labour through and through.

THIRTY-SEVEN

Melanie was pissed off with Pete's working all the time and anxious to start her precious weekend. Pete, as a result, wrote the first draft more quickly than usual, revising while she cooked. He emailed it in just after eight. The paper would fact check but, given how both Sarah Bone and her mother had cooperated, were bound to go big on the story. This was a proper scoop, the sort you held back from first editions so the competition couldn't nab it for their second editions.

Pete had written Sarah up sympathetically. *MP's paternity shock*. The story was more tabloid than the ST usually ran with, but you didn't look a gift horse in the gob. For the following week's series opener (presuming it was ready to run by then), he'd agreed to leave out Sarah's affair with Paul Morris. The affair was only relevant to the drugs story if Sarah was in league with Morris. But all he could really report was that Sarah Bone had had an inappropriate relationship, much as her grandfather had done decades ago. Didn't make her corrupt.

Pete hadn't agreed what to reveal or not reveal about Nick Cane. Sarah's association with Cane was so ancient, their current connection so tenuous, that her urge to protect him looked more like misguided loyalty than naked self-service. Her affair with Morris had already demonstrated that she was no judge of character.

He replayed the tape of their conversation.

'As for Cane, I can't keep him out of the story. He supplied Morris in the early '90s. He was in prison during Morris' ascendancy, so he's not tied to the big network I want to expose, but if it turns out he got back in with the network after his release, I'll have to write about that.'

'He didn't. Nick's loyal. That's why he stayed friends with Andrew Saint. But he didn't work for him. The opposite. He worked for an advisory service getting people off drugs.'

'Just like Frank Davis.'

Davis had run CAT – the city's Crack Awareness Team – and used it as cover for dealing. The stuff of legend: but that was before Nick Cane's time. Davis was also the former owner of the flat where Nick now lived, the one that Geraldine owned. Hard to figure how that came about. Pete always found it hard to believe in coincidences.

There was one other part of the conversation Pete wanted to remind himself of. He rewound the tape to where Sarah was talking about Morris, off the record.

I had no idea. Nobody did. I talked about this with Eric Turnbull, who was the Chief Constable during the period. The police didn't suspect that Morris was dodgy. As soon as he became a county councillor, Paul went on the police committee. Not typical behaviour for a dealer.

That kind of chutzpah suggested someone in the know, a player with the confidence to make outrageous moves. Which, in turn, suggested that Morris had protection higher up. But who? Not Sarah Bone. MPs had precious little influence over national policing. It might be worth chasing the local perspective. Pete wondered what Eric Turnbull was doing these days. The ex-Chief Constable couldn't be that old. Police could retire at fifty, on a full pension, if they chose. Now Pete had an extra week to nail this story, he would take the opportunity to do some supplementary interviews, and Eric Turnbull was at the top of his list.

He opened Alta Vista on his laptop and looked up Eric Turnbull, OBE. The ex-Chief Constable had remarried recently, to a solicitor called Mary Harris. They lived, the article said, in The Park. He'd bet that the copper and the solicitor had a rather more salubrious pad than Sarah's.

Sure enough, after a bit of searching, he established that the couple had moved into a penthouse, a new development on the site of the old Nottingham General Hospital, wedged between The Park Estate and Nottingham Castle. The same set of searches revealed that Mary Harris was the solicitor for Nazia Khan, an interesting coincidence. The inquest into her husband's death was imminent.

Pete had his work cut out for tomorrow. First, Turnbull. Then, depending on what he heard from him, Cane. This story kept getting bigger, juicier. The double murder in Majorca was important enough. But if he could also establish who murdered Paul Morris, this might become the sort of story that won prizes.

THIRTY-EIGHT

'What are you going to do about Pete?' Jerry asked Nick when she phoned on Saturday morning.

'The story's been delayed.'

'How come?'

'Your friend was offered something better. He's going to hold back the stuff about her and Paul Morris.'

'She's off the hook, then. What about you?'

'I've got a feeling I'm only the bait. He's after something else.'

'Do you think he suspects how Paul died?'

'I reckon he thinks what everyone who remembers the case thinks, which is that Paul Morris was killed by associates from the underworld. The motive's unlikely to be clear unless Pete tracks down his so-called kingpin and they talk.'

'Any idea who that is?'

'Jerry, I don't even know if he or she exists. The drugs world is full of gangs with shifting alliances. Whoever was behind Andrew and Nancy's killings is probably out of the picture by now, enjoying their spoils in a villa by the med.'

'Is there anything I can do to help?' She sounded so concerned, so loving, that Nick avoided his natural reaction, which was to dismiss her offer.

'Just keep your ear to the ground. And bear in mind that if Pete finds out you stole those files, he won't trust you again.'

'I don't think he trusted me before. He just wanted to fuck me.'

Nick sighed. Jerry's sexuality, in particular her penchant for older men, perturbed him. The doorbell rang. His portable phone meant he was able to carry on the conversation while he walked down two flights of stairs, albeit the sound became cracklier.

The doorbell rang. Nick looked at his watch. Nearly midday. Not often canvassers came out on a Saturday. Still, it was the last week of the election.

'I wasn't expecting to see you.'

'Sorry to turn up out of the blue. I've got a few questions that won't wait.'

Phone still in hand, Nick thought for a moment, then told Jerry, 'I've got to go. A journalist just turned up, wanting to interview me.'

'Is it him?' Jerry asked, in a quiet voice.

'It is.'

'Be careful what you tell him and ring me when he's gone.'

'I'll do that.'

He clicked off the phone and turned to Pete. 'You'd better come in.'

This time, Pete got a good look at Nick's flat. It was on the shabby side but the rooms were a fair size. He had a good view over the city. A better place than Pete's, in London. Pete still couldn't work out how Jerry came to own this flat, or what her connection was with the previous owner, Frank Davis. He wasn't going to ask Nick this, not unless it came up. He'd ask Jerry, when the time was right.

'What can I do for you?' Nick asked.

'Have you seen the story?'

To Nick's credit, he didn't ask *what story?* He smiled, then seemed to consider before replying, 'Sarah consulted me about it, yes.'

'You don't know how she happened to have seen something that I hadn't sent to the paper.'

'You'd have to ask her that.'

'But you've read it?'

A moment's hesitation. Cane was not a natural liar.

'I'm aware part of it's about me, let's put it that way.'

'I offered you your say. Sarah's got the story delayed until after the election, so I'm here to repeat the offer.'

'Look around this place. The only expensive stuff is computer paraphernalia, and I need that for work. Does it look like I'm Nottingham's Mr Big?'

While he was talking, Pete took the micro-recorder from his pocket and put it on the table between them.

'You also own a very large house in Notting Hill. Could be

worth a million. How did you pay for it?'

That stopped him in his tracks. Nick looked at the recorder for a moment, then spoke carefully.

'Where did you get your information?'

Pete didn't reply. No point in dropping Jerry in it.

'If you got the information legally, you'd have found out how I came to own the property. An old friend left it to me in his will.'

'Andrew Saint?'

'Yes.'

'And why would he do that?'

'Out of friendship. What else is there? Andrew had been dead six months when I heard. His sister contacted me. I don't think she was particularly happy about my getting the house, but she inherited everything else.'

'You own the house through a limited company?'

'Andrew's business was… complicated. You'd have to ask an accountant. Something to do with corporation tax.'

'The point I'm getting at is that you now own a business that Andrew Saint funded from the proceeds of crime, a business which you helped him build up.'

Nick spoke carefully. 'The first thing you said is speculation, the second slander. I'm not a drug dealer. Yes, I used to grow weed and sell it, but I served my sentence. I admit that Andrew helped me find people to sell to, but that was over a decade ago. Andy wasn't Nottingham's biggest drugs baron. Neither am I.'

Sam took Ahmad and Tamazur to see a movie, giving Bilal a chance to talk to his sister. Naz had only just got up. She wore leggings and a baggy, grey sweatshirt. Hardly mourning gear, but she wasn't seeing visitors. What she wore was up to her. Bilal repeated the question she'd refused to answer the night before.

'Who is he?'

'Doesn't matter.'

'Are you going to be with him after the baby is born?'

'I don't know.'

'Suppose he wants to raise the baby with you, where does that leave me and Sam?'

201

'He won't want to bring up our baby. I doubt he'll even want to be with me. We don't have that kind of relationship, never have. It was always more… carnal.'

It made Bilal uncomfortable, hearing her talk like that.

'*Always*? How long has this been going on?'

'I told you, I knew him before I got married.'

Was she saying they'd had sex before she met Omar? Surely not.

'The sooner you move,' Bilal said, 'the better. That's what I came to say.'

'I'm talking to Sana about places in Birmingham. It needs to be near a good school. There are options. After the inquest, on Thursday, I'll make a decision.'

'The inquest will be inconclusive, you do know that? It won't say natural causes, it'll say "cause unknown".'

'Mary explained.'

'That'll be enough for Fahd to carry on a vendetta against you. There'll be more paint on your doors. Ahmad and Tamazur will get hassle at school. That's why I think you should consider leaving town as soon as the inquest is over.'

'I could go to Birmingham tomorrow, I suppose, start looking seriously. If I did that, would you and Sam have the kids again? I know it's a lot to ask.'

'You're having a baby for us,' Bilal told her. 'Ask whatever you like.'

'One other thing. I wrote a will. Mary said it was a good idea.'

'Does she know you're pregnant?'

'Not yet. I didn't want to confuse her with the surrogacy issues. I named you and Sam for the guardianship of Tamazur and Ahmad. OK?'

'Say again?'

'Guardianship of the kids. Sell this house to pay for their upkeep. It's just a precaution, in case I crash my car or whatever. Is that all right with you?'

'I suppose.'

She gave him a plaintive smile.

'When are you meeting him again? Your lover.'

'Maybe tomorrow. Maybe never. It's nearly over, I think.'
'Does he even know about the baby?'
A small shake of the head.
'Why not?'
'Things are complicated enough without him knowing.'

M ary Harris and Eric Turnbull's penthouse had superb views over the city centre. Pete glimpsed Mary, hunched over a laptop at a long desk. She did not look up.

'What can I do for you?' Eric gestured for him to sit on a smart, Eames-style chair. Turnbull was in his mid-fifties, thin and generally well preserved, with a soft, unmistakeable voice and pale blue eyes that met Pete's unflinchingly.

'I'm trying to put together a story about something that happened under your watch. I'd be grateful for any help you can give me. Paul Morris's murder.'

'I knew Paul Morris, and that happened while I was Chief Constable, only it didn't happen in Notts, but in London. Near Kings Cross, as I recall.'

'Morris was stabbed in the shower. His assailant didn't break in. They seem to have had a key to the flat, meaning that they were trusted by the victim.'

Turnbull poured coffee from a Gaggia-style machine. 'Give me a moment.' He took an espresso cup through to Mary, giving Pete time to check out the art on the walls. Abstract. Colourful. More imaginative choices than your average senior police would make but, when you looked closer, they had no depth, no edge to them. There were a bunch of framed photos too. Honeymoon shots. Mary Harris could rock a bikini. Eric wore a baseball cap emblazoned with the name of the exclusive-looking resort they were staying at. Pete made a mental note of it.

'*The Sunday Times*, you said?' Turnbull handed him his coffee.

'Yes, do you read it?'

'I'm a *Telegraph* man myself.'

'Each to their own.' Pete did not mention the story about Sarah that he'd written for today's paper.

'Why your interest in such an old case?'

'There's another, linked story. It's about the drugs trade in Nottingham and a double murder in Majorca.'

'Andrew Saint and Nancy Tull.'

'Saint was a major player in the Nottingham drugs trade, I believe.'

'We arrested Saint once, at a brothel. That was the closest we got to him. His connection there was Terence Tailor. The brothel was run by Tailor, who's now serving fifteen years for rape and drug-related crime. His sentence would have been shorter had he named names. But presumably he preferred to stay alive.'

'Unlike Saint. Who do you think killed him?'

'Someone he owed money to.'

'The same person who killed Paul Morris?'

Turnbull leant forward. 'The same organisation, possibly. I'd heard rumours about Morris, but no behaviour I saw suggested anything untoward. He was on the make, certainly. Also a womaniser. That could have been his downfall.'

'How do you mean?'

'A jealous husband or a woman spurned, take your pick.'

'There's one other name I need to ask you about. Nick Cane.'

'I know who Cane is. Have you spoken to him?'

Pete made a calculation. If he was going to get anything remotely indiscreet out of Turnbull, he needed to share.

'Cane was cagey, but told me that he used to supply Paul Morris, who, at the time, was working for Andrew Saint. Cane claims to have been clean since he got out of prison four years ago.'

'Maybe he has. We never caught him doing anything. Cane says that Morris worked for him? Interesting. Though it's easy to tell lies about dead men.'

'What would be Cane's motive for that?'

'To protect himself and his business. I've been retired for more than a year. I'm out of the loop, but I always had the sense that Cane was a bigger player than he let on. It wouldn't surprise me if he picked up the reins from Saint after he got out of prison. Nancy Tull, the woman who was murdered alongside Saint, she used to be Cane's girlfriend. Cane might well have been involved in Saint's death.'

Pete tried not to show his disbelief. 'For romantic reasons?'

'More likely business. What was Saint doing in Majorca? Who

was he running from? That's what you need to work out.'

'Who was his boss? The Kingpin, if you like…'

Turnbull considered. 'That's a fundamental misunderstanding. We don't have underworld kings. No Moriarty, no master of crime. We have deep seated corruption with shifting alliances based on mutual advantage and provisional trust.'

'How does that connect with the establishment? The police, for instance?'

Turnbull gave an expansive shrug. 'At every level. Sometimes covertly, sometimes overtly. Politicians, police, local government, big business, banks and, ultimately, the legal system: they're all compromised, to some degree.'

'Doesn't that scare you, or, at least, worry you?'

'You can't take that attitude because the world has always worked that way. People do bad, selfish things. It's in their nature. Society legislates against the bad for the greater good. But the greater good is a nebulous concept and individual greed will often outweigh it. That's the game of life.'

'Eric, I'm ready to go out.' Mary Harris was in the doorway, hair brushed, white blouse, almost as tasty out of a bikini. Pete decided that he'd got as much out of Turnbull as he was going to get. He stood.

'I'm sorry to have taken up so much of your time on a Sunday, but you've been very helpful. Thank you.'

'The pleasure was mine. Good luck with your investigation.'

'How did your meeting go?' Mel asked later that afternoon.

'Better than expected, not that I was expecting much.'

'Why did you go, then?'

'I wanted to hear the sound of his voice.'

When Sarah came in from canvassing, her answering machine was full. She couldn't face listening to all the messages but asked Hugh to triage them while she had a shower.

'There's only a few you really need to hear,' he said when she returned. 'I've deleted the rest.'

The first was her mum. 'My phone's been going non-stop.

Why'd I let you talk me into this?'

Sarah tried to call her back, only to get a busy signal. She listened to the rest, quickly deciding to ignore all the TV and radio requests. There was only one call she felt obliged to respond to. She gave Brian from the *Nottingham Post* a few words.

'This won't affect my relationship with my mother. If anything, the revelations make our family bond stronger. Politicians are always under pressure to keep their private lives from interfering with their public ones. That comes with the territory. Trouble is, non-politicians can get caught in the middle. That's what happened to my mother. We're both glad that the secret's finally out.'

'What about your half-brother?' Brian asked. 'How do you feel about Kevin Bone now that you know he wasn't your father?'

'To be honest, I haven't even begun to come to terms with that part of the story. All I can say is that life was hard for gay men in the early sixties. Kevin shouldn't have been put in the position he found himself in. I'm sorry that he's no longer here for us to talk about it. The thing is, I thought of him as a bad... not so much a bad but an exasperating father, when, in many ways, he was a good brother to me, given the impossible position he found himself in.'

'Perfect,' Brian said. 'Thanks. We'll be going big on this tomorrow. I don't think it'll hurt your campaign one bit.'

'I hope you're right,' Sarah told Brian.

'There was a message I didn't understand,' Hugh said, when she'd put the phone down. 'The chairman of the Police Federation says his thoughts are with you and this doesn't make any difference to anything.'

She'd known that giving her boyfriend access to her communication devices would cause a problem sooner or later.

'There's something I ought to tell you,' Sarah said.

'I read your story,' Jerry told Pete when he rang her on Sunday night. She was stoned and randy and surprised that he'd called. With any luck, she could talk him into coming over for a quickie. 'Wasn't that what they call *a scoop*?'

'It's getting a lot of attention. The morning talk shows all covered it.'

'I'll bet they did. Celebrating?'

'On my ownsome, nobody to celebrate with.'

'Why don't you come round here then?"

'Can't. I've had to stay in Nottingham.'

'Then take your hard-on to your school-teacher.'

Pete gave a soft, sexy laugh. 'She's gone out. I'm supposed to be working.' 'You deserve to have fun. I'm putting my fingers into my panties, pretending that they're yours. I'm already a little bit wet. Oh, that's nice…'

'You sound really stoned,' Pete told her. 'Wish I was. I've run out. Don't know where to get any in Nottingham.'

'I could give you my friend Shaz's number. She'd sort you out. In more ways than one, if you know what I mean.'

'Tempting,' Pete murmured, 'but Melanie might come home.'

'She'll do you a threesome if the money's right. Shaz is on the game.'

'Interesting people you hang out with.'

'Shaz was my best mate in the home. Still is, in some ways. She's a proper friend. You can't hold it against her, what she does. Not everyone has choices.'

'I don't hold anything against her. In fact, give me her number. If she's your only friend, I need to know it, in case anything should ever happen to you.'

'Aah, so you do have a sentimental side.' Jerry didn't know what Pete's game was, but tonight she was beyond caring. She gave him Shaz's mobile number. Pete had his pervy side. It wouldn't surprise her if he checked out Shaz, though she doubted Shaz was his type: too fleshy and too mouthy. If he wanted to score off her, or screw her, Jerry wasn't bothered. She tried to remember why Pete had called in the first place. Maybe, she told herself while she rolled one last spliff to help her sleep, he was just lonely.

FORTY

Pete found himself spending more time in Nottingham than he did at home. Monday morning, after Mel had gone to work, he planned his week. He was sure that Nick Cane, his first priority, was holding something back. Cane might not know who'd killed Andrew Saint and Nancy Tull. Or paid to have them killed, which amounted to the same thing. But he knew more about Paul Morris than he was letting on.

The Omar Khan inquest was this week. Shrewd of the coroner to schedule a controversial inquest on the same day as the General Election. That gave Pete a reason to talk to Rebecca Allen again. She would know the post-mortem result, which wasn't yet public.

Rebecca's mobile went to voicemail, so he left a message. Then he rang the office in London and made a request that would help him with his other lead.

'I'll put Ted Burley onto it,' his editor, Karen, promised. Ted was old school, not far off retirement, but still reliable. 'Do we need to save you a slot this Sunday?'

'I might need an extra week.'

'No worries. You bought yourself extra time with the Sarah Bone exclusive. In fact, we might do better with the story if it isn't buried by election coverage.'

'Most boring election ever. We need to give the reader a few distractions.'

'Here's a thing,' Karen said, 'looking at the latest projections, according to our modelling, your girl is one of the only Labour MPs to lose her seat. Since you're there, might be worth a follow-up sob story.'

'And if she wins?'

'Shorter piece but the human interest angle remains. Maybe voter sympathy re the paternity exclusive helped her retain what would otherwise be a Tory seat.'

'I'll see what I can do.'

For his next call, he used the number that Geraldine had given him.

'Yeah?' Shaz had a thick Nottingham accent. Pete introduced himself.

'What is this? I don't do house calls.'

'I want to buy you a drink. I'll make it worth your while.'

'I could meet you in The Vernon,' Shaz conceded. 'Six tonight.'

'You're on. How will I know you?'

'Oh, you'll know me.' She hung up.

'I've slept on it,' Hugh said in bed on Monday morning.

'And you're still talking to me?'

For the first time since Hugh started staying over, they hadn't made love the night before. He'd not been sulking, not exactly, but his sense of betrayal was manifest, reminding Sarah how much younger than her he was.

'You really think you're going to lose?'

Sarah sat up. 'I don't *think* anything. You have to believe in victory while you're fighting an election. You also have to be realistic. I'm odds on to lose. Therefore, when an opportunity presented itself, I prepared an escape plan.'

'How long ago?'

'Before we started... you know.'

'And does our... *you know* change anything?' He was using his most civil, cultured voice, which, despite his being naked, turned him into a member of the ruling class. Sarah, with only a skimpy T-shirt covering her chest and little roll of belly fat, felt uncomfortable. Maybe that was his intention. She took a deep breath.

'This is an office romance, Hugh. We're having an election affair. It's intense, but that doesn't mean it's going to last. Neither of us knows that.'

'And neither of us knows that it won't.'

'Odds are, in time, you'll end up with someone nearer your own age. And that's all right. We're enjoying ourselves.'

'You don't want me to accompany you when you start the new job?'

'I'd keep on my London flat, for now at least, come and see you at weekends. We'd find out how we got on without my being your boss. It might be good for us.'

She'd started looking at the floor while she spoke, her mind whirring away. These were ideas that she'd been trying to keep at bay until the election was over.

'What about the other alternative? That you win?'

'Then we're in clover, aren't we? I wouldn't have started seeing you if I thought I was going to get back in, but now that I am… now that *we are*, we'll find out where this leads us. If that's what you want.'

'Shall I tell you exactly what I want?' Hugh said, getting out of bed.

She couldn't help but admire his taut, tall body. He even had a sweet-looking penis, lightly freckled, the head just slightly twisted, giving it a little personality. Hugh went down on his knees.

'As soon as you get back in – because *you will* get back in, I'm sure of it – I want you to agree to marry me, as soon as practicable. Then, whenever you're ready, I'd like us to start a family.'

'Bloody hell,' Sarah said.

Shaz was hardly the full-on tart Geraldine had led Pete to expect, maybe because she wasn't in all her working gear. Jeans rather than fishnets, thighs a little on the fat side, plump tits poking out of a deep red basque under a denim jacket. Neither tall nor petite – 5' 3" or thereabouts. Fair bit of make-up and bright red lippy. Ripe then, but hardly excessive, not for a city like this. A few drinks in him and Pete definitely would. If he hadn't known that she was nineteen, the same age as Jerry, he'd have said twenty-five, at least. Old enough to choose what she did for a living.

'Here you go.' She'd asked for a rum and coke and he'd ordered a triple to loosen her tongue. Not to open her legs. She charged for that, and Pete had never paid for it, not once. Nor had he any interest in buying dope off her. He hardly touched the stuff, except when he was with Geraldine.

'If you aren't here to fuck me, what are you here for?' Shaz asked.

'I'm interested in Geraldine.'

'Nobody calls her that. It's Jerry. Like in *Tom and Jerry.*'

'In that case,' Pete asked, 'who was *Tom?*'

'Ooh,' Shaz took a deep gulp of rum and coke. 'Good question.'

Her phone buzzed. From the way she frowned at the text, he knew it was her pimp.

'I'm not meant to be on yet,' she told Pete.

'Tell him you're working.'

'He'd expect to see the money.'

He checked his wallet. 'I can afford another round and still give you forty quid. Will that cover it?'

She gave him a cheeky smile. 'I like you.'

'Back to the question. The one who... her first, he was older, right?'

'A lot older. Spoiled Jerry for lads her own age.'

'And he was a dealer?'

'If you say so. I thought he had some sort of council job.'

'But he pretended to be teaching her English.'

'You're getting mixed up.' Shaz laughed. 'I wasn't talking about Nick. He was a bit of a softy, always giving Jerry lessons for free. She offered it him on a plate once, but he wasn't interested. Not all blokes like fresh meat.'

Pete signalled to the barman, who was watching them closely, the pub being otherwise empty. Same again for her. When he brought the drink over, Shaz grinned and put her hand under the table, ran a finger up and down Pete's crotch. He watched her text a single word. *Working.*

'Who was her tom, then? This older guy.'

'All the girls knew him. Most of us fancied him too. Black guy, built. But married, which is why it had to be really hush hush. His name was Paul. I say "was" cos Jerry told me he'd carked it.'

'Paul Morris?' Pete was on full alert now.

'That was it.'

'Did she say how he died?'

212

'Not sure. She was off her tits and so was I. Stabbing, was it?'

'It was. Did she know who did it?'

Shaz seemed to think for a moment. 'I reckon we'd taken some e, too. She was upset about it, I remember that. And Nick Cane helped her, she said.'

'Helped her how?' Pete tried to conceal his excitement. 'Was he involved?'

'You'd have to ask her. You're her friend, right? I texted her and she said I could trust you.'

'That was good of her,' Pete said and left a silence, which was often the best way to get information you weren't expecting.

'Come on,' Shaz said. 'While he's in the other bar.'

She took his hand, leaving her drink on the table, but taking her bag. Shaz led him into the lady's loo, where she locked a cubicle behind them, then gave him a blow job that was worth every penny of the forty quid he slipped her later. Which was on expenses. So, technically, he'd still never paid for it.

FORTY-ONE

O n the day before the election, council estates were key. Get the votes out there and Sarah had a fighting chance. Nick gave the day over to campaigning, even though he hardly saw the candidate. Nor did he talk to Tracey, beyond a passing hello. That was one thing about staying single until you were forty: a scrapbook could be filled with images of ships you'd passed in the night. He wondered how many of those Sarah had. He kept picturing her in bed with her secretary, or parliamentary assistant, whatever he was.

Nick had had one relationship with someone a lot younger than him. Chantelle, two and a half years ago. Despite the fourteen years between them, he'd wanted to believe they could make it work. Despite his criminal past. Despite her being black and him being white. And look how that had turned out.

His mobile rang. Bilal.

'I want to talk.'

They arranged to meet at a pub on Nick's cycle route home. He was mounting his bike when Sarah's car pulled up alongside. Winston – Sarah's agent – was in the driver's seat, rather than young Hugh. Sarah bounded out of the car in full candidate mode, shaking his hand as though she were after his vote.

'I really appreciate your coming out so often, Nick. I know you have plenty of paid work to do.'

'My work's a pretty moveable feast.'

'I wondered whether you'd like to come to the count tomorrow.'

'Oh.' Nick was taken aback. 'Might that not be… awkward?'

'If you mean your conviction, that's behind you now.'

'I didn't…'

She smiled awkwardly. He remembered that embarrassed smile, though he hadn't seen it for a long while. She lowered her voice.

'Do you mean awkward because of Hugh? He's had to go back to London. That's why I've got an extra place at the count.'

'I'd love to come,' Nick said. 'Thanks.'

'Winston will text you the details.'

Fifteen minutes later, Nick was with Bilal outside *The Plough*, an ancient, boozer hidden away at the back end of Old Radford on St Peter's Street. Nick rolled a cigarette.

'There's something I need to know,' Bilal said. 'I won't go off on one if you tell me what I don't want to hear, but we can't stay friends if you lie to me.'

'Sounds fair,' Nick told him, tearing the stray strands of tobacco from the end of the roll-up and returning them to his packet of Golden Virginia.

'I've asked you this before, and – honestly – I'll understand if you felt you had to lie when I first brought it up. My sister's been having an affair with someone. There's no doubt about that, because she admitted it to me. Is it you?'

Nick lit his cigarette and considered his reply. 'Does she say it is?'

'What she says doesn't matter, I want the truth.'

'It's not me. I've never slept with Nazia. She was still a virgin when we split up.' He made sure to look Bilal in the eye throughout this statement. 'OK?'

'I trust you, so, yes, OK.'

'I can't believe she let you think it was me.'

'She didn't, at least not directly, but... she also told me that he's white.'

'Why would Naz tell you that?'

'Doesn't matter. Also, someone claimed to have seen you at her house.'

'I've never been to her house. I don't even know where she lives.'

Bilal told him. 'You were seen getting out of a car.'

'I don't own a car. I mostly get around by bicycle. As you can see.'

He pointed through the window where his bike was locked to railings.

'She's moving away,' Bilal said.

'Probably a good idea. When?'

'Straight after the inquest. There's something else.' He scratched his head, plainly trying to decide whether to tell Nick what it was.

'Take all the time you need,' Nick said.

'Just between us, OK?'

'Just between us.'

'Sam and me, we've been trying to have a baby for years. A few months ago, Nazia offered to be a surrogate for us.'

'That sounds more like the Nazia I used to know.'

'Only now she tells us she's pregnant, by this white lover. She's going to have the baby and give it to us, tell people that she was acting as our surrogate.'

'How does that kind of thing go down in your community?'

'Not well. But better than if people were to find out she was screwing around while her husband was alive. Thing is, I have to know who the father is.'

'Then ask her.'

'I've asked and asked. She won't tell.'

'She probably has a good reason. What does Sam think?'

'Sam really wants a baby. She'll do whatever needs doing.'

Sam, Bilal told him, would fix the paperwork to ensure that the baby would be legally theirs, even though to do so might put her job at risk.

'I hope it works out,' he told Bilal. 'In time, perhaps Naz will tell you.'

'Keep this to yourself, yeah? I had to ask.'

'You did,' Nick said, 'and I will.'

BOOK FOUR

Nazia

Fahd

Jerry

Caroline

Pete

Bilal

Nick

Sarah

FORTY-TWO

Nick took Nazia to the *Trent Navigation Inn*, a short walk from Notts County's Meadow Lane ground. She wasn't a football fan but Nick wanted her to see his brother, Joe, play. Neil Warnock, County's new manager, had bought Joe from Sheffield Wednesday. So far, the move was working out well for both men. Joe was scoring goals. Fans were talking about County winning promotion next season.

Wanting to make a good first impression, she'd picked a short, black, biker-style leather jacket to wear over the tightest top she dared wear in public. Not low cut, not when there was a chance someone from the community would spot her.

Joe sauntered in while Nick was at the bar. He was her age and shared his brother's strong features. People slapped him on the back, moved aside to let him by. She gave the footballer a big smile. He grinned back.

'My name's Joe.' The way he said it made her tingle between the legs.

'I know who you are,' she said. 'I'm Nazia. Call me Naz, if you like.'

She couldn't believe a girl like her was in a public house, dressed like this, flirting with a footballer.

'Can I buy you a drink, Naz?'

'No need,' she said. 'Your brother's at the bar, getting me one. I think he's getting one in for you, too.'

'You're with Nick?' He took the setback in his stride. 'You don't look old enough to be a teacher.'

'I'm having a gap year, looking after my little brother. Nick teaches him.'

'What happened to your parents?'

'They both died.'

'Sorry to hear that.' He put his hand on hers for a moment, gave it the tenderest of squeezes. 'What do you plan to study?'

'Social work.'

'In Nottingham?'

'That's the plan.'

'Good plan.' He glanced over her shoulder. 'Ey up.'

'You two have already met, I see.' Nick put two pints and a vodka tonic on the table, then sat on a stool between them.

'Were you at the game?' Joe asked Nazia.

She nodded.

'Her first football match,' Nick said.

'Not the last, I hope.'

'You played well,' Nazia told Joe.

'I should have scored.'

'It was a good save.'

A teenage girl came over to get his autograph. Nick went to the loo.

'How long have you been seeing Nick?' Joe asked.

'Depends what you mean by seeing.'

'You and him, you're not...' He didn't finish the sentence, which made the question much more dangerous. She wasn't sure whether to finish it for him. Some words stumbled out anyway.

'Boyfriend/girlfriend? Not exactly, but you know your brother better than I do. He's not always clear about what he wants. To be fair, neither am I.'

'I'm the opposite,' he said, glancing over in the direction of the Gents. 'I always know what I want and I know how to get it. I'd like to go out with you soon, just the two of us. Could we do that?'

'Somewhere people don't keep asking for your autograph?' Another girl was coming over. While Joe signed her programme, Nazia wrote on a beer mat.

'I have to be very careful,' she told Joe when the girl was gone, 'who I see and who I'm seen...'

She stopped speaking because Nick was pushing his way back through the packed pub. Joe glanced round to see what she was looking at. Not yet decided, Nazia slipped the beermat into a pocket. Why was she so tempted? A third division football player was hardly a huge catch. Nick could be arrogant, but Joe had a different level of conceit. That said, he did have things to be conceited about: his firm body, those brown eyes, that thick, tousled hair. His rich, suggestive voice.

The brothers began to banter and tease each other, showing off. Nazia joined in now and then, but was happy to observe, still making up her mind.

Things between her and Nick had begun to plateau. Nick often implied that he was serious about her, but he held back. He didn't want to spoil her marriage prospects, he said. That was honourable of him, but it was also boring. She was nineteen, she was on a gap year, and she wanted to have fun.

The three left the pub together. A group of youths, too young to go in, sat on top of a wall, sharing a cigarette. Seeing Joe, they began to chant.

2-4-6-8, who do we appreciate?
Joe Cane!
2-4-6-8, who do we appreciate?
Joe Cane!

Joe gave the kids a cheery wave. While Nick unlocked his car, Nazia slipped Joe the beer mat, still warm from being pressed against her bum.

'Just between us.'

'Just between us,' he repeated, with a charmingly sincere smile. 'Can't wait.'

FORTY-THREE

2001

N obody knows anything. This was the conclusion Fahd had come to. Nobody was better than anyone else. Pray twice a day and live a devout life or go whoring and drink yourself stupid most nights, the way he had in his twenties. Meant nothing.

For a few years he'd tried politics. He'd wanted to build an identity that distinguished him from his big brother, the successful dentist. But he'd soon found out that it was all vanity. Those who were on the council to line their own pockets disgusted him. Others were there because they wanted people to admire them. He despised them even more, because he'd been one of them himself.

In the end, family was all that mattered. He'd hoped, after Omar died, that Nazia would see sense, agree to marry him. If she had, he'd never have treated her the way Omar did. Omar was always too soft. He'd forgiven Nazia for saddling him with another man's child. He would probably – in time – have forgiven her for going back to her old lover. Fahd had told Omar about the affair just before he died. His brother's reaction was more sad than angry. He'd neglected Nazia, Omar said. Fahd would not neglect her. He wouldn't take any nonsense from her, either.

Women were the weaker sex. Fahd still meant to step into Omar's shoes. He'd pretend to forgive Nazia. He'd make her see him as her protector. Fahd would've been a better match for Nazia in the first place, had he known her then.

Fahd had not even met his sister-in-law until after the wedding. Ever since, he'd fantasised about Omar dying young, him marrying the bereaved widow. He'd imagined the respect that would bring. Twelve years later, the dream seemed to have come true. Until, after the funeral, when he had said to Nazia – too soon, he should have known it was too soon – that, once her *iddah* was over, he'd do the right thing and take Omar's place. And she'd laughed. Actually laughed.

The same day she'd deserted the wake while the mourners were still gathered, rejecting them too. He'd convinced himself she'd gone off to see her lover. Angry, he'd looked in her bedroom for evidence, wanting to show Fahd and her uncle that he was right. He hadn't been thinking of murder. Then he'd found what he found. He should have left the needle where it was for the police to uncover. In the circumstances, nobody could blame him for not thinking straight.

Fahd wasn't alone in suspecting Nazia. It wasn't him who'd written those words on the garage door. Not the first time anyway. But after Bilal washed the first lot of graffiti off, it had been Fahd who replaced it. Keep the pressure on. He wanted Nazia to confess. It did him good to know that other people suspected her as much as he did. Including Uncle, who was her blood relative.

Earlier in the day, after hearing that the post-mortem had not come to a definitive conclusion, he'd gone to Uncle for advice.

'Let the law take its course,' Uncle insisted. 'All that stupid painting on the doors, do you think that helped anything?'

'The exhumation wouldn't have happened without me doing what I did. There'd have been no inquest.'

'And what good will the inquest do, apart from stirring up trouble?'

'Nazia deserves trouble. She deserves…'

Uncle wagged a finger to shut him up. 'You always liked that woman too much. So jealous of Omar. If the police say she did not kill him, she did not kill him. If they're wrong, it is for Allah to judge, not us. Let her go to Birmingham.'

'It *is* wrong.'

'You were at fault, coveting your brother's wife. She says you asked her to marry you when her iddah ended. She says you only started your accusations after she refused.'

'I made no accusations until I found that syringe.'

'You searched a diabetic's house and found a syringe, what of it?'

Tonight, Fahd meant to prove the old fool wrong. He timed his arrival in The Park so that he was waiting when Nazia got back from taking the children to Bilal and Sam's. The kids were staying in Wollaton until their mother found them a new place to live in Birmingham. Nazia meant to leave Nottingham as soon as the inquest had delivered its verdict. Tomorrow.

Fahd was on foot. He did not want any witnesses to his arrival. Cars could be tracked by multiple cameras. People said that phones could be tracked, too, so he'd left his at Jamal's. Jamal and two other friends would swear blind that Fahd had spent the evening playing cards with them. When they found out what he had done, they would not be happy, but they would understand that it was a matter of family honour. They would keep their word.

He descended the steep Park steps. Before reaching the bottom, he put up the hood of his jacket. He had a pile of red leaflets under his arm. It was the night before the election. There were plenty of leafleters around. Nobody would give him a second look.

A taxi parked by Nazia's house. The driver walked up the steep driveway. Fahd recognised him. Like Fahd, he had a key to the house. Cane went inside.

That complicated matters.

If only you could choose who to love, who to desire. Nazia had loved her husband the best she could for twelve years. Not in the way that she'd loved Nick Cane, but at nineteen she'd been naive and pretty stupid, though not stupid enough to think she'd end up marrying Nick, or, indeed, any non-Muslim. Nick had treated her with respect. Too much respect. Then his brother, Joe, came along, and he had no respect, only lust. Which was mutual. She'd allowed herself a fling before entering adulthood. Joe was her reward for looking after Bilal and delaying university. She thought they'd been careful. Then she fell pregnant.

Had it been any other man, she might have gone to Nick for help. Instead, she'd gone to Uncle, explained the situation without telling him who the father was. She'd made up a story. He'd pretended to believe it. Uncle found Omar, sent them both back home until she could return as a respectable new wife and mother.

She and Omar did make it work for more than a decade. Omar was a good father but an inconsiderate lover, a workaholic who, after the kids went to bed, had little time for her. Once the kids were both at school, she became more frustrated.

Two months ago, Omar took Tamazur and Ahmad away for the weekend. She'd been out with some friends and found a familiar face behind the wheel of the taxi taking her home. That night, she wanted him just as much as she'd wanted him the day of her twentieth birthday, when he'd come over after training and asked if he could use her shower. He'd always withdrawn, or used a condom, but neither method was reliable. Now she'd been caught out twice. This time, she was going to tell Joe. But not about Tamazur, that would be too much to throw at him.

It would be easiest not to tell him, like before. If she stopped seeing Joe after tonight, broke off all contact the same way she had in 1989, he needn't know. Time had caught up with them. Joe was no longer the handsome young footballer who could have any woman he wanted. She was no longer the lithe twenty-year-old he'd flattered into giving up her virginity behind his brother's back. Even then, she'd known Joe's faults – selfishness, arrogance, laziness (off the pitch) – all plain to see. But you couldn't choose who to desire.

These days, the twinkle in Joe's eyes had faded and his body had become flabbier. He was still exciting in bed. She hadn't decided whether to sleep with him tonight. One last orgasm to remember each other by. A lot of pressure to put on a tumble between the sheets, but it might take her mind off the inquest.

Nazia drove past Joe's cab, which he'd parked a little up the road. It pleased her that he was already waiting inside. She must remember to ask for her key back. She parked the Alfa, noting that Joe had closed the curtains in the living room. She'd wanted blinds but Omar had insisted on velvet curtains. They kept the house warmer, he said. Why had Joe closed them? Paranoia about the neighbours, or maybe he wanted to have sex in the living room? She and Omar had never done it in there, but she'd still feel Omar's presence. The idea didn't appeal.

Nazia checked her hair in the rear-view mirror and freshened up her lipstick before getting out of the car. There was a light on in the living room. She pushed the door open and saw Joe, staring at her. His eyes were wild. He couldn't move, because his arms and waist were tied to the back of a dining chair. And he couldn't say anything because he had one of her favourite scarves tied around his head, gagging him. There was only one person who could have done this. She turned to face him.

'Surprise!' Fahd said.

FORTY-FOUR

J erry saw a missed call from Nick on her phone but didn't
return it. Shaz had left a message, and she wanted to catch her
first. But Shaz didn't pick up. She always set her phone to silent
when she was working. Jerry left a voicemail.

At weekends, Jerry missed Nottingham. She didn't mind her
placement – she was learning how the world worked – but
summer weekends in an empty house dragged. In Nottingham,
even when none of her mates were about, there were places to go
out on the cheap. London was too spread out, too expensive.

Shaz returned her call between jobs. 'What's up, girl?'

'Thought I might come to Nottingham this weekend, catch up
with you.'

'That'd be good. Have to be in the day though. Sonny won't
give me nights off on a weekend.'

'Saturday's good. Let's see a movie, go to the Chinese banquet
place, yeah?'

'Cool.'

'You tried to ring me, by the way.'

'I was probably off my tits. When?'

'Yesterday.'

'Oh yeah. I wanted to tell you about the drink with that guy
you sent to me.'

'What guy?'

'Old guy. Good looking, in a weasely sort of way. Asks lots of
questions.'

'Pete Carlson.'

'That's what he calls himself.'

'What was he asking questions about?' Jerry felt ill at ease.
Why on earth had she given Pete Shaz's mobile number?

'That guy you used to shag back in the home. Paul Morris.'

'You told Pete about me and Paul?'

'Ancient history, innit?'

'What else did he ask?'

Pete had asked about Paul's murder but Shaz didn't know any

details.

'And he asked about your friend Nick.'

'How did Nick come into it?'

'Think I said he'd helped you out with Paul. What difference does it make?'

'Helped me out *how*?'

'I didn't say 'cos you never said.'

'I didn't want Pete to know about that.'

'Why'd you give him my number if you didn't want me to talk to him?'

'I thought… I don't know what I thought. Did you fuck him?'

'Sucked him off for forty quid. Have you fucked him?'

'You know my type.'

'He's quite fit, isn't he, for an older bloke?'

'He's not bad.' Not a good man, but not a bad one, either. Even so, if he'd worked out what Jerry had done to Paul, she'd have to do it to him, too.

Joe was bleeding from the side of his head and looked dazed. Her brother-in-law looked manic. The last time she'd seen Fahd was after the funeral. When he'd made his proposal, Nazia had responded with a nervous laugh that he'd mistaken for mockery. She'd never have dared mock Fahd to his face, he was too dangerous. Even Omar used to say that his brother made him nervous.

'What do you think you're doing?' she asked the madman.

'Finding out if he killed my brother,' Fahd said.

'He didn't,' Nazia's voice came out thin and hoarse, 'nobody did. If anyone's responsible, it's you. You told Omar about me and him, didn't you? You must have been following me, is that how you found out?'

Joe coughed and made a panting noise. Nazia hurried over to help him. The knot that attached him to the chair looked difficult to untie. She recognised Omar's tow rope from the garage. Joe's glasses were steamed up but she could still make out the fear in his eyes. Blood continued to drip from the wound on his head.

Before she was able to untie the scarf that was gagging him,

Fahd grabbed her. He flung her across the room so forcefully that she slammed onto the floor. Her left thigh would be badly bruised. She managed to pull herself upright. She needed to talk Fahd out of this, to play for time.

'How did you get in?' she asked.

'I took a key when I was at the funeral.'

'After you'd planted that needle.'

'I didn't plant anything.'

'How else did it get there?'

'Maybe your friend Nick here hid it.'

'This isn't...' Nazia started to say, then realised it made no difference to Fahd who Joe was. Fahd, she saw now, had a knife in his hand. It was her biggest, sharpest Sabatier from the knife block in the kitchen. She tried to stay calm.

'Just get out of here,' she said. 'I'll see if I can stop him calling the police.'

'I'm not going anywhere until you give me what I want.'

'Which is what?'

'The truth.'

'I've already told you the truth. Neither of us killed Omar. He just died.'

'Stand still.' He stood so close, she'd no choice but to breathe his stale, sweaty body odour. Fahd tapped her chin with the knife's long, sharp blade. Humiliating tears formed in her eyes and she could do nothing to stop them falling.

'It was him, wasn't it?' Fahd whispered in her ear. 'Tamazur's father.'

'Yes,' Nazia said. 'It was him.'

'And you've been fucking him ever since.'

'No,' Nazia said.

He grabbed her blouse, pulling the fabric away from her chest. Then he began to cut, slicing open the front so that her breasts were exposed. Fahd stared, then, with his knife-free hand, cupped each breast in turn. She flinched.

He slapped her across the face.

'Strip.'

She screamed.

Fahd pushed her back onto the floor.

He placed the knife against Joe's chin.

'Strip or I slash his throat.' A trickle of blood ran down Joe's neck.

Shaking, she took off her clothes.

Fahd inspected her.

'You were beautiful once', he said. 'Look at you now. All that extra weight around the hips and waist. The bag you're growing beneath your chin. You're still fuckable, but you won't be for long.'

Nazia shivered.

'I hate it,' Fahd said, 'when attractive women act like their bodies, their pretty faces are something they earned. Expecting praise for an accident of birth. It's a false, conceited way of looking at the world. Yet you women get away with it. All because men want to fuck you. You, you're well past your prime, but you still act like you're special – it's pathetic. Nick Cane must be fucking you out of nostalgia, there's no other explanation.'

'That's not Nick,' Nazia said. 'You've got this all wrong. Get out his wallet, take a look at it.'

Fahd gave her a wary glance.

'Get on the sofa, or I slice his throat.'

While she did as he asked, he reached into Joe's pocket and took out the wallet. Joe tried to kick him but the rope allowed little room for movement.

'Joseph Cane,' he muttered. 'Was it him all along?'

She nodded.

'Makes no odds. Enjoy the show, Joseph Cane.'

Caroline parked outside Nazia's home in The Park. Kath, the babysitter, understood the situation. She had a story ready should Joe came home before Caroline did: a family emergency. Joe, neither of whose parents were living, had never shown much interest in Caroline's family, who lived two hours away.

This was the same house she'd followed her husband to four weeks before, near The Park steps. Stupidly, she'd believed his story about a meeting with a restaurant owner. A smart area, though this was not one of The Park's prime properties. The nondescript bungalow dated from the 70s. At least, being set back from the road, it didn't disfigure the tree-lined avenue of Victorian villas.

Half ten. Joe's car was parked near the bottom of the drive. She walked up the driveway. Nazia's four by four sat in front of a badly painted garage door, the word *whore* still legible beneath grey primer. She thought of ringing the doorbell, but doubted Nazia would answer it. If Caroline were to bang on the door, she was bound to wake the children. They didn't deserve to find out that their mother was a slut. Though they were bound to be told by someone, sooner or later.

Joe and Nazia. She wondered how long it had been going on. Did Nick know? No. Nick was a decent man. He'd never have asked her to let the family stay with them if he'd known that Joe was fucking his ex. She wondered whether Nazia and Joe had done it in the house after she'd gone to bed. Would they be that brazen? It was luck that she had seen Nazia's message flash up on his mobile yesterday, while Joe was in the loo. Later, when she checked his texts, it wasn't there. No messages from him to her either. All deleted. Joe was good at covering his tracks. He'd probably had lots of practice.

Her thoughts turned to murder. She wanted to know whether Omar had been poisoned, and, if so, who had injected the sleeping man. She couldn't see Joe injecting anyone. He hated needles. Could have been his idea, though.

Which was Nazia's bedroom? Behind the curtains in the front room, a light went off, signalling that they'd finished their business. Caroline decided not to confront her husband – not tonight, anyway, not until she'd worked out what she was going to do. Time for her to go.

Before she could leave, the front door opened. Caroline stepped behind Nazia's car. The man leaving was not Joe, but an Asian. He wore a grey kagoule. The hood was up, though it wasn't raining. There were a wodge of Labour Party election flyers under his arm. Head lowered, he hurried down the drive, onto the road, where he looked quickly to his left and right before setting off toward town.

At the bottom of the drive Caroline looked around. She saw the man in the grey kagoule turn up The Park steps. Across the road, a man putting out his bin gave her a suspicious glance. Neighbourhood watch. You weren't meant to park here without a permit. She had left her car much further up the road so that Joe wouldn't notice she was there. She returned to it. No warning notice. Good.

'Well?' Kath asked Caroline, after pouring them both a glass of Semillon Blanc.

'I don't know. He was there, but so was somebody else, an Asian with a beard. I can't work it out.'

'Maybe you shouldn't jump to conclusions on the basis of one text.'

'Maybe.'

When Kath was gone, Caroline had another glass of wine to help her sleep, then went to bed. Half eleven. Late for her. She'd have expected Joe to be back by now, whatever he'd been up to. He wasn't there when she woke up in the night to use the loo, either. She called his mobile. It went straight to voicemail.

'Where the hell are you?' she asked, then hung up.

She didn't get much more sleep after that.

FORTY-FIVE

T his election, most pundits agreed, was dull. Even '87, the second Tory landslide, when Labour pulled back only a tiny percentage of the votes that Foot had lost in '83, had been a more interesting campaign than this. Party leader Neil Kinnock held onto his job in '87, but, after today, the Tories were bound to need a new leader. Last time round, they'd gone for youth, then undermined this by choosing a bloke who was Sarah Bone's age but behaved as though he were a generation older. He made Tony Blair seem fresh and vital by comparison.

'Feeling confident?' Pete Carlson asked the candidate. She smiled with what, in journalese, he would describe as 'aplomb'.

'Quietly optimistic,' Sarah Bone said.

'The paper wants a follow-up after the splash last Sunday. Can you give me five minutes?'

'At some point. There'll be lots of hanging round at the count. Coming?'

He hadn't planned on going, but calculated that a close-up view would add colour, especially if Sarah lost.

'You bet,' he said.

She was whisked up the street. Pete's mobile rang. The office. Ted Burley had been doing some research for him. Ted knew his way around property registers, tax offices, even the Charities Commission. He had contacts everywhere. You wouldn't think it to look at Ted now, overweight and gone to seed, but he'd come of age in the swinging sixties. Back then, he'd once told Pete over a drink or two, he'd done his share of swinging, both ways.

'Your questions about Cape Verde,' Burley said, in his rich, well-educated voice. 'It took a little time, but I got some interesting results.'

The inquest was at two. Bilal had told Naz that he would arrive by half past one and walk with her to the Council House. The night before, she'd dropped off the kids at his, bringing all their stuff, ready for the escape to Birmingham. The idea was that Sam would collect Ahmad and Tamazur from school, then Bilal and Naz would join them in Wollaton once the inquest was over.

He parked in her drive and rang the doorbell. No response. Odd. He was a little early. Even so, where could she have gone? The curtains were still drawn from the night before.

He rang her mobile. It went straight to voicemail. He rang the landline and heard it ringing through the door. Bilal might be a few minutes early, but this felt all wrong. He got the spare key out of his pocket. If she'd fallen or hurt herself somehow, he'd feel bad about the two minutes he had waited outside. Even so, it went against the grain, entering the house without her permission.

The burglar alarm tone didn't sound, which meant it hadn't been activated. She never went out without turning it on. He called her name. Twice. No response. Then, by instinct, he went into the living room, which was in darkness and smelt... bad. He felt his way to the window and tugged at the chord until the heavy curtains opened, suffusing the room with sunlight.

At first, Bilal thought that the guy in the chair was Nick Cane, but he had never known Nick to wear glasses. The dead man was tied to the chair with a thick piece of rope. His throat had been slashed.

Nazia's body was on the sofa, opposite the dead man. She was naked. Bilal found it hard to look but, nevertheless, looked again. Red marks ringed her neck. She'd been strangled. The man in the chair must have been forced to watch. Then he, too, had been killed.

A terrible calm descended on Bilal. Anger would probably come later, but he knew what he had to do. He called the police, then Sam, saying only that something dreadful had happened. Nazia was dead. Then he phoned Nick Cane.

No reply on Nick's landline. He would be on his way to the coroner's court in the Council House. Bilal tried him on his mobile and it was picked up at once.

'Bilal? Shouldn't you and Naz be here? Everyone's waiting to go in.'

'Is Fahd there?'

'Funnily enough, no.'

'My uncle?'

'Heavy-set bloke in his sixties?'

'That will be him. Please would you give him your phone.'

In Punjabi, he told Uncle what had happened. The replies were monosyllabic. Then he asked Uncle to return the phone to Nick.

'What's going on? Your uncle looks as though you gave him a death sentence.'

'Nazia's dead. Murdered. The police are on the way. You need to come to the house. Whoever did it killed her lover, too. The dead man, I think he's your brother.'

Sometimes it was best to catch people off guard. This was Pete's chance. Mary Harris checked her watch, impatient for the arrival of her client, then left the ante-room, presumably to look for Nazia Khan. Pete joined her in the corridor.

'Mrs Turnbull, if you've got a minute?'

'I don't use my husband's name. I'm sorry, do I know you?'

'Pete Carlson. I visited your flat recently. I'm a reporter for *The Sunday Times*, doing a piece on Nottingham crime syndicates.'

'Crime isn't my area.'

'No, but it used to be your husband's. When I was in your home, I couldn't help but notice your honeymoon photos. Cape Verde, wasn't it?'

'That's right. I don't see…'

'You stayed in a complex called High Sierra, I believe.'

'We have a flat there. Why do you ask?'

'And do you know who owns that estate, with all six of its villas?'

Mary looked irritated, but at least she didn't clam up. 'Why would I know that?'

'The company that owns the complex appears to be owned by your husband, Mrs Turnbull.'

'I find that highly unlikely.'

'I agree. They were pricey, even for someone on a senior police officer's salary. But a colleague traced the company that owns it to your husband.'

Mary Harris remained stony-faced. 'Why come to see me, rather than Eric?'

Pete hesitated, choosing which half-truth to respond with.

'I hoped there might be a simple explanation. If there was, you'd know it.'

'If you have any questions for my husband, put them in writing. I'll be advising him not to speak to you in person. Excuse me, I'm waiting for a client.'

Pete returned to the ante-room in time to see a seventyish Pakistani man hand Nick Cane a phone. Nick listened, his face turning pale. The elderly Pakistani left, his heavy footsteps echoing from the corridor's wooden floors. Nick approached Mary Harris and whispered in her ear. She, too, looked shocked.

The Coroner was coming. Mary hurried over to him and spoke urgently. When Pete turned to look for Nick, he was no longer there. The coroner returned to his office. Mary Harris hurried down the stairs. Pete knew better than to accost her again. He went back to the antechamber, where only a handful of journalists remained. Two minutes later, the coroner's clerk came in.

'There have been unanticipated developments that require the postponement of this afternoon's inquest. All jurors will be sent home and we will reconvene at a date and time to be announced in due course.'

The reporter from *The Nottingham Post* began to ask questions, but it was clear she wasn't going to get any answers.

Nick decided not to phone Caroline yet. Bilal might be wrong. He walked rapidly down the wide Council House stairs. He'd never been to Nazia's house but knew where it was. Not far from Sarah's flat. He hurried out of the Council House and crossed Market Square before climbing Friar Lane. At the ringroad, he went down into the subway beneath Maid Marian Way and up onto the other side of Friar Lane. The road went past Nottingham Castle into The Park estate. Despite his distress, Nick couldn't help but notice that, even in this, the richest, most Conservative area in Nottingham, there were plenty of Labour posters in windows. Another landslide was on the way.

Joe and Nazia. He'd known that Joe had once had a thing with a Pakistani woman but it had never occurred to him that Joe might seduce a grieving widow who was under his protection. Bilal must be wrong. Unless they'd begun an affair before Omar's death. In which case, Nazia would have had a motive for murdering her husband. Which, in turn, meant that his brother must have been involved.

Only, Joe wasn't a killer. Neither was Naz. Both were victims. Fahd had created a chimera out of his twisted suspicions. Fahd must have known how the inquest was likely to go and decided to get his revenge in first. Joe, though. Joe was dead. Where did that leave Caroline and the kids? Who was going to tell them?

Maybe it wasn't Joe, Nick reminded himself as he charged down the hill, onto Newcastle Drive. There were three police cars on the road outside Nazia's house, so he had no difficulty working out which one was hers. The police had yet to close off the crime scene. Nick was able to walk halfway up the drive before an officer stopped him.

'One of the victims might be my brother. I've been asked to identify him.'

He was waved forward. At the door, after repeated explanations, a DI came and spoke to him. He'd seen her before somewhere. She introduced herself as Rebecca Allen.

'We have to respect the integrity of the crime scene. I'd like you to come to the window with me and see if you can identify your brother from there.'

Nick followed the DI to the back of the house. Through a wide, double window, he took in the terrible tableau. What must be Nazia's legs. Mercifully, he could not see the rest of her body. Blood on the floor. A bespectacled figure was tied to an upright chair, head slumped, neck slashed open. Joe.

'It's him. Have you any idea how…?'

'He appears to have had a heavy blow to the head, after which he was tied to the chair while unconscious. We don't know whether he was awake when his throat was slashed. I have to ask: when did you last see him?'

'A few days ago.'

'Are you… were you close?'

'Pretty close. He's my only sibling.'

'Was he having a relationship with Mrs Khan?'

'Not to my knowledge but…' He explained how Nazia had come to live with Joe and Caroline for a while.

'Caroline will be devastated. I need to…'

'That's for us to do. We will need a family member, though, to look after Mrs Cane's children while we're talking to her. Would you be the appropriate…?'

'I'm all she's got. The rest of her family live down south.' He looked at his watch. 'She'll be setting off to collect Phoebe from school in fifteen minutes or so.'

'Maybe best if we time it for after she's got home.' Rebecca put a hand on his wrist and he realised that he was shaking. 'I think you're going to need some time to take this in before you're in a state to help other people.'

'I know who must have done this. Nazia's brother-in-law, Fahd Khan.' He started to explain about the murder and the inquest, but DI Allen stopped him.

'I know the background. We're already trying to locate Mr Khan. I must urge you not to make contact with him.'

'I wouldn't trust myself.'

'What I think you should do now is sit down, take a few breaths and let us get on with what we have to do. Then I'll drive you to your sister-in-law's house.'

He did as he was told and sat on one of the patio chairs, shivering in the sun. After a while, Rebecca came over and took him to her car.

'We have a mutual friend,' she said, making conversation when they were stuck in traffic on the Mansfield Road, 'Sarah Bone. I was at Ryton with her.'

'Right.'

'Do you think she'll get back in?'

'I'm hoping so. Sarah ought to be told about all this. She had an interest.'

'She'll have other things on her mind today. We're going to

keep a lid on what's happened for as long as we can. It'll make the investigation smoother.'

They were early. The old estate was full of children walking back from school, their paths covered by blossom fallen from the late-flowering cherry trees that lined the road. Caroline appeared, a child holding each hand, Phoebe chatting away. Nick and Rebecca got out of the car. Phoebe let go of her mum and ran to greet her uncle Nick. DI Allen took out her warrant card. Caroline's face fell.

'Is it Joe?'

Nick nodded.

'Why don't you let Uncle Nick take you inside?' Rebecca said to the children. 'I need a few words with your mummy.'

FORTY-SIX

'I knew,' Caroline said. 'I knew there was something going on. For weeks. Longer.'

'Before Omar Khan's death?'

Caroline ignored the question. 'When did it happen?'

'Some time last night. We can't be more specific yet. When did you last see your husband?'

'Yesterday morning. He didn't come home last night, I left messages. But…'

'Had that happened before? Did you ever report him missing?'

'No. But… as I told you, I thought he was having an affair. I thought…'

Nick held her and she began to cry. He'd just returned from leaving Phoebe and Oliver with a neighbour.

'And where were you last night?' Rebecca asked. Caroline didn't reply, so Rebecca tried again. 'At home with the kids?'

Caroline half nodded.

'You'll be contacted by support services in due course, but if you would like me to arrange a bereavement counsellor to visit soon…'

'I've got Nick,' Caroline said.

'We'll come and talk to you both again tomorrow,' Rebecca told Nick, then handed him her card. 'Until then, if there's anything you need, call me, regardless of the time.'

When she'd left, Nick asked Caroline what she wanted to do about Phoebe and Oliver.

'Leave them for a while. I don't know how to tell them.' She turned to face Nick. 'Did you see his body, are you sure it was him?'

'I'm sure.'

'How did it happen? She wasn't clear.'

'It looked like a single knife slash to the throat. It would have been quick.'

He didn't mention how Joe had been tied to the chair, nor that he had probably been made to watch his mistress being raped and murdered. He did not tell her what Bilal had told him the last time they met: that Naz was pregnant. By a white guy. By Joe.

'There's a problem I need your help with,' Caroline said, in a timid voice.

'Anything,' he told her.

'I went to her house last night. I didn't go in. I had no idea. But I may have seen the man who did it.'

Melanie was rattled.

'When I came home,' she told Pete, 'There was a man watching the house. He was sat across the road, in a black Audi. When he saw that I'd seen him, he drove off.'

'Probably coincidence,' Pete said. 'Nothing to worry about.'

He hoped this was true. Surely it was too soon for Pete's conversation with Mary Harris to have provoked a threat from her husband. Yet, if Eric Turnbull was what Pete suspected him to be, he would be capable of rapid response.

'I'm going to have to go back to London tomorrow,' he told Mel. 'Get this story written up. And I'll be out late tonight. This might be the last time you have to put up with me for a week or two.'

She looked disappointed. 'A week or two, or for good?'

'That's up to you,' Pete said, conscious that only a few days back he'd let a nineteen-year-old scrubber suck him off. On top of which, he'd been fucking her best mate. He spoke more tenderly. 'Where do you want us to go?'

She sat on his lap and kissed him softly on the lips. 'We're neither of us getting any younger. Play your cards right, maybe it's time for us to go all in.'

Later, Mel made cheese omelette with oven chips and baked beans as a late supper. Pete turned on the TV, caught the regional headlines after the 9PM news.

Police confirm that one of the victims in a double murder in The Park area of Nottingham last night was mother-of-two, Nazia Khan. This killing follows the unexplained death of her husband less than a month ago. The inquest into Omar Khan's death, due to be held today, has been postponed indefinitely. The other victim, who died of stab wounds, has not yet been named.

Pete rang Rebecca Allen.

'You're late to the party,' she said. 'I expected you to call hours ago.'

'I was having a nap to help me stay up all night for the election.'

'I'd forgotten about the election. Finding two bodies will do that.'

'I'd appreciate some background,' Pete said. 'I'd owe you big time.'

'Most of it's already out there,' Rebecca said. 'What did you want to know?'

'The other victim, who is he?'

A dry laugh. 'Want to guess?'

'It'll be either Fahd Khan or Nick Cane.'

'Wrong. It was Cane's brother, Joe, ex-footballer and taxi driver.'

'What happened?'

'We're still putting it together.'

'I just want your thoughts, off the record.'

'You know Fahd Khan accused the wife of having an affair?'

'Nick Cane told me that wasn't true.' Nick, Pete was beginning to realise, had always told him the truth.

'She wasn't sleeping with Nick, as Fahd suggested, but now we understand why he was in the frame. Nick and his brother look similar, superficially at least.'

'So you think that Fahd Khan…'

'Not Fahd, evidently. He has a rock solid alibi.'

'Who then?'

'The wife. Caroline Cane. We have a witness who saw her leave shortly after the murders had taken place. She was arrested an hour ago.'

'Has she confessed?'

'No, but her story's so full of holes, it's only a matter of time.'

S arah was exhausted. She'd packed in canvassing at nine, then gone home to get her head down. Unable to sleep, she rang Hugh in London. She felt bad about how awkwardly they'd left things. He was unfailingly civil, as always.

'I hear that the exit polls are going to show turn-out down but the percentages almost the same as last time. You're in with a chance.'

'If I get back in,' she told him, 'you still have a job. Nothing's changed there.'

'I'm not sure I can continue,' he said, in a neutral tone.

'Our not seeing each other socially shouldn't interfere with your work. Stay on until you've got another job, at least. I'll give you all the help you need.'

'There'll be plenty of jobs to go round in a new parliament,' he assured her.

'Oh, Hugh...' She didn't know what to tell him.

'Don't worry, I'll not make the mistake of falling for my next boss.' He said this in a half teasing way, so she forced a chuckle before saying goodbye. Sarah ought to ask Gill Temperley how to successfully manage office affairs. Did they all end as inelegantly as this? Married Gill's toy-boys knew where they stood from the start, that was key. They weren't going to ask her to move in with them, much less propose marriage and children. Sarah should have been clearer with Hugh.

She turned on the News at Ten. The exit poll said what Hugh had told her it would. There were three new messages on her mobile. One was from Nick.

'I'm not going to make it tonight,' he said. 'My sister-in-law's been arrested for murdering her husband and Nazia. It's preposterous. Caroline saw Fahd Khan leaving the house. But he has an alibi that says he was several miles away with three other blokes and she admits to having been there. Good luck.'

Sarah rang Rebecca, who would know what was going on. The call went straight to voicemail. Then she called Winston, who filled her in on the cancelled inquest, the double murder. He hadn't heard about the arrest until she told him.

'A woman scorned,' he said. 'Strongest motive going. Good thing you didn't get more involved in the Omar Khan case. Don't give out any quotes, alright?'

'All right.' Winston arranged to pick her up at midnight for the count. Party scrutineers would soon be starting their work, but Sarah was entitled to more rest. None of the Nottingham results ever came in before three in the morning.

'Do you think she did it?' Bilal asked Nick, when they met in Wollaton.

'Not a chance. I saw how shocked Caroline was when they told her. Trouble is, they have a witness who puts her there. Her, but not the person she saw leaving.'

'Who she thinks was Fahd.'

'She's never met Fahd, but she identified him from a photo.'

'Fahd has a very strong alibi, Uncle tells me. Several corroborating witnesses.'

'And does Uncle believe them?'

'Probably not,' Bilal admitted.

Nick checked his watch. Gone ten. Caroline's solicitor had promised to call when the interrogation was over. His sister-in-law was represented by Charlene Jagger, head of the partnership that Mary Harris had recently joined. Jagger was an assured, articulate woman of Afro-Caribbean heritage and came highly recommended.

Caroline and Joe's kids were still at a neighbour's. Julie was not a close family friend. She'd already gone beyond what could be expected of her. If Caroline was not released tomorrow, Nick would need to move into her house to look after the kids. Otherwise, they'd be shipped off to Caroline's parents down south. Was Nick up to caring for an infant and a toddler? He didn't know.

'How are you managing with Ahmad and Tamazur?' he asked Bilal.

'We've told them that their mummy's had to visit someone in

hospital, so they can't go to Birmingham yet,' Bilal said.

'What will happen to them?'

'Nazia changed her will recently. Just in case, she said. We'll be their guardians. She was going to... she was going to...'

Nick didn't know what to say. They'd each lost their only sibling. He squeezed the young man's arm.

'It was going to be our baby,' Bilal said. 'Me and Sam were going to pretend she'd acted as a surrogate for us. He killed her baby too. Our baby.' He paused, then looked Nick in the eye. 'Your nephew or niece.'

'I'm trying not to think about that.' Nick hadn't told Caroline that Nazia was pregnant with Joe's baby and he didn't plan to tell her, not yet. If the police thought Caroline knew, it provided her with even more of a motive for murder.

His phone buzzed. A text.

'They're letting her out tonight,' he told Bilal. 'I have to go pick her up.'

'Leave Fahd to me,' Bilal told him. 'This is family business. I'll work out how to deal with him. OK?'

'I suppose.'

'Please give my condolences to your sister-in-law.'

Caroline hardly spoke.

'They haven't charged her,' Charlene Jagger told Nick. 'She's agreed to return at midday tomorrow to continue the interrogation. Can you bring her in?'

'I can. Is it good that they haven't already charged her?'

'Neither good nor bad. It probably means they're waiting for forensics.'

Nick took Caroline back to Sherwood, where she phoned Julie, who had long since put the kids to bed. They had not been told about their father. The story had been on the TV news, but Joe hadn't been identified. His name was bound to be in tomorrow's papers, though. Soon, everyone on the estate would know.

Nick made Caroline some cheese on toast and mixed her a stiff gin and tonic. They watched some of the election together, hardly taking anything in.

'You'll stay the night?' Caroline asked, finishing her drink.

'Course I will. Is the spare bed made up or shall I get some…'

Caroline began to cry. He held her.

'What is it?'

She dried her eyes before she replied.

'Would you mind getting into bed with me? I can't face being alone.'

Half an hour later, he lay alongside her, wishing he were at home. It felt weird, being in his brother's bedroom, sharing his marital bed. Nick was in his boxers, Joe's widow in a pale pink, cotton night dress. He couldn't remember the last time he'd been in bed with a woman he'd no intention of having sex with. No, he could: Sarah, the night of the 1997 election. She'd been so tired and drunk, she'd passed out before he got his clothes off. He'd hoped that they would make love in the morning, but she'd woken to a call offering her a job as Prisons minister, a job that made their relationship impossible.

'Hold me,' Caroline asked, and he realised that she, too, was wide awake. He did as she asked. For a long while, they lay closely entwined. Good to feel the closeness of another body against his. He was drifting into sleep when he felt her lips press against his. He kissed her gently back, the automatic response, only to feel an urgent, exploratory tongue. She squeezed one of his buttocks and whispered.

'Please. I need you to.'

She rubbed against him and they kissed again. He helped her pull his boxer shorts over his half erection. There should be no awkwardness. They were old lovers. Yet the act, once they began, felt unreal. He tried to remember the excitement with which they had made love when they were in their twenties. Her body felt very different from when they were last together. He found that the only way he could keep himself aroused was by remembering his afternoon with Tracey. The unexpectedness of that union, the gloriously dirty way it made him feel, had permitted him, for a time, to forget about seeing Sarah with her young lover.

Caroline's shudders when she came were familiar, taking him back in time. Nick withdrew without finishing. Afterwards, she lay in his arms, eyes moist, but asleep at last. When he was sure that she was well away, he eased himself out of her arms and went downstairs to watch the election results.

Election counts turned out to be boring. In the Harvey Hadden stadium, three of the four Nottingham constituencies had already declared resounding majorities for the Labour candidate. Graham, John and Alan, the returned MPs, had long since gone to the celebrations. Only Sarah remained. Pete could see the MP huddled with her agent, trying to decide something: whether to ask for a recount, perhaps.

Electoral politics wasn't Pete's thing. He had only a loose idea of how recount rules worked. If it were down to under a few hundred, he understood, a recount could be requested. But the time was getting on for four in the morning. Wouldn't it be better if they all went to bed and came back tomorrow when minds were fresh? Better still if everybody in the country voted electronically and all of the results could be declared at once, a few moments after ten in the evening, rather than condemning people to wait around in an echoey, draughty sports hall.

The returning officer approached the Tory candidate, a fiftyish GP whose metal-rimmed glasses gave her a stern appearance. Tories liked to look bossy and they had a point. Dress for the part you want to be cast in. Maybe it was time for Pete to move away from the leather-clad, cool-if-slightly-sleazy look he'd affected for the last twenty years. If he was going to spend more time in Nottingham, move in with Mel, he ought to change his image. Chinos rather than Levis. Longer hair. Button up shirts instead of T-shirts. Tweed? No. Even a sports jacket would be going too far. Shoes instead of boots, maybe. Start dressing like a grown-up.

The Tory seemed satisfied and the returning officer called all of the candidates to the stage. The remaining party workers began to gather at the front. Pete got out his note of the votes cast in '97, when Sarah had unexpectedly won.

Sarah Bone. Labour and Cooperative Party. Nineteen thousand, four hundred and ninety-two. Bad news. She was down by nearly two thousand, the size of her majority.

The Liberal did about the same as last time. The Green did a bit better. Finally, the Tory. *Nineteen thousand, one hundred and…*

The hall erupted into cheers. The Tory vote was down a couple of hundred, enough for Sarah to hold on by the slimmest of margins. Just under four hundred votes. But hold on she had. The MP began her speech with the obligatory thanks to the returning officer and the police. Party workers came next.

'I want to thank everybody, every last volunteer, from those who came out once or twice to those who came out day after day. I couldn't have done this without all of you. And I promise that I will go back to Westminster with renewed vigour, to fight for the interests of Nottingham West. I assure that I will always put principle – *socialist principles* – above all else when it comes to casting my vote. I couldn't be more excited to be elected for the third time in this, which was once the most Conservative of seats. Thank you. Here's to the next Labour government!'

FORTY-EIGHT

'There's someone outside the house again,' Mel told Pete.

Pete got out of bed and looked through the window. A green Astra was parked opposite Mel's front door.

'Same bloke as before, as if he wants to be seen,' she said. 'Makes me nervous.'

'You're probably imagining it. I'll deal with him if he stays much longer.'

He'd only had three hours sleep. Five minutes later, he watched Mel leave the house. The green Astra man was a slaphead, with brutish looks that Pete associated with a particular type of working-class drug dealer. The kind who, when asked, claimed to be a bouncer. Local heavies like this one, together with the Jamaicans south of the Trent, ran the city's cannabis trade. They used illegal immigrants to tend grow houses in derelict factories or former council houses. Easy to deny, easy to move on. All that was widely known, yet high level prosecutions were non-existent. Which meant that these big boys had protection at the very top.

It was time for Pete to get out of Nottingham.

The audacious move, he told himself, after he'd showered and eaten a slice of toast, would be to approach the watcher, ask him for a lift to the station. But you didn't take the piss out of these people. You showed respect. Bag over his shoulder, Pete left the house and tapped on the car window. The watcher wound it down.

'Yeah?'

'You can tell your boss I'm leaving. My work here's done, so you can stop watching this place. The woman and I are through, too.'

He walked away quickly, before the slaphead had time to respond. He'd done his best to protect Mel. By the time Pete came back to the city, all this should be over, one way or another. Pete would either have proved that Eric Turnbull had been allowing drug dealers to flourish, at massive profit to himself, his former police cronies and underlings, or he'd have moved on to another story.

When Pete got home, he'd file the Sarah Bone human interest piece. Revelations about an MP's paternity helped Labour hold onto its most vulnerable seat. Then he could get on with his big story for the following week. He needed to see Geraldine again. She knew something about the death of Paul Morris, he was sure. Discovering that Morris had been Geraldine's first lover explained a lot.

Who was her father? Geraldine never discussed family, only saying her mother died while she was in care. He'd assumed a drugs overdose, suspected her mum was on the game, her father an unknown punter. Yet that might be prejudice painting the most familiar picture. The girl remained an unknown.

Pete needed something concrete to tie Eric Turnbull to the drugs money. According to Ted Burley, Turnbull's owning property in Cape Verde, was not, in itself, proof. The charm might be the murder of Paul Morris. Why did Morris move to London, abandoning a career in Nottingham, to become a home office advisor on drugs policy? Chances were, he moved to get away from someone. Geraldine? Hardly. She was a succubus of sorts and bloody hard to resist, but not a threat. He might be escaping the wife, but his intelligence said that the Morris marriage was strong, regardless of his infidelity, and Morris was a doting father.

Which only left Eric Turnbull and his operation. Suppose Morris wanted to clean up his act? Or perhaps he'd tried to take over, then realised what he was up against, left the city in order to regroup. One thing was certain, his had been a professional killing. The knife wound was a clean hit. Stabbed in the shower, from behind, with the water left running. No forensics. His flat showed signs of having been wiped clean too. The police would never have known that Sarah Bone had been there had she not been spotted leaving, not long before the killing occurred.

Sarah Bone hadn't known that Morris was a drug dealer. Had Geraldine? She might know much more than she had so far let on. Time to text her. *Back in London later. Want to come round tonight?*

He had a spare set of keys to Nick Cane's flat. Geraldine's. He'd pinched them from her the last time she stayed over, thinking they might come in useful. He had a sudden inspiration about the best place to hide Andrew Saint's incriminating cassette. An insurance policy. He'd sort that out on the way to the station.

'I hope I haven't woken you.' Eric's suave voice reminded Sarah, just out of the shower, that she owed a phone call to the chair of the Police Federation. 'It seems congratulations are in order.'

'Wonders never cease, eh?' Sarah wrapped a towel around her wet hair.

'Are you pleased? When we last had lunch I sensed that you were conflicted about which path your future would take.'

'The electorate made up my mind for me. Sorry I wasted the Federation's time. And yours. Soon as I've got some coffee down me, I'll ring their chair and-"

'-no need, no need. He and I have already spoken. They're delighted to have you back in high places.'

'I'll call him anyway,' Sarah said. 'And, since Nottingham's not getting rid of me, we can have lunch again soon.'

'Maybe more than lunch. Something I've been meaning to tell you. Since Mary and I paired our resources, we've been in a position to run a second home.'

'I didn't know.' Sarah had assumed that the divorce had hit Eric hard, hence the downsizing. If you called a penthouse flat near Nottingham Castle downsizing.

'An apartment in one of the Cape Verde islands, just off Africa. Two bedrooms, ocean view. Mary would welcome company there. As would I. We only see ourselves using it for three or four months of the year. Once we'd shown you the ropes, if you ever wanted to make use of the place when we're not around…'

'That's incredibly generous of you,' Sarah said. 'Mary does know that…'

'She knows that our relationship, while affectionate, never went beyond the platonic, if that's what you're asking.'

Not for want of trying on his part. 'Then thanks again,' Sarah said. 'Let's discuss it next time we have lunch.'

Odd that Eric should throw an offer like that into a phone conversation. He must have an ulterior motive. Eric nearly always had an ulterior motive. Used to be getting into her knickers. Maybe it still was. Sarah would get to Cape Verde and the wife wouldn't be there.

While she had the phone in her hand, Sarah decided to call an old friend, ask for an update on yesterday's tragedy.

'Caroline Cane's about to continue her interview,' Rebecca concluded.

'You can't seriously think-'

'-do you know Caroline?' Rebecca interrupted.

'I went to a party at her house once. I met Joe a couple of times when I went out with Nick. He was living in Sheffield then. Are you going to charge Caroline?'

'We're waiting on forensic and DNA results,' Rebecca said. 'The friend watching her kids says Caroline saw a text that led her to think hubby was having an affair. Friend insists that Caroline was only out of the house for half an hour. Hardly gives her time to commit two murders and a sexual assault.'

Sarah agreed. 'I wanted to tell you that Fahd Khan came to one of my surgeries not long ago, making threats connected with his brother's death.'

'We're keeping very close tabs on Fahd Khan,' Rebecca said.

'You're not going to tell me anything concrete, are you?'

'You're too close to the family. It's not wise to get involved before charges are brought. I hear you got back in. Congratulations. Never in doubt, I'm sure.'

Sarah tried Nick, but he didn't pick up. He'd be with Caroline. She'd missed Nick last night. She would have liked someone close with whom she could share both her jubilation and her ambivalence about the result. She couldn't tell Tony, while Hugh thought she should be elated and couldn't understand why she wasn't.

Time to begin her duty calls. No point leaving the landline open for the PM's office to ring with the offer of a job. She'd no hopes in that direction.

Pete rang Jerry just before seven. The pub was noisy and she had to go into the street to take his call.

'You haven't answered my texts.'

'I've been run off my feet all day.' Working at a high-class solicitor's meant that she was learning a range of upper-middle-class excuses.

'I need to see you.'

'I'm a bit tired for a booty call,' Jerry said, playing hard to get.

'It's about a story.'

'What story?' A lorry rumbled by. She had to get him to repeat his answer.

'The murder of Paul Morris.'

A bolt of ice sliced Jerry's spine. 'What about it?'

'Your friend Shaz told me all about you and him.'

'She doesn't know what she's talking about.' Jerry snapped. She'd learnt to push what happened with Paul to the back of her mind. Nick had sorted it out, that was what she chose to remember. In a way, it hadn't really happened.

'Calm down,' Pete said. 'I'm not judging you.'

How much did he know? Had Jerry let Shaz guess how Paul died? Surely not, even if she was off her face. But Pete was clever, could read between lines.

'That was a long time ago,' she said.

'Two years. It's part of my story. I know about Paul and Nick Cane, too.'

'What do you mean?'

'Nick used to supply Paul with dope, back in the day.'

'You're saying that Paul was a dealer?' This was news to Jerry. It must be bollocks. 'Come on! His job was stopping dealers.'

'Ask your friend Nick about the dealing. He confirmed it to me.'

Pete had spoken to Nick. That was worrying. Still, Nick would never give her away. Also, he'd thrown the knife into the river for her. He was implicated.

'I don't know anything about Paul except he had a wife and

253

three kids who are getting on with their lives. It seems a pity to rake all this up and hurt them.'

'You probably know more than you think you do. Let me ask you a different question,' Pete said. 'Ever heard of Eric Turnbull?'

'No.'

'Pity. Look, I need to see you. Apart from anything else, I've missed you.'

'I've missed you too,' she whimpered, because she might yet need to keep him onside. 'But I really am whacked out tonight. How about in the morning?'

'OK. By the way, you know when we were in your Nottingham flat?'

'Nick's flat. Yeah?'

'There was a box under your bed. Had old cassette tapes in it.'

'I know the one you mean.'

'If anything should happen to me, look for one with the word 'chestnuts' on the label.'

'You what?'

'Just remember that, please.'

'You're weird. But I'll remember.'

They agreed that she'd be at his by eleven.

FORTY-NINE

When the police released Caroline for the second time, her solicitor said it meant she was unlikely to be charged.

'You admitted being outside the house, which neutralises their witness. Long as there are no forensics showing you inside, they won't charge you with murder.'

'I've never been inside her house,' Caroline told her, 'but suppose Joe accidentally transferred some of my hair, or skin, or....'

'That's highly unlikely,' Charlene Jagger assured her. 'Let's get out of here.'

Nick was waiting at the Central Police Station's front desk. Caroline took in the flash of interest when he first saw Charlene. She remembered that Nick's last girlfriend had been Afro-Caribbean, but Nick shouldn't be looking, not when they were both meant to be grieving. Maybe Nick and Joe weren't so very different: each too handsome for their own good and hard-wired for promiscuity.

They stopped at Julie's to collect Phoebe and Oliver.

'Do you want me with you when you tell the children?' Nick asked.

'Maybe you can look after Oliver while I talk to Phoebe.'

His mobile rang and he looked at the screen. 'It's Sarah. I left a message. I'll call her back later.'

Nick watched TV with Oliver while Caroline talked to Phoebe, who already seemed to know that something was seriously wrong. Joe's name had been released to the press this afternoon. So far, school had kept the news from spreading.

After five minutes, Phoebe charged into the living room and gave Oliver a big hug, which scared him. Caroline had asked her to be strong and look after her brother. She found simpler words to tell Ollie that Daddy wouldn't be coming home. Soon, the four of them were sat together, watching a DVD of *The Clangers*.

Later, Kath visited to see how Caroline was. Nick used this as an opportunity to go out.

'There are a couple of people I need to see.'

'You'll be back later, won't you?' Caroline asked.

'Before you know it. With fish and chips from Captain Cod for supper, yes?'

'Yes, please,' Caroline said, although she had no appetite whatsoever.' 'I'll make up the spare bed for you.'

Fahd wasn't answering his door to anyone, but the knocking didn't stop, each thump louder than the one before. Eventually, he cracked and went downstairs.

'Who is it?' he called.

'Uncle. Let me in.'

Uncle wasn't his uncle, not by blood, but Fahd felt obliged to open the door. He must look a mess. His dhoti was stained and his hair unwashed. The family elder wasn't the sage, stern figure that Fahd had gone to a few weeks ago, bearing news of his niece's infidelity. Tonight's Uncle was dead-eyed and determined. He must be here for vengeance. Fahd mumbled a pleasantry, offered tea, conscious of the paper peeling from the wall by his front door, the threadbare carpet.

Fahd led Uncle into the spartan living room and gestured for him to sit down. The older man hadn't been to the house before. He glanced around the shabby room. This was not the home of a highly observant Muslim. The only Islamic artefact was an aerial photograph of Mecca in a clip-frame above the sofa, which Uncle shunned, taking the upright chair. Fahd only half opened the kitchen door, not wanting Uncle to see the mess inside. 'Can I offer you some tea?'

'I don't want to drink, I want to talk. I want you to listen.'

He gestured for Fahd to sit, which he did, on the lumpy sofa, opposite Uncle.

'Are you ready to confess?' the elder asked.

Fahd said nothing.

'You did not even wait for the inquest result.'

'I knew which way it would go.'

'You don't know the favours I had to call in to make that exhumation happen. There was no new evidence, but once you started spreading lies about Nazia, I had to lance the boil. The coroner found no proof of foul play.'

'Lack of proof doesn't mean she didn't do it. Her or her lover.'

'Did either of them confess to you?'

'No, but…' He stopped himself. How easily he had fallen into that trap.

'You will go to prison for the rest of your life,' Uncle said. 'You know this.'

'I have alibi witnesses.'

'Of course. Men willing to perjure themselves in court. Each prepared to go to prison themselves after you are found guilty, keep you company in there.'

Fahd brushed Uncle's sarcasm aside. 'She was a slut! And Joe Cane deserved to die, too. He was the father of her daughter!'

This didn't seem to throw Uncle. 'How do you know that?'

'Omar admitted it to me when I told him about the affair. The pregnancy was the only reason she agreed their match. Omar arranged for the wedding to be in Pakistan. That confused people about the timing of the pregnancy.'

Uncle nodded. Again, this wasn't news to him. 'Or did you arrange their wedding?'

'What does that matter now? Go on.'

'She'd never say who the father was. Omar assumed it was this Nick Cane she'd been seeing. Turns out it was his younger brother, the footballer. Nazia admitted it to me.'

'And you have admitted to me what you did to him and to Nazia.'

Fahd feared that Uncle was about to hit him, but the older man merely stood his ground. 'I will give you until Monday to put your affairs in order.'

'It is not for you to judge,' Fahd said.

Uncle crossed the room and slapped him hard across the face. His cheek stinging, Fahd knew better than to retaliate. Uncle was getting on, but he was still connected. Fahd should have known that he was behind the exhumation order. Uncle must have suspected murder, too. He'd wanted to be sure how Omar died. But he hadn't found out. And neither had Fahd.

Uncle reached into the pocket of his jacket. He pulled out a small, brown glass bottle and handed it to Fahd. The bottle rattled in his shaking hands.

'When the time comes, and it will come very soon, you must take these, all of them. Diamorphine. They act quickly. No pain.'

Without a word, Fahd took the pills from Uncle.

'Insh'Allah,' the old man said.

When he was gone, Fahd considered flushing the morphine pills down the toilet. But he might decide to use them, so did no such thing.

'We want you to join the government.'

It wasn't the PM calling, but the Chief Whip.

'In what role?'

'East Midlands Regional Whip. We need new blood. You're experienced enough now. People trust you. They see you as independent, which is useful.'

Sarah considered. The Whips Office was a useful source of influence. True, it was a step down from the junior ministerial role she'd been given four years earlier. That said, five years ago she'd have leapt at it.

'I'm not sure,' she said after a while. 'My priorities have changed. I want to concentrate on my constituency. Maybe I've more to offer from the back benches.'

As a whip, she'd be bound to support the government. In this unexpected third act, she decided, she wanted to be free to speak her mind.

'Take a couple of days to think about it,' she was told. 'We need a new Midlands whip and we need more women whips. This could be good for you.'

She agreed to defer the decision. Then she rang Nick again. This time, he answered his phone. He wasn't himself, she could hear that in his voice, which sounded numb, artificial.

'Terrific news about your victory. Congratulations.'

'It was too close for comfort,' she said. 'How are things?'

'I'm in the queue at the chippy, so I can't really talk. Have you heard anything about… you know?'

'I spoke to someone involved with the investigation. I doubt that they seriously suspect Caroline, but the police have to wait for forensics. I'd like to see you. We could talk all this over then. But I know it's a difficult time.'

'I'm staying at Caroline's until Sunday, when her parents are coming to help. Until we know whether she's being charged, it's hard for me to make plans.'

'Understood. Why don't I call you on Sunday?'

At the end of the conversation she felt more distant from him than she had before the call began. No matter how much Sarah might think she wanted it to happen, this weekend wasn't the time to broach their getting back together.

Captain Cod was the biggest and best chippy for miles. Also, the busiest, especially early evening on a Friday. If you ordered your fish as soon as you came in, it would be cooked by the time you got to the front of the queue. Nick watched a new batch of chips hit the fryer and asked for two cod, one large. His mobile rang again. This time, it was Jerry.

'I need to talk to you. Pete's doing a story about Paul Morris. He's trying to find out who killed him.'

'Whoa,' said Nick. 'Hold on and let me think for a minute.'

Jerry didn't know about Nazia and Joe's murder. Nick wasn't going to tell her about that while he was stood in a queue at the chippy. He stepped outside.

'OK,' he told Jerry. 'I can talk now. There's no way Pete can find out how Paul died. Not unless you tell him.'

'He knows about me and him. He says that Paul was a drug dealer.'

'He was. I thought you knew that.'

'Maybe you told me after… a lot of what happened back then is a blur, to be honest.'

'Don't tell Pete that.'

'I don't know what to tell him.'

'Say you heard about Paul's death and were upset but got over it.'

'Pete's after some big conspiracy story. He thinks whoever

killed Paul or had him killed is his missing Mr Big.'

'And he intends to pin it on me.' Nick tried to fake a chuckle, but it came out as an awkward laugh. The whole thing felt unreal. Yet he was in it up to his neck: he'd covered up how Jerry, in a jealous rage, had stabbed Paul Morris to death. He'd thrown the murder weapon into the Trent. Back then, Nick was not long out of prison and still had a prisoner's mindset. What seemed reckless and irresponsible today hadn't even felt like a choice then. A kind of altruistic determination had taken him over. Any way you looked at it, he'd helped her get away with murder.

'I'm seeing him tomorrow,' Jerry said. 'I'll find out more then.'

He went back inside just as their dinner came out of the fryer. 'One large fish, one medium fish. Any chips?'

'Large chips. Two fritters. One fish cake. Large mushy peas.'

Dinner for four and change from a tenner. While the food was bagged up, Nick phoned Caroline to say that he was on his way, get the kettle on. Important to stick to the routine. Drinking strong tea with fish suppers was the Sheffield way. Joe must have made the same call many times. His cheating bastard of a brother.

FIFTY

Quarter past eleven and Geraldine hadn't shown up. Pete must have her rattled. He wondered if she'd done a runner. Until their conversation the night before, he hadn't even considered what he now suspected. But he'd heard the panic in her voice when he suggested that he knew how Paul Morris died.

Geraldine didn't like Pete's knowing that Morris had been her lover – both before and probably while he was also screwing Sarah Bone. Jealousy. It was the oldest motive on earth. He'd been stupid not to seriously consider it before.

He rang her mobile and she answered after eight rings.

'You're meant to be here by now.'

'Soz,' she sounded bleary. 'Kerri at work lent me *The Man Who Fell to Earth*. Stayed up late cos I had to watch the whole thing in one go. Total masterpiece.'

'I think I've worked out how Paul Morris died.'

'You have?' Suddenly, Jerry sounded wide awake.

'If you want your name kept out of it, get over here.'

'I don't understand why I can't answer your questions on the phone.'

'Because when I look you in the eyes I can tell if you're lying.'

Someone rang his doorbell. Probably the post.

'Get over here,' Pete repeated.

'Give me time to get dressed. I'll call a minicab, all right?'

'All right.' Pete's doorbell rang again, more insistently this time. 'Gotta go.'

He hung up and pressed the intercom button.

'Parcel.'

'Bring it up, please.' He pressed the buzzer to let them in.

'Are you sure you want Mr Cane here?' DI Allen asked in the interview room.

'He's an old family friend,' Bilal told the DI. 'His brother was killed, too.'

Earlier, he had explained to Nick that, as the legal guardian of

Nazia's children, he'd given permission for their blood to be tested. He'd also told Nick how he'd seen Joe going into Nazia's house weeks back and initially assumed that Joe was Nick.

'I must ask you both to keep these results to yourselves,' Rebecca Allen said. 'Their implications affect the ongoing investigation.'

'I understand,' Bilal said.

Nick kept schtum. He wouldn't promise not to tell Caroline something she might need to know. At least she hadn't been brought in for interview today. Yet.

'The blood tests show that Omar Khan was the father of Ahmad,' the DI said, 'but not Tamazur. There is a near hundred percent likelihood that Tamazur's father was Joseph Cane.'

'Jesus,' Nick said.

'My brother-in-law, Fahd, was aware of this,' Bilal told the inspector.

'Why didn't you tell me?' Nick asked.

'Fahd only told my uncle yesterday. Uncle told me last night.'

'Why did your uncle go to see him?' Rebecca Allen asked.

'To ask if he'd done it, of course.'

'And did he confess?' Nick asked.

'He didn't deny it. Fahd knew that Nazia agreed to marry Omar because she was pregnant and needed a husband. They married in Pakistan and didn't return until Tamazur was born. The Khan family has strong ties to Pakistan. My fear is that Fahd will escape there before you're in a position to charge him.'

'He's being watched very closely,' DI Allen assured him. 'But we need evidence. So far, all we have is Caroline Cane's statement that she saw a man who looked like Fahd leave the house. His face was obscured. It's not enough.'

'Is my sister-in-law still under suspicion?' Nick asked the Inspector.

'No charges are imminent. Was Caroline in the picture when your brother got Nazia pregnant?'

'No. That was before they met. Nazia was going out with me back then.'

Rebecca frowned. 'I'm afraid that makes you a person of

interest, too.'

'What happens next?' Bilal asked the inspector.

'Be patient. We're interviewing all of Fahd's alibi witnesses again. As soon as one of them cracks, everything will fall into place. That is, presuming he did it. Until we get some firm evidence, or a detailed confession, it's an open case.'

Nick was staggered. Joe had been having an affair with Nazia while Nick was seeing her. Nick had behaved honourably. He'd resisted having sex with Naz, although he knew she was persuadable, only for Joe to sweep in and take her virginity. Nazia didn't dump Nick because she'd yielded to family pressure to marry a middle-aged dentist. She'd dumped him because she'd opened her legs for his brother's greedy, restless, unthinking dick and got herself up the duff.

The way Nick felt at this moment, Joe deserved to be dead.

While waiting for the taxi, Jerry selected the push-up bra and black leather motorbike jacket. The outfit was too warm for the time of year, but made her feel sexy and confident. She added leopard skin effect leggings which would be easy for Pete to slide off. The knife was the one she took for protection on nights out. She didn't want to hurt him. The girl who, in a jealous rage, had killed Paul Morris wasn't the young woman she had become. But if she had to use the knife to protect herself, or Nick, she would. Pete said he needed to see her eyes, but she could lie for England. He'd no proof. Nick got someone to clean up Paul's flat before the police came. And no way could Pete know how Nick got rid of the knife for her.

'Here's fine,' she told the taxi driver, fifty yards before the flat, a first floor walk-up on a crowded, shabby main road where every other shop was a takeaway.

'Something wrong?' the driver asked when she didn't get out after paying.

'Just give me a mo'.'

Two men were leaving Pete's building. One was heavy set, the other more wiry. The big one wore a woollen cap, with no hair showing beneath; his partner had a crew-cut. Both were in their thirties or forties, hard to tell. But Jerry knew what kind of people they were, and she could see that they were in a hurry. Only when they were well down the road did she leave the cab.

Once the men were out of sight, she rang all three doorbells. Somebody let her in. The door to Pete's flat, on the first floor, was ajar. She pushed it open. She could have called his name, but didn't want to draw attention to herself, not when there were other people in the building, not when she feared what she might find.

Pete was on the floor of the living room, his head twisted backwards at an unnatural angle. His neck was broken. The bruises on his face indicated that he'd been beaten up first. If the doorbell that went when she was on the phone had been rung by the thugs who'd done this, they'd had a good twenty minutes to interrogate Pete, then search the place.

Shock, it must be, turned her super-rational. She needed to remove all evidence that she'd been here. She needed to remove any indication that she knew Pete. She needed to see what he had written about her and Nick on his laptop and perhaps destroy that, too. Only his laptop wasn't there. Nor was his phone.

Pete used to keep his laptop in plain view, on the table where he did his writing. Did he have any back-up? An external hard drive of some kind, a USB stick? Through an open window, she heard a siren. Pete had neighbours. They might have heard something, called the police. Pete's killers, she reckoned, would have done a thorough clean-up job. Time to leave before she was seen.

Outside, she walked at a steady, purposeful pace, without looking back. Only when she was two streets away did she breathe freely. She looked around to see if anyone was watching her. Didn't seem to be. No more sirens. Sirens were a commonplace on the streets of Clapham anyhow. Pete was dead. The thugs she'd seen must have murdered him to kill his story. They knew what Pete knew, but not what Jerry knew. They'd find that he had texted her, and called her, but not that she was coming to see him today: there was no record of that. If the thugs came after her, she could plead ignorance, say she thought

Pete was an old perve who was after her body, the news story a mere excuse. They might believe her. They might kill her anyway.

Where could she run to? She only felt safe with Nick in Nottingham. But when the killers read Pete's story on his laptop, they'd know about Nick, too. He might be the first place they would look.

Nick. She'd better warn Nick.

'She cheated on you with Joe all those years ago?' Caroline was bewildered.

'I'm still taking it in,' Nick told her. 'That he could... that she could...'

'Joe was God's Gift back then,' Caroline said. 'He acted his age. Joe always took what he wanted. He was hard to say no to. Which doesn't excuse what Nazia did. I can't begin to tell you how disgusted I am. Did Joe know about Tamazur?'

'I don't know. Maybe. Probably. If she didn't tell him back then, surely she would have after she got pregnant by him for a second time.'

Caroline shook her head in disbelief. 'How will I tell Phoebe and Oliver that their dad...'

He held her while she cried. Over the years, Nick had become inured to his brother's smaller betrayals: selfish acts; small lies; petty thefts he remembered from childhood. Yet he'd thought that he was the one who had seriously cheated – by secretly sleeping with Caroline after Joe had dumped her. But he had hardly behaved badly. When Joe decided that he wanted her back, Caroline had sworn Nick to silence. For years, Nick had felt guilty about breaking some stupid, unwritten code, yet he'd done nothing wrong. His brother, meanwhile, had ruined Nazia's life, forcing her to enter an unloving marriage, bringing tragedy in its wake.

'Do you think he was going to leave me for her?' Caroline asked.

'I think she was going to move to Birmingham, have her baby there. After that... I don't know.'

'If I didn't have a strong enough motive to kill them both

before, I do now.'

'Don't say that, even in jest. You're not cleared until they charge Fahd. The police still need evidence. Their best hope is that one of the alibi witnesses cracks.'

His phone rang and the number calling showed on the screen. Jerry.

'I'd better take this.'

'Nick, I need… I don't…' He'd not heard Jerry like this in an age, not since… It took a while to understand what was spooking her. Pete Carlson had been murdered – for the story he was working on. Jerry had found the body.

'Are you still at his flat? Have you called the police?'

'The police? No, of course not. I don't want to be tied up in this.'

Calling the police wasn't in Jerry's nature, but Nick insisted it made sense.

'Were you seen?'

'Only by the taxi driver.'

'How good a look did you get at the men leaving?'

'A pretty good look.'

'I really think you should go to the police.'

'No! From what Pete wrote in that article I sent you, these people could well be connected to the police. If word leaks and they find out I saw them, can identify them, I'm as good as dead myself.'

She made sense.

'OK, scrub that. You'd better get out of London for a while.'

'I have work on Monday.'

'Call in sick from Nottingham. If the killers have Pete's phone and computer, they know who you are, where you live and where you work.'

'If they've read Pete's story, they know who you are, too. They know that I own your flat and they know where it is.'

'Pete didn't send his story to the paper, though, did he? These men aren't going to be bothered about me, or you. They wanted to end Pete's investigation into their boss, whoever that is. But we'd better play this safe. I'll find somewhere for us both to stay until we know they're not coming for us. Pack a bag, get on a train.'

'What was all that about?' Caroline asked when he was done. He told her, leaving out how Jerry had murdered Paul Morris and he had helped cover that up.

'She can stay here,' Caroline told him.

'Your parents are coming tomorrow.'

'I'm going to put them off. It's too much disruption. I'd rather you stayed. I don't have to explain things to you. And this Jerry sounds like she needs help.'

Bilal and Uncle met at the Shah Poran Islamic Centre, a mosque on Gregory Boulevard, near the Forest.

'Have you heard from Fahd?' Bilal asked.

'I don't expect to. He knows that no man of religion can accept what he did,'

Uncle's hooded eyes drooped. 'Is it true she was raped?'

'I believe so.' Bilal tried to explain. 'He wore a condom, so there's no firm evidence, but he tore…' He couldn't get the words out.

Uncle patted Bilal's arm. 'We must let the law take its course, as Fahd should have done with his brother's death.'

'I don't think Nazia had anything to do with Omar's death.'

'We will never know for sure. How can we? Fahd is a very troubled man.'

'A troubled man with a lot of alibi witnesses.'

'Justice will find a way.'

'How?'

Uncle's words, when they came, were measured. 'Some say suicide can be an honourable act. Others that only Allah has the right to say when a life ends.'

'Fahd's convinced he has the right to do whatever he wants,' Bilal argued. 'He'll never kill himself. Where does that leave me – am I supposed to kill him to avenge my sister?'

'Killing is never justified. And you're responsible for two children. Nazia would not thank you for abandoning them in order to fulfil your foolish pride.'

A pity, Bilal thought, that Uncle had not counselled Fahd against impatient behaviour. But Bilal was his blood. Fahd was not. Uncle held little sway over him.

'I will go and see him again if you wish,' Uncle said. 'Urge him to confess.'

'He won't.'

'If he doesn't, he knows what is expected of him. He has the means at hand.'

Bilal understood. Uncle was right about his responsibilities. Tamazur and Ahmad were distraught, Tamazur especially. At some point, he and Sam would have to explain to her that her father was not her father, that Nick Cane – who she had hardly met – was her uncle, the same as Bilal, just as Uncle was to him.

The girl at the door was not yet twenty, according to Nick, but looked at least twenty-two, and was a knock-out. Caroline wouldn't have let Joe anywhere near her. Nick treated Jerry as he might a sixth-form student, or a step-daughter, but Caroline had eyes. The way Jerry looked at Nick was anything but filial.

'This is very good of you,' Jerry told Caroline. There were traces of Nottingham in her voice, mixed with University Everywoman: an idiom Caroline was fluent in. She showed Jerry to the spare bedroom that Nick had vacated earlier.

This morning, Oliver had visited her room while Nick was there, joined them in bed for a comforting cuddle. Later, before Jerry arrived, Caroline had explained to Phoebe that Nick was staying in her room because she got upset in the night. Phoebe shouldn't let that stop her coming in if she was scared of anything.

People said you couldn't change the past, but they were wrong. Knowing what she now knew changed how Caroline felt about everything. She wanted what she should have settled for all those years ago. She wanted to hang onto Nick.

Caroline watched crap Saturday evening telly with the children while Nick and Jerry talked. They seemed to have an urgent, precarious situation to deal with. Whatever it was, Caroline didn't need to take it on board. She was in a desperate enough situation of her own. She rang home to assure her parents that she didn't need them to come before the funeral after all. Her brother-in-law was helping. There no longer appeared to be any imminent risk of her being charged.

'They know who did it, Dad. They just need the evidence. My solicitor reckons they only took me in to give the killer a false sense of confidence, encourage him to make a mistake.'

'How do you stand it?' Dad asked, 'knowing that the man who

did this awful thing is walking free?'

'You've got to have faith in the justice system,' she said. Her feelings of vengeance and hatred for Fahd Khan felt oddly muted. Hard to hate a man she'd never met. It was her husband and his mistress that she was learning to loathe.

On Sunday morning, Nick rang Bilal, then Sarah. Before he could explain why he was unable to meet her later, Sarah launched into a breathless piece of news.

'Have you seen the papers? Pete Carlson's been murdered.'

'Really?' Nick tried to act surprised. 'How?'

'Police think he interrupted a break-in. *The Sunday Times* says it's possible he was killed by the criminals he was writing about. The story even mentions me.'

'Christ, what have they got?'

'Just that his last published piece was about my unexpected re-election. They mention he had a girlfriend in Nottingham but not what he was investigating here.'

So far, the police had not tried to contact Jerry and Nick didn't plan to mention the girl to Sarah. The police didn't have Pete's phone or laptop. Carlson was unlikely to have told his Nottingham girlfriend much about Jerry, not given that he was clandestinely screwing her. The police, therefore, probably had no way of knowing that Jerry existed. The killers, on the other hand, knew her name and, if they'd read her texts, they also knew the nature of her relationship with Pete.

'I'd like to see you,' Sarah said.

'It's difficult,' Nick said. He explained why he was still at Caroline's.

'Just for an hour. I'll come to the house if you want. I need filling in on what's happening with the murder case. And I'd like to talk about us.'

That *us* was ominous. Nick had hoped there might be an *us* after the election, particularly if she lost. But that was before he found out about Hugh and discovered that, were she to lose, Sarah had a job lined up down south. Before Joe and Nazia's murder, which changed everything. Since seeing Sarah with

Hugh, he'd stopped allowing himself to hope. Maybe that explained why he'd been with two different women in the last fortnight. For a long time, he had, whether consciously or subconsciously, been saving himself for Sarah. No longer.

'I'll call you later,' he offered. 'Maybe we could meet for a drink after all.'

In the front room, Caroline was doing a jigsaw with the kids. Nick went through to the kitchen, where Jerry was finishing a bowl of Rice Krispies.

'How long has it been going on, then?' she asked.

'How long has what been going on?'

Jerry gave him a condescending but amused look. 'You and Caz. I'm a light sleeper. I heard her come, big-time, about three in the morning.'

'Oh, that.'

'I'm jealous, obviously, but mostly I'm confused. Yesterday you told me she was heartbroken because hubby was playing away and got bumped off for it.'

'What you heard has only happened a couple of times, since the murder.'

'So, twice in four days.'

'She and I… we have history. We had a thing, before she married Joe.'

'Of course you did,' Jerry said. 'I reckon you've slept with every woman I've ever seen you with. Except me. You're making me wait.'

Nick said nothing in response. Safest way. Jerry went on.

'I know you. You get a sense of obligation. You're going to be landed with Caz and her kids. You'll end up marrying her because you think it's your duty.'

'My brother's just been murdered and we haven't started planning his funeral yet. Don't go mapping out my whole future for me.'

Jerry gave him a stern look. 'Shagging her every other night might determine your future. All actions have consequences.'

'Not all actions,' Nick said, thinking of Paul Morris. Jerry got away with that. Pete's death was convenient for her, too. He'd

271

been digging into her affair with Paul. What if Jerry had killed Pete? The story about the thugs could be a complete pack of lies, one he'd been gullible enough to fall for. Everyone chose who and what to believe. Sometimes the choice was unconscious. Sometimes it changed.

'Did you remember anything else from yesterday morning?' he asked.

'Not really,' she said, 'but I do remember something Pete asked me on the phone. He wanted to know if I knew a man called Eric Bull.'

Nick thought for a moment. 'Eric Turnbull?'

'That was the name.'

'And did you?'

'I've never heard of him. Have you?'

'I know who he is, but I've not met him, except in passing.'

He knew someone who had, though, and he'd be seeing her later.

'Is he a dealer?'

Nick laughed. 'Hardly.'

'What's so funny?'

'Until a couple of years ago, he was Nottinghamshire's Chief Constable.'

'I understand. Yes. You must do what your conscience tells you. I understand.' Fahd put the phone down. Huzaifa was the second alibi witness to call. The police were piling on the pressure: re-interviewing witnesses on a Saturday night.

He'd told Huzaifa that he didn't plan the rape, but had to admit, when pressed, that he'd taken a condom with him, making it hard to claim the assault as a spontaneous act of revenge. He had to explain why he'd left his phone at Jamal's. He didn't explain how, that night, he'd made his sister-in-law's lover watch, taking off his gag, telling him he'd only stop if he admitted helping Nazia murder Omar, explained how they did it. He couldn't forget Joe's tormented pleas. Nazia, by contrast, hadn't said a word. She'd squirmed, then groaned, then played dead.

Eventually, Joe had confessed, as he was bound to. Fahd had pressed him for details: where, how, when? The taxi driver was unconvincing. Fahd, to punish them both, continued the act he'd fantasised about for so long. It wasn't satisfying. After defiling Nazia that way, strangling her was an act of mercy. Cutting her lover's throat afterwards was the work of mere moments.

Possibly, he'd told himself on his walk home, Nazia acted on her own. It was even possible that Omar had died of natural causes. Fahd's phone call to Omar telling him that Nazia was being unfaithful could have brought on a fatal heart attack. If so, it was on him, but Nazia still deserved to die. Omar's death had ruined three more lives, the third being Fahd's. Five, if you counted the children. Eight, when you included Joe Cane's other children and widow.

Nazia's brother, Bilal, and her uncle had right on their side. Fahd accepted that. He accepted that his friends were right to desert him. He would go to prison. Easier to end it all now than go through a trial, then tear up sheets to hang himself in a prison cell. Two murders and a rape meant a life sentence. He'd be seventy before he got out, should he live that long.

There was a third of a bottle of vodka left and there were

three cigarettes in the packet. He ought to get it over with before the police came. He didn't think about writing a note until he'd started taking the pills. By the time he'd washed all the pills down he'd drunk so much vodka that he didn't know what to write, or who to write to. He barely knew how to sign his name. But there was a pen in front of him, so he pulled the cardboard inner out of his packet of Marlboro Reds and managed a single word before he passed out, lit cigarette in his mouth.

Sorry

Nick and Sarah had arranged to meet in The Fiveways, a pub just off the ring road, a short walk from Caroline's. Nick arrived late, looking tired and numb. Sarah bought him a pint. He drank the first half very quickly. She tried to talk about Joe, but he was clearly still in shock and didn't want to engage. Instead, he asked about the election aftermath.

'Were you offered a job?' he asked.

'East Midlands whip. A test to see if I want to get back on the greasy pole.'

'If you'd wanted to climb the greasy pole, you'd have taken the offer of Benn's safe seat in Chesterfield. Tony Bax says you could have had it on a plate.'

'Good thing I didn't,' Sarah said. 'It went Lib-Dem.'

'You're kidding!' A spark of life in Nick's eyes.

'One of the only seats we lost. Everyone thought Nottingham West was a goner but we worked hard and hung on. In Chesterfield, there were local schisms and the campaign was well below par. There was lots of tactical voting by Tories. The Lib Dems took it by nearly three thousand.'

'Might have been different if you'd been the candidate.'

'Maybe, but I'm glad I didn't have to find out. Turn-out was down everywhere. Labour actually got fewer votes this time than when we lost in 92. Anyway, Nottingham's stuck with me for four or five more years.'

'You should be happy,' Nick said. 'I couldn't see you living down South.'

'What's London, if not down South?'

'It's two hours on the train. That's nothing. Remember that girl I used to tutor, Jerry? She's at university there but comes back all the time.'

This was an odd lurch in the subject. Sarah wanted to talk about herself and him, not some teenager.

'I remember her, yes.'

'The thing is, she was having a fling with Pete Carlson.'

'Christ. How did that happen?'

'Pete got to know Jerry because he was looking into me. He interviewed her and… Anyway, Jerry's pitched up with me and Caroline, completely freaked out by Pete's death. She thinks that whoever killed him might come for her.'

'Why would she think that? Does she know who did it?'

'Not as far as I'm aware,' Nick said, somewhat cagily. 'Have you any news?'

'I phoned Pete's editor. She said Pete kept promising something big but not delivering. She's assigning someone to cover his murder.'

'Pete was looking into everyone who worked with Andrew Saint.'

'Whoever killed Pete took his phone, his laptop, computer discs, the lot. According to the police, they did a very clean job. Professional.'

Nick scratched his chin. 'There was one odd thing. According to Jerry, just before he died, Pete asked her if she'd ever come across Eric Turnbull.'

This threw Sarah. 'Why would he ask her that?'

'She thinks it was to do with identifying a Nottingham Crime boss.'

'Well, it's hardly going to be the Chief Constable, is it?'

Nick didn't respond to this point. 'Are you still friendly with Turnbull?'

'Sort of. Less so since he remarried. Before that, he kept trying to get me into bed. Eventually, he gave up on me and married a solicitor.'

'I've met her. Mary.'

'Seriously, you think Pete was investigating *him*?'

'You never know.'

'That's nonsense, Nick. You're getting more cynical in your old age.'

'You're not that far behind me,' Nick reminded her.

'Thanks for that,' Sarah said, then tried to shift the subject. 'Getting older does make you consider what you really want from life.'

'And is this what you want, turning forty, to stay in Parliament?'

Sarah gave a wry smile. 'Funnily enough, it is. Not to get into government, but to do things. Casework. Helping people. Making a difference where I can.'

She tried to formulate a way to say that, since she no longer had cabinet ambitions, it didn't matter if she dated an ex-con. Every lead-in she could think of was crass. Anyway, Nick was looking at his phone. He swore.

'Text from Bilal, Nazia's brother. Fahd Khan has killed himself.'

Sarah felt little surprise and less sadness. 'Did he confess?'

'Suicide's a convincing confession, isn't it? I have to go and tell Caroline. She's been going out of her mind with worry about them arresting her.'

'Of course,' Sarah said. 'I'm in my car. Let me run you back.'

Caroline heard Nick open the door. He'd only been gone half an hour. Maybe Sarah hadn't shown up. She hoped that was the case. She needed Nick. The last thing she wanted was for him to be distracted by Sarah Bone. If those two were ever going to get back together, it would've happened a long time ago.

Sarah was with Nick, heavily made-up, doubtless to hide how washed out the election had left her. The MP was only Nick's age, but the forties were harder on women than they were on men. What was she doing here?

'I've had some news,' Nick said. 'Can we go in the back room?'

He put an arm round Caroline's shoulder and ushered her into the quiet room, where he sat her down on the sofa and spoke gently.

'I just had a text from Bilal. Fahd took his own life today. Sarah's spoken to a friend who's working on the case, DI Allen. She says the police are regarding this as a confession of guilt. Evidently Fahd's alibi witnesses were starting to back out. He knew it was only a matter of time before he was charged. Hey...'

Only when he gave her a tissue did Caroline realise that she was crying.

'He couldn't live with himself,' she said. 'That's something.' He held her while she cried. 'Sorry. You know I'm not normally like this.'

Caroline needed what she needed and she knew that she had to press him now, while she was weak and he'd find it impossible to refuse her anything.

'You won't leave us yet, will you? Phoebe and Oliver like having you here. It makes things feel more normal. You're all that's holding us together.'

'I won't leave you,' Nick promised. 'I'll stay as long as you need me.'

Hearing Nick return, Jerry came downstairs. He wasn't in the hall, but the MP for Nottingham West was, standing there like a spare part, looking at her phone. Jerry decided to take control.

'I don't know if you remember me,' she said. 'I'm Jerry. Can I help you?'

'Nick had to give Caroline some news. Thought I'd stay in case she needs to ask me anything. Not that I know much more than I've already told Nick.'

In other words, she wasn't waiting for Caroline, but for Nick. Jerry had seen Sarah Bone before, but never up close. She was Nick's age and showing it, make-up not quite concealing the tired lines beneath her eyes. Older than Caroline then, but also better looking with a great figure and, probably, in the long run, more of a threat. It was time to see Sarah Bone off.

'They may be a while. You know those two have a thing going on, do you?'

'Pardon?' The MP looked confused.

'They used to be a couple, before Caroline dumped him for

his younger brother. But now he's gone, Nick's back in her bed every night.'

'Her husband's just been murdered.' Sarah smiled awkwardly, as though waiting for Jerry to admit that this was some kind of wind-up.

'You know what Nick's like, always a sucker for needy people. He's helped me enough over the years. He's family. Her kids' closest male relative. She'll get him to stay here while she sorts herself out. Knowing Nick, he'll never leave.'

Before Sarah could react to this, Nick returned, without Caroline.

'What is it?'' Jerry asked him. 'What happened?'

'Fahd, who killed Joe and Nazia, has killed himself.'

Jerry swore. 'How's Caroline taking it?'

'Relieved, I think, but freaked out.' He turned to Sarah. 'I'm going to be staying here for the foreseeable, helping Caroline keep things together.'

Sarah glanced at Jerry, a shrewd look that acknowledged her earlier insight, then gave Nick a politician's compassionate smile. 'If there's ever anything I can do to help, you know where to find me.'

Before she left, Nick kissed her on the cheek.

'So that's her,' Jerry said, when she'd gone. 'The big love of your life. She still likes you, you know.'

'She's got a boyfriend nearer your age than mine. She doesn't need me.'

The toy-boy info surprised Jerry. Probably just using him for sex, the way she'd been using Pete.

'Had she heard anything about what happened in London?' Jerry asked.

'No. When I put it to her that Eric Turnbull might be involved in something dodgy, she said it was nonsense.'

'She's right, isn't she? Paul Morris being a drug dealer is one thing. The Chief Constable running a drugs cartel, that's another.'

'In that case, why did Pete ask you about him?'

'No idea.' Jerry decided that now was the time. 'There's something I've been waiting to tell you. Pete borrowed my keys to your flat. He hid something there.'

FIFTY-THREE

July 2001

Today was the house's last sitting before the summer break. Sarah and Hugh sat opposite each other in her office. He had not, as far as she knew, applied for any new jobs. Since her promotion, she had a second desk, in the whips' office. That meant they saw less of each other at work, which made things less awkward. Whips weren't allowed to speak in the Commons. As a result, Hugh had less research to get on with but more constituency casework to handle. They'd been to bed twice since her re-election, each time after she'd invited him to supper in her flat. Today, they ought to discuss how often he would visit Nottingham over the summer.

'Any urgent messages?' she asked.

'Some bloke from the Sunday Times, Ted Burley, he said his name was. He's working on a piece about that dead journalist, needs your input.'

'I'll call him when I have time.'

'Actually, he's waiting in the lobby.'

While Hugh went off to collect the journalist, Sarah sorted out the paperwork she meant to take home. Her life in Nottingham felt thinner than it used to. She was considering asking Hugh if he'd like to move in over the summer. Sod what prudes in the local party thought. They could hardly deselect her. Sarah would need to set conditions. No talk of marriage or kids. No long-term commitment – not at first, anyway. But she didn't know if he'd be up for it.

Nottingham was lonely without Hugh. Sarah hadn't seen Nick since Nazia Khan's funeral. She didn't know if he was still living with Caroline. Eric was spending all of his time in Cape Verde and hadn't repeated his offer for her to visit him and Mary there. Maybe because Mary had stayed behind in Nottingham.

Hugh poked his head round the door. 'He's here. Want me to stick around?'

'No, but there are things we need to discuss. Like to come up to Nottingham with me this weekend?'

'Very much,' he said, with that beguiling grin, then let the journalist in.

Nick wanted to visit the family in Wollaton but Bilal kept putting him off.

'How do the kids feel, knowing that Fahd did what he did?' Nick had asked last time they met.

'Ahmad is angry. Tamazur keeps it all in. She was always scared of Fahd anyway. At some point, I'll have to explain that Joe was her father. And that…'

'That I'm her uncle,' Nick said. 'I'd like to be involved in her life, Bilal. I'd like to stay friends with you and Sam.'

'We're family,' Bilal said, 'but families are always complicated. Be patient.'

Nick left it a month before calling again. This time, he was invited over. Hard not to think about how, last time he was in this small, suburban home, Nazia was here, too. Sam left the two men alone in the front room.

'How are your sister-in-law and the children?' Bilal asked Nick.

'The kids are doing pretty well. They're very young still, which is a mercy. As for Caroline, she has good days and bad days, but she's talking about selling the cab company, going back to teaching.'

'You still living there?' Bilal asked.

Nick wasn't sure if he'd guessed that he and Caroline had been… whatever they had been, in the madness of grief. The physical side had only lasted a couple of weeks. They'd put a stop to it after the funeral, by mutual agreement. He'd told Caroline that they weren't right for each other. If they were, Caroline would never have married Joe. She'd agreed, kind of, and that was how they'd left it.

'I'm back in my flat,' he replied. 'But I do spend a lot of evenings and weekends in Sherwood, help out with the kids and stuff. I enjoy it, really.'

'You've always loved children,' Bilal said.

'Have I? Yes, I suppose I have.'

Sam brought them both a brew.

'How are the kids?' Nick asked her.

'Ahmad sits with his head in the TV all the time. Cartoons mainly. Tamazur stares into space a lot. At least she reads. That's something, right?'

'It is. Can I speak to her?'

'She's in the kitchen. Why don't you come through with me?'

Nick found his niece reading a novel called *The Rag and Bone Shop*.

'Remember Nick?' Bilal asked her. 'He used to be my English teacher.'

'I remember,' she replied without looking up.

'How are you getting on with the story?' Nick asked.

'It's good.'

'Would you like me to read some of it to you?'

'I can read for myself.'

'I know you can, but I like to read out loud. It's one of the things I miss about being a teacher. Will you let me?'

Tamazur handed Nick the novel. He began to read, doing all the voices, the way he used to back in the 80s, when he'd been Bilal's teacher. Sam leant her head on Bilal's shoulder. Together, they listened to the older man read to the young girl.

Ted Burley looked like an old school hack: balding and overweight, in an off the peg suit that had become too tight on him. None of which should have dented Sarah's confidence in the journalist or his paper's investigation. But it did.

After Hugh had shown Ted in, then cleared off for the day, they got down to business. Ted told her that the police investigation into the murder of Pete Carlson was at a dead end.

'Whoever killed Pete also took his phone, computer, the lot. All we have are short summaries he gave his editor in emails. Hardly any detail.'

'You must have some leads.'

'Pete was investigating the deaths of Andrew Saint and Nancy Tull. Do you have any idea what conclusions he had come to?'

'None whatsoever, I'm afraid,' Sarah said. 'But there is somebody you ought to talk to. Pete suspected him of being involved, because, back in the day, he used to supply Saint with cannabis. Pete finally accepted that he'd been going straight since he got out of prison, four years ago. This person is a friend. I'll ask him to talk to you, as long as you promise to treat him fairly. He's had to put up with a lot from the press and police in the past.'

'You're talking about Nick Cane,' Ted said. 'I've spoken to him already. He gave me a cassette of a recording that Pete hid in his flat.'

This took Sarah by surprise. 'A recording?'

'A secret recording made in the mid-90s. Evidently Pete found it in Saint's old home with the help of a girl called Jerry.'

'I know who she is. How did it end up in Nick's flat?'

'Jerry is Cane's landlady and used to be Pete's lover. For some reason, she lent Pete a key to Cane's flat. He hid the cassette there as insurance. After the murder, she told Cane about the cassette. Cane got in touch with me when he saw a piece I wrote about the murder. There are two voices on the cassette. Nick Cane identified one of them. I hope you can help with the other. May I play it to you?'

'Whenever you're ready.'

Ted got out his machine and pressed 'play'. Sarah listened carefully. Ted sat in silence, watching Sarah's face fall.

'The voice with the northern accent is Andrew, obviously.'

'Nice to have another confirmation. The second voice?' Ted asked.

'You really need me to tell you?'

'This is a secret recording. It isn't evidence, or proof, but it's the best I'm likely to get. I need to hear you say it, so that I can publish when the time is right.'

'The other voice, the one offering protection for a fifteen percent cut, that's Eric Turnbull. In 1996, he became Nottinghamshire's Chief Constable.'

'Gotcha,' Ted said.

EPILOGUE

O n Daddy's bedside table was a note. The words were in English. Ahmad didn't understand all of them. He knew *Whore* was a bad word. In the note, Daddy said that Mummy was one. He said that now she could be with her lover.

Ahmad pushed aside the duvet and felt Daddy's body. It was cool. There was a hypodermic needle by his right hand. The plunger was down. Ahmad understood what Daddy must have done and he knew the word for it. *Suicide.* Suicide was against Islam. Life was God's gift, not yours to take away. Suicide brought shame on the family and shame was worse than death.

Ahmad had to tell Mummy. She was with Tamazur in his sister's bedroom. He could hear them talking. But Daddy's note was nasty about Mummy. Ahmad didn't want Mummy to see it. And he didn't want Daddy's death to bring shame on the family. There was only one thing he could do. Get rid of the note.

He took the pale sheet into the bathroom and flushed it down the toilet. What about the needle? Best get rid of that too. Not in the bin. He'd hide the needle somewhere else, throw it away later.

Ahmad took one last look at his father. He had to protect Daddy from people saying bad things about him. Would Daddy go to hell? Would Mummy? Ahmad didn't like to think about that. He went into Mummy's room and tucked the needle into the back of her wardrobe, behind some old shoes. Then he pushed open the door of Tamazur's room without knocking. His words stumbled out.

'It's Daddy. He won't wake up.'

ACKNOWLEDGEMENTS

Thanks to Meg Munn and Emma Rixon for their help with research on this novel. I'm more than grateful to Graham Caveney, Al Guthrie, Di Peasey, Paddy Stamp, Jane Urquhart and Nahem Yousaf for commenting on different drafts. Thanks to John Lucas for everything, most especially his rigorous editing.

As ever, any errors are entirely my own.

www.davidbelbin.com